HALO

POINT OF LIGHT

HALO®
POINT OF LIGHT

KELLY GAY

BASED ON THE BESTSELLING VIDEO GAME FOR XBOX

G

GALLERY BOOKS

New York London Toronto Sydney New Delhi

G

Gallery Books
A Division of Simon & Schuster, Inc.
1230 Avenue of the Americas
New York, NY 10020

First Gallery Books trade paperback edition March 2021

GALLERY BOOKS and colophon are registered trademarks of Simon & Schuster, Inc.

For information about special discounts for bulk purchases, please contact Simon & Schuster Special Sales at 1-866-506-1949 or business@simonandschuster.com.

The Simon & Schuster Speakers Bureau can bring authors to your live event. For more information or to book an event, contact the Simon & Schuster Speakers Bureau at 1-866-248-3049 or visit our website at www.simonspeakers.com.

Manufactured in the United States of America

10   9   8   7   6   5   4   3

Library of Congress Cataloging-in-Publication Data is available.

ISBN 978-1-9821-4786-0
ISBN 978-1-9821-4787-7 (ebook)

Hello again, Reclaimer

PROLOGUE

"**F**ind what's missing. Fix the path. Right what my kind turned wrong."

I have rolled these three sentences, these twelve words, in and around and through my internal processes like nimble, devoted fingers on prayer beads, coaxing out their secrets and meanings, wading neck-deep into an ancient past clogged with wrongs.

They are simple words, mostly unremarkable on their own, but strung together exponentially problematic.

An imprint of the Librarian, the esteemed ancient Forerunner, the Lifeshaper, with her uncanny ability to anticipate and plan and manipulate Living Time, gifted me these words and a key a year ago deep inside a mountain in Africa. Had I known then what it led to, I might not have taken it.

Her faith in me is both humbling and devastating.

After all this time, why couldn't she let me be?

Our old friends and enemies are gone. There is no one left to share in the shame of the past. No one left to shoulder the burden she places upon me. Nothing good can come from opening the deep, dark wounds of history.

Sometimes dipping your toe in still water does not go unnoticed.

A lesson taught to me by my mother over a thousand centuries ago in Marontik, along the mud banks of the slow river Sahti, where the crocodiles slumbered with one eye open.

Back then, I was Chakas. Back then, I was human, blissfully unaware on my backwater planet of Erde-Tyrene—Earth, as it is now known. Such brief time I had there . . . Before the Flood reemerged and threatened all sentient life. Before the Forerunners launched weapons of last resort to cleanse the galaxy. Before I was swept up into the fray, losing my humanity to become 343 Guilty Spark and tasked with firing one of those awful weapons and then monitoring it for the next one hundred thousand years alone.

Alone. Alone. Alone.

Waiting for life to creep back into a silent galaxy . . .

As I grew from child to man, I thought I knew better than to listen to silly warnings from my mother. Adventure, thieving, trickery, foolish bravery—those were the foods that nourished my soul, and I devoured them with enthusiasm, those wild and heedless thrills, which filled my lungs like a rare cold wind and left my skin tingling and my chest heaving.

For a very small speck of time, I knew what it was to be truly and recklessly and fragilely alive.

Until the young Forerunner Manipular, Bornstellar, arrived in Marontik seeking his own adventure and treasure. His presence ignited within me and my small Florian friend, Riser, a geas—genetically imprinted predispositions and commands placed in us since birth by the Librarian—to guide Bornstellar to Djamonkin Crater and release her husband, the dreaded Didact, from his cryptum.

Ancient gods playing games with mere mortals . . .

We were linked, the three of us, our fates entwined far more tightly along the world-line than any of us could have imagined.

And all that remains of us now is . . . me.

And while the thrills of my youth, the wind in my lungs, and the tingling of my skin are lost, never to be experienced again, only remembered and simulated, I endure. A superior artificial intelligence, now with my human memories restored, in command of a fully functioning armiger construct, one that gives me the body I lack and the ability to shape and mold and re-form to my liking.

She said I was a singular marvel, and she was right.

But what good is a singular marvel without a purpose?

A question I did not have to ponder long, apparently. She knew I would take up her cause before I knew myself—as all good mothers do.

If not me . . . then no one.

A dramatic sigh builds within me.

I went looking for a gift, and I got one. With it and those twelve words, along with a crew of human salvagers, and a hybrid starship, I am here.

We *are here.*

Gathered on the bridge of the Ace of Spades, *in the Sagittarius Arm of the Milky Way galaxy, staring beyond the floor-to-ceiling viewscreen at a monstrous technological wonder suspended in space and outlined in blue.*

I never wanted to see a Halo again.

Especially *this one.*

THREE WEEKS EARLIER

CHAPTER 1

There wasn't a single exhaust trail or cloud in the atmosphere, nothing to spoil the deepest blue sky in all the colonies. Field after field of intense green stretched in giant waves straight to the cobalt horizon. The wind rolling down from the highlands bent the tips of waist-high florus crops, revealing an emerald shimmer beneath slim upper leaves, a shimmer that mirrored the wind's path, racing up and down the hills like a shiny green ribbon loose in the breeze.

It was hypnotizing.

The scene soothed Rion Forge's soul. It was an affirmation and a reminder. She counted herself lucky to witness and explore far more of the galaxy than most ever would: the stars and their systems, planets and moons, biomes and landscapes, and plants that bowed to the wind and revealed their glittery underbelly. It had been easy to forget her passion for exploration and space when most of her time in the last year was spent running and grieving and trying not to get herself or her crew killed.

If only today were about exploration, and not the cold, hard truth. . . .

She wasn't sure which was more amazing—the view or that her mother had chosen to call this place home.

Laine Forge had never been a nature lover, never liked to take walks in the local park back home or get her hands dirty tending the few container plants Rion's granddad insisted on having around. Yet here she was, living her life in the very environment she'd always avoided. Granted, people changed all the time, but this change was hard for Rion to wrap her head around. That her mother had left Earth for an idyllist community on an Outer Colony ag planet made Rion realize that she might never have truly known her mother at all.

Rion shifted on the old Mongoose ATV to look behind her. The cargo bay doors were just closing, the *Ace of Spades* engaging her shiny new bafflers and rendering the ship nearly invisible. *Ace* was still the same sleek *Mariner*-class vessel she'd always been, but she'd also had one hell of a makeover, thanks to a Forerunner upgrade seed. The seed had been custom-designed by Spark to integrate Forerunner technologies with *Ace*'s existing framework and operating systems, creating a unique retrofit and comfortable user interface that gave Rion and her crew greater flexibility to navigate the stars quicker and more safely than ever before.

They'd set down on Sonata at the edge of a florus field, one of thousands, with a swath of dense forest at their backs. To the south, a dirt road edged the field and would eventually lead to the community where Laine lived on the outskirts. South was the way to go, but Rion couldn't seem to make the quad move.

Out in space, light-years from home, it was easy to lose track of those left behind, easy for the days and weeks to stretch into months and years. The longer the gap widened, the harder it became to reach out and reconnect, as though time created its own wall, every passing moment adding strength to a barrier that now seemed impossible to break.

She'd faced Brutes, hinge-heads, Hunters, and Jackals; toxic landscapes, mutiny, starvation; had built one of the most successful salvage operations along the Via Casilina, and yet she couldn't seem to muster the courage to put the damn quad in gear and face her mother. No matter how Rion spun it, there was no getting around it or out of it, no excuses good enough to abort this particular mission.

News like hers deserved to be heard face-to-face. Family to family.

Upon arrival in the Helice-12 star system, she and Spark had completed a sweep of the area and then a thorough evaluation of Sonata's orbital defenses and communications array. It was your standard Outer Colony complement for an agricultural world. Besides the population and pristine beauty—at least on this side of the planet—the real thing of value here was Florus Corp's one and only export—refined florus—which provided all-natural, good-for-you, non-glucose-based sweetener to the entire galaxy. Florus's green stalks had long ago been studied and synthesized, but those other competitors just couldn't compare to the organically grown real deal. And that only happened here in Sonata's rich blond soil, where Florus Corp reigned supreme.

Standard defenses or not, she and Spark had taken great care with their approach into the planet's atmosphere.

After fleeing Earth a year ago with what the Office of Naval Intelligence believed was *their* high-value asset, the organization had been relentless in their pursuit. Rion had no doubt that ONI had tracked down every member of her and the crew's families—friends, customers, rivals, all of them. Every known associate would have been interviewed and put through a series of neural markers and psych evaluations. Surveillance would have been initiated for a time and was perhaps still ongoing, depending on the relationship.

That's what happened when the newest member of your crew was an artificially enhanced human mind housed in a technologically advanced armiger construct. ONI knew him as 343 Guilty Spark, former monitor of a Halo installation. Rion and crew simply knew him as Spark, a being whose knowledge and abilities were unparalleled assets that any civilization would kill to get their hands on.

Now that the dust had settled, a few things were working in her favor. ONI would know based on interviews and interrogations that Rion hadn't seen her mother in sixteen years and that they hadn't spoken in twelve, and there was nothing to suggest a change in the status quo; the chances of her turning up here were slim to none.

And as broad and far-reaching as the UNSC's intelligence organization might be, ONI simply didn't have enough resources to station effective teams to monitor everyone known to Rion and her crew on a long-term basis. And they *certainly* couldn't sideline dozens of capable starships across Rion's vast stomping grounds in the hopes that one day she might turn up. It just wasn't feasible— the galaxy was too damn big to spread the fleet so thin.

A sleeper agent or two at prime locales was a possibility, but the most likely scenario was general surveillance via tech, paid informants, and locals. Good thing Rion had her own advanced surveillance. If anything should go wrong, any messages in the area sent, any ships suddenly dropping out of slipspace, Spark would initiate immediate evac. They'd be off planet and into slipspace before ONI had a chance to assemble.

In reality, though, Rion knew the biggest risk they faced from ONI was the hefty reward they were advertising across the galaxy. That kind of outsourcing was the real headache and caused all manner of self-serving opportunists and experienced pros to crawl out of the woodwork.

Another current of wind flowed in from behind her, the florus leaves bending once more to reveal their shiny underbelly, and off the ribbon of green raced. . . . She could watch the effect all day—and would if she could get away with it—but she had stalled long enough.

Putting the quad in gear, Rion began the journey south, and tried to focus on the pleasant feel of warm wind against her skin instead of her growing apprehension.

The small farmhouse was just off the road, set in the slope of a gentle hillside, behind a dark indigo-colored stone wall and a wide patch of short, leathery grass. White and pink cone-shaped flowers lined the front of the house, the blooms brushing against the windowsills. The residence was made of the same striated indigo stone as the wall. Wispy green bushes and potted flowers were set on either side of a sturdy pale-wood door.

In the sloping yard, a pair of overalls, three towels, and a white blanket hung on lines strung between two T-shaped poles. There wasn't a vehicle parked in the dirt driveway, though she spied two old ag-carts in the shed as she pulled in, parked, and cut the quad's engine.

The simplicity was staggering.

For a long time, Rion stared at the house, preparing what she'd say and working up the courage to do what needed to be done.

John Forge, United Nations Space Command Marine Corps sergeant, crew member on the *Phoenix*-class warship *Spirit of Fire*, son, husband, father . . . was gone.

He'd been gone for a very long time.

In the early stages of the Covenant War, the *Spirit of Fire* had pursued a Covenant destroyer into slipspace and was never seen or heard from again. For the next twenty-six years, its disappearance remained a mystery, a thorn in the heart and soul of every family member of those eleven thousand crewmembers on board.

But the *Spirit* hadn't been lost with all hands like the UNSC told the families years ago. The crew had survived the journey through slipspace and come out the other side to a Forerunner shield world, one that held an entire fleet of technologically advanced warships sought by the Covenant. Had the enemy acquired that ancient fleet, it would've ended the war before it ever really began. Humanity wouldn't have stood a chance.

If things had felt off the last few months—and they certainly had—it was because Rion had little interest in this new reality. At least in the previous reality her father was out there somewhere, still alive, still existing among the same stars and systems that she did. There was comfort in that. Far more than she'd realized.

Leaving Earth, running with pirates, scavenging the leftovers of one battle after another, buying her own ship, becoming a respectable salvage captain . . . the good and the bad—it all began with John Forge. Sharing the news of his passing, putting the words and knowledge out there, was final and irrevocable.

And delaying the inevitable was only making her nerves worse.

Resolved, she swung her leg over the seat, hopped off the quad, and straightened her shoulders before heading around to the front door.

As she cleared the corner, a woman appeared around the other side of the house.

Rion froze at the sight of Laine Forge.

Aging, she had expected, but this version of her mother had done a complete one-eighty. Gone was the carefully cultured city girl, and in her place was an overall-wearing, loose-braid-over-one-shoulder, bare-arms-with-biceps, middle-aged farmer with a steely glint in her eyes, no makeup, and a smudge of dirt on her brow.

Laine's step faltered at Rion's sudden appearance and her face drained of color. "Lucy?"

Clearing the tightness from her throat, Rion dipped her head in greeting, surprised she'd managed to hear her given name over the pounding of her heart. "Hey, Mom."

CHAPTER 2

When Rion dressed that morning, she'd stared at her reflection, trying to see her adult self through her mother's eyes. A teenager's face no more, but one hardened by time and conflict. Frown and laugh lines had worked their way into smooth skin. Bright, hopeful eyes were now jaded by life experience. Her lithe body had become hard and solid and strong. And there were scars too. Plenty of those to go around . . .

Rion had chosen her worn-out fatigue trousers, utility belt, and light jacket over a tank top, braided her long dark hair into a low knot, and armed herself with the usual light accompaniment: utility knife, stun gun, and M6.

Tiny green songbirds with blue beneath their wings flitted back and forth from the two blond-barked trees near the house, furiously chattering, singing, and bringing much-needed noise to the silence that stretched between mother and daughter.

Seeming to recover from the shock, Laine moved toward the front door with a stiff gait. "What are you doing here?"

A warm welcome wasn't expected, but Rion had hoped for one nevertheless. She wanted to smile, to laugh, to breathe easier and know her mother had missed her or was at least glad to see her.

But there was no hug. No smile. No gladness.

Laine gestured to the front door. "Here, why don't you come inside." She continued to stare at Rion with confusion, as though she couldn't believe what she was seeing.

Rion ducked through the doorway into a small, well-built house with an open concept—small living room to the left, stairs in the center, and to the right a kitchen, which Laine entered, going to the sink to wash her hands. After drying them on a dish towel, she turned and gave Rion the once-over. "Last time I saw you in person, you were just a girl."

"I was sixteen."

Laine leaned against the sink and reiterated her point, "Like I said . . . ," though Rion hadn't been disputing it. "What are you, thirty . . . three now, right?" Rion dipped her head as Laine's gaze became more critical. "You look like him," she noted. "Even more now than you did back then. You always carried yourself like him too. Like a soldier."

If only those words were a compliment or simple observation, but Rion knew them as the insult they were. Turning tail and getting back to the quad was starting to look like an excellent idea.

Laine's eyes softened somewhat. "Please. Sit down. I just made some fresh *agani* juice. We grow them here on the farm." She picked a green fruit from a bowl on the wood counter and tossed it.

Rion caught the small oval on the fly. It fit neatly into the palm of her hand, the fruit's rind thin and covered in tiny dull spikes. She brought it to her nose and caught the scent of citrus and lemon and apple all rolled into one.

"It's like a lime, only sweeter. Do you remember . . . ?"

"Granddad used to bring limes home from the commissary

every once in a while." A rare treat. "Don't think I've had one since." Rion rolled the *agani* around in her palm, watching as Laine retrieved a glass pitcher from the counter and poured two glasses of a pale liquid. "So, Sonata," Rion said, attempting to fill the quiet with idle conversation. "Didn't peg you for a farmer."

Laine set the glasses on the table and pulled out a chair. "Didn't peg you for a wanted criminal, but here we are."

Nice to see her mother's comeback game was still going strong. Rion sat and tried the drink, finding it more sour than she expected.

Laine snorted. "You get used to it."

"If you say so. I hope the authorities didn't cause you too much trouble."

"They were . . . thorough. Not like I had much to tell them." Laine shrugged. "Barely know you anymore and said as much. So what did you do? They wouldn't say."

"They claim I took something that belonged to them."

"Did you?"

"What I took was never theirs to begin with, so, no, not really."

As Rion took another sip, Laine's expression grew shrewd. "Why are you here now, after all this time? If you think I'm going to hide you or have the money to—"

The sip went down with a cough. "I have more than enough money. And the entire galaxy at my disposal. Believe me, there are better places to hide than this."

Stay calm. Don't let her get to you. Rion eased her grip on the glass. She'd learned a long time ago how to let Laine's comments bounce off—simply stop caring and the easier it was to exist in the same space as her mother. How stupid of her to hope things would be different, that time might have dulled the sharp edges. . . .

She steadied herself and got on with it. "I have some news. About Dad."

Laine's whole body stilled. Several seconds passed before she shifted back in her chair and let out a sharp, disappointed laugh, as though Rion had failed some test she hadn't known she was taking. "Suppose I shouldn't be surprised that *he's* the one to get you here. Always him . . ."

It didn't have to be that way.

It was on the tip of her tongue to voice the thought, to remind her mother that, *Yes, it was always him, because you chose to keep me at arm's length.*

"He's dead then, I take it."

A gasp escaped before Rion could stop it. Her heart gave a hard, painful bang. She stared straight ahead, in total disbelief, wondering if those words uttered so offhandedly had really just come out of her mother's mouth.

Laine's shoulders slacked and guilt clouded her eyes, showing a sliver of humanity at least. "I knew if I ever laid eyes on you again, it'd be one of two things. Either you found him, or he's truly gone. And by the look on your face . . ." Abruptly Laine stood. "Is that all, then?"

"Isn't that enough? Don't you want to know what happened, how he died?"

"Lucy." A tired expression crossed her mother's face and seeped into her tone. "Your father died a long time ago. I've made my peace with it."

"Yes, I know you have. You never believed he might have survived, never had the tiniest bit of hope."

"Because I used it all up year after year when he was off on deployment, when I thought he'd change his ways." Grief and emotion warred with anger, anger at admitting she felt anything at all. "I gave every last bit of hope I had to that man, so, no . . . I had nothing left after he went missing."

And you had nothing left for me either.

"He died saving the crew. . . ."

"I don't want to hear it. I'm plenty busy right n—"

Rion lurched to her feet, her chair scraping loudly. Her father deserved acknowledgment. He deserved to have everyone know of his sacrifice, not to have his memory cast aside so readily. And damned if she was going to stand by and say nothing.

"Your husband—my *father*—stayed behind on an alien world and manually detonated the *Spirit of Fire*'s fusion reactor to destroy a fleet of enemy warships that most likely would have led to our extinction. He saved you . . . me . . . and everyone else in this goddamn galaxy. You can hate him all you want, but it will *never* change the fact that he was a hero, and a good father."

The bang of a side door echoed from down the hallway. Loud footsteps preceded a tall kid with disheveled sandy-brown hair and grease-stained overalls. He drew up short as he entered the kitchen. The easy half grin he wore died as he glanced from Laine to Rion. The pause lasted only a few seconds before he continued into the room, first going to Laine and kissing her cheek, then opening the refrigerator door and pulling out a can.

He popped his drink and drank deeply before eyeing them again.

Clarity snapped through Rion like lightning. Laine actually had the nerve to look irritated as the kid finished his drink in long, thirsty gulps. He swiped his forearm across his mouth, then regarded them both with curiosity.

A second later, he choked and coughed. "Oh, shit. Is this her?"

Laine's frown worsened.

He moved closer and stared eye level at Rion, thoroughly and unabashedly. A wide smile spread across his face and into his eyes. "My big sister—we meet at last."

It felt like the whole goddamn planet had flipped upside down, then right side up.

Laine went to the sink. "You might have known about it had you ever kept in touch."

"Pretty sure it works both ways," Rion responded without missing a beat. "Had I gotten married or had a child, I sure as hell would have shared that with you. Not waited you out to see if you'd ever contact me again so I could drop the news."

"I think that's my cue to leave," the kid said slowly. "Nice to finally meet you. You're taller than I thought you'd be. . . . I'll be in the shed," he told Laine as he left the kitchen.

The room went silent. The outside door banged. The birds' relentless chatter beyond the kitchen window filled the space once more. Now that he was gone, the revelation, the *betrayal*, began to sink in. Rion's emotional fortitude was shot, leaving her raw and exposed. How could one person be so unbelievably spiteful?

"So . . . how old is he?"

"Sixteen."

The answer shouldn't have hurt more than anything else that had transpired so far, but it did. "You were pregnant when I left home?"

"Ran away."

"What?"

"You ran away from home. Don't say *left* like you were going on some extended trip or off to college."

"So what, this is payback? I ran away, so you cut me out of all the important events in your life?"

"You left me, Lucy. Just like your father did. And I don't owe either of you anything."

And there it was—the truth, settling hard and ugly right in those raw spots. "I was just a kid—your *daughter* . . ." Not some shrink who could've seen and understood her mother's pain.

All this time, she'd thought she was alone, an only child. Maybe she would've kept in touch more if she'd known. . . .

Her mother seemed to read her mind. "Don't do that."

"Do what?"

"Pretend you'd have been any different if you knew. You still would've stayed away. You think I wanted my son to pine for his big sister the way I did for your father? To know you, only to watch you go away over and over again and wonder why 'up there' meant more to you than the people down here?"

"You don't know that."

"Yes, I do. And so do you, if you want to be honest with yourself."

"I gave you my waypoint. You never once left a message in all these years, that you left Earth, that you had a new family—not *once*." Not even the last time they'd spoke. Goddammit, now her eyes were starting to sting. "Dad is gone," she said, suddenly overwhelmed and tired and not knowing what else to say. "I just wanted to let you know." She made for the door, but hesitated. Her mother didn't reply. "Take care, Mom."

Every step out to the quad became a mantra. *Stay calm. Don't let her get to you.* One thing Rion knew for certain: she was never readier to get off solid ground.

Her new half-brother was pushing one of the old ag-carts she'd seen earlier from the shed into the driveway. He stopped when he saw her approach. "You leaving?"

She gestured to the vehicle. "She's seen better days." The single operator's seat was in the back left of the vehicle overlooking a wide flat bed in the front. Carts like this one were used all over the colonies, for a variety of purposes.

"Big on understatements, are we?" He grinned. "Your quad has some age on her too. Straight M247 . . . guessing '42 or '43?"

One had to be a true wheel hound to know the variants down to the year. "Impressive. She's a '43. Can definitely take a beating."

"I can tell." He reached into the bed and pulled a toolbox to the edge. "Don't mind her, okay? She's always been a hard-ass."

Even though he was young, he had an easy way about him that reminded her of Cade. Like her former first mate, he wasn't afraid to really look at a person, to see past the clutter and to the heart of the matter.

"If you want to know," he continued, "she did miss you. I mean, she'd die before admitting it, but it's true. That's how I found out about you—caught her looking at old photo logs a while back. Told me all about you and your dad, about how he went missing and you took off to find him. . . . *Did* you? Find him, I mean."

A well of grief rose up, but Rion managed a weak smile. "Took a couple decades . . . but, yeah, I found him." And in the process lost Cade, the man she might've spent the rest of her life with.

"So what you're saying is you suck at finding things."

Her laugh was instantaneous. If only the kid knew that's how she made her living. "Yeah . . . you could say that."

A sheepish grin tugged at his lips. "Sorry. You looked so sad."

It was sweet of him to cheer her up.

"You gonna come back, now that you know about me?"

"I would like to. . . ."

"Well, if you do or you don't . . ." He reached into his pocket and tossed her a cheap data chip. "Here's my info. Message me sometime, if you want." He tipped his gaze to the sky. "Always wanted to see what it's like up there . . ."

"You've never been off world before? Even in orbit?"

"I wish. It's not like we have a ship and fuel just lying around. No one around here has that kind of money." *I do*, she wanted to say, gripped with the sudden desire to give the kid anything he asked for. "Who knows—maybe one day, she'll let me go for a spin with you. . . ."

Their amusement ran parallel, both knowing Laine would never allow it.

"You should probably head off now," he said with a slight wince. "And please don't hold it against her. I think she thinks she's doing you a favor."

"What do you mean?"

"Those guys from ONI. They came by a while back; seven or eight months ago now, I guess it was, put the whole community through interrogation—no, no, it wasn't like that," he hurried to assure her. "It was the most interesting thing that's ever happened around here, trust me. Well . . . except for today. They gave her a transponder to use if you ever showed up. I'm guessing she hit it the minute you came outside."

"They have people nearby?"

"They used to, but gave up after a few months. No surprise— too boring out here. They have an office up in Lanchessa, so I'm guessing it'll take them another fifteen, twenty minutes to get here, give or take."

As Rion absorbed that bit of news, he reached across the quad and held out his hand. She took it, holding on for a moment, connecting. "Glad we finally met," he said.

"So am I."

They let go, and he went to grab a wrench from the toolbox when she realized something completely obvious had been forgotten. "Hey. I just realized I don't even know your name."

"Oh, yeah, sorry. It's Cayce."

"Cayce." She gave him a smile and a nod. "See you around, kid."

"Hope so."

CHAPTER 3

ONI Axon Relay D-2713 / Lanchessa / Sonata / Helice-12 System

The alert blared from the comms console, waking Crewman Lowell from his afternoon nap with all the shock of a cold-water dousing. His entire body jerked, feet coming off the console so quickly it almost sent him backward in his chair.

The alarm never went off.

Shit!

The alarm never went off.

He steadied his shock. The moment had come. The very reason he'd been reassigned to this mind-numbingly boring outpost in the first place. He grabbed the console and pulled himself close to scan the data populating across the screen.

"Steady now, Lowell," he muttered.

Damned if he'd mess up his chance at redemption. Not when Rion Forge was being served up on a silver platter. Quickly, he entered a command to connect the station with the closest orbiting GPS satellite and then followed up with coordinates to find his target. Real-time satellite images built on a second screen, and soon Lowell found the Mongoose parked in the farmhouse's driveway, along with two individuals, one male and one female, standing with an old ag-cart between them.

Despite his shaky hands, his fingers flew across the panel, alerting the main office and then entering engagement codes to activate HI-JACK Protocol. Once codes were entered, Lowell stilled and waited for Bullet to come online, his eyes glued to the screen, heart racing.

Green reception. Bullet was hot.

He entered coordinates to target the Mongoose.

The miniature stealth drone installed on the farmhouse's roof—one of three placed around the community—had only one job: to tag whatever Lowell told it to.

As the female began to move toward the Mongoose, Lowell's finger hovered over the firing command. "Not yet . . ." He zoomed in with Bullet's targeting vector. A few steps more and the wanted salvage captain was throwing her leg over the vehicle. From the satellite's position, he could only see one of her hands grip the handlebars, but that was all he needed—that and the puff of exhaust as she started the quad.

"Fire."

Tag employed.

His heart was racing.

There seemed to be no reaction on the ground. The quad reversed and left the driveway. Adhesion was good. The tag had found its home.

Going dark in three . . . two . . . one.

And done.

"Holy hell." With a resounding exhale, Lowell leaned back and linked his fingers behind his head. He'd played his part, and now it was up to the technology in orbit to do the rest.

The main Lanchessa office had already scrambled the one light prowler they had at their disposal. If it reached the *Ace of Spades* in time, it would be a miracle.

Not that it mattered. He knew the real miracle was HIJACK, specifically designed with that rogue salvaging ship in mind. The ins-and-outs were far above Lowell's pay grade, but he did know ONI was playing the long game and deploying Bullet was only step one.

And he'd done his job perfectly.

Now maybe he could get the hell out of this crap assignment and back to doing something worthwhile.

CHAPTER 4

Bungalow 14 / Lapis Bay Resort / Emerald Cove / Alpha Imura System

Niko knew one day his past would come back to haunt him. He'd always had a feeling, a strange sense of knowing, or more to the point, he knew the odds. And every once in a while, it sucked being right.

His leaving Aleria hadn't been forgotten. Courier guilds weren't known for letting even the slightest snub go unpunished. One way or another, eventually, everyone paid their price. Cross Cut was especially diligent in that regard, and Niko had done more than simply snub his old guild; he'd left with unfinished business, unpaid debts, and unfulfilled contracts.

His absence had been a huge blow to the guild. Valuable folks with advanced tech experience like his were rare in a place like Aleria. There were no advantages for educated scientists and researchers and technicians to relocate to a drought-ridden, dying world with a collapsing government, abandoned by the Unified Earth Government, with no real prospects of rejuvenation. So the guilds recruited from the existing population to run the trade and manage their fleets of slipspace-capable starships. If someone like Niko wasn't there to maintain and repair drives and fusion engines, the guilds' entire livelihood ground to a halt.

Lessa had just returned from shopping and was now in her room packing. Ram was on the wraparound balcony of their treetop bungalow, his rocker moving back and forth, his tanned bare feet propped on the railing, a fine tendril of cigarette smoke trailing up past his tattooed shoulder. The view beyond the balcony was holocard perfect—clear turquoise water as far as the eye could see, dotted by sails from a dozen leisure craft, and framed on both sides by steep forested slopes. Their unit had the best comms signal and the easiest escape route should they need it.

And they wouldn't.

Still. It was hard to be relaxed and enjoy this last day in paradise because his heart was pounding and his knee wouldn't quit bouncing. He'd already bitten all of his fingernails to the quick and couldn't shake the agitated energy running through his body. They had an hour before meeting the *Ace of Spades* at the rendez-vous point, and he needed to figure this out.

Three years ago, he and Lessa had left Aleria in a hurry following the promise of a better life, a freer life, one with prospects as part of Rion's crew. They weren't hustlers anymore or slaves to the mines or indentured to the guilds. They could leave *Ace* whenever they wanted and plot their destinies as they saw fit. In Triniel, they had an entire hidden and untouched Forerunner planet as a source of immeasurable wealth should ever they need it, and in Spark they had a nigh-invulnerable ally and a mind rich in Forerunner locations and information and technology.

Aleria had held no future for them. It never would. It was in its death throes, and everyone knew it. Yet here he was, being called back home. No, more like *blackmailed* back home, and he wasn't sure what to do about it.

He ran a hand down his scruffy face and let out a troubled sigh. Less would worry her curls straight out if he told the truth. Rion and Spark would want to go fix things immediately. And Ram? He'd probably vote to take a hit out on the blackmailer and call it a day.

The problem was, Niko had a history with the blackmailer, and allowing anyone to help him meant revealing a truth he'd sworn would never get out. And, unfortunately, Bex knew it.

After creating a temporary backdoor access into his old Waypoint profile, one that ONI was monitoring, along with all the others, he'd found the message waiting in his mail folder. Innocuous, but he had read between the lines, saw Bex's alias, and knew where to go to get the real message.

Another server. Another account. Another back door. Simple enough.

And there it was, straight from the one person he never imagined would turn on him and use the truth against him, especially for her Courier guild, Holson Relay. He supposed he couldn't blame her. He'd left without so much as a good-bye, though he had tried to make amends over the last couple of years, to keep in touch.

But his attempts paled against the fact that he had gotten away from Aleria and Bex hadn't. They'd been partners of a sort, Holson Relay and Cross Cut aligning for a time. She'd been their resident tech expert and he'd been theirs.

If Bex didn't get the tech she was asking for now, she threatened to spill the truth they'd uncovered and it soured his gut. They'd made a pact. How could she have swung a one-eighty so quickly?

He had one month to get his hands on a bank of midsize

slipspace capacitors. Talk about one hell of a deadline. Too pricey to buy outright . . . though, if he gathered his income from the Forerunner tech they'd sold earlier in the year along with a loan, he might be able to pull it off. But even then, he'd have to forge the necessary paperwork and bypass sales regulations. There wasn't time to go to Triniel, salvage, and then sell the goods to raise funds. Nor was there time to recover a bank of capacitors from salvaging a decent wreck. The black market was looking like his best option.

Or you could ask for help . . .

No. He had a good situation now. The best, in fact. He wasn't going to jeopardize it by letting the truth get out. Sometimes you had to hold those past deeds and truths close to your chest, bury them down deep where no one could find them, where they'd be forgotten, where it was better for everyone.

After burning his trail, Niko used a new encryption key to make a new account, addressed a reply to Bex, and hit send.

Fine. I'll do it.

He burned the account and prayed to God this was a onetime deal. He sat back in his chair, wanting to vomit.

CHAPTER 5

Ace of Spades / Slipspace to Emerald Cove

Like faint breath on the back of one's neck, I feel them.

I know they are there.

Not errant bits of data or misplaced logs. They are old memories, I am sure of it. So old I am certain they do not belong to me.

At times, quite suddenly and unexpectedly, these deep things will stir and stretch, about to wake and reveal themselves only to settle back down to their slumber and deny me once again.

Such inability to recall that which I know is there is completely unacceptable. It prompts me to run diagnostics and sector scans to no avail.

During my transformation from human to machine, Bornstellar said I was becoming a keeper of the biological records of my race. "That seemed the best way to salvage your memories and your intellect, and to safely contain the most dangerous components of the Librarian's experiments."

For so long these words were forgotten. Now I ponder them, and their meaning, more and more.

Patience, however, is the key. More or less.

Waiting—though I never liked to do so in any form, human or ancilla—has become a special talent of mine. Patience never fails to produce the response I desire. This would be true for most beings, but then, most beings are biological and, sadly, they simply run out of time.

This musing gives me pause.

I might, once again, outlive the majority of life in the galaxy— a quite conceivable and troubling notion, one I do not wish to repeat.

Or . . . do I?

All this knowledge and power curtailed in order to exist in this technologically unimpressive time period. Perhaps the next age will be more challenging, and I should indeed practice patience. . . .

Rion enters the bridge with a cup of steaming drink, Casbah coffee, no doubt—it is her favorite. She sets it on the arm of her captain's chair and then walks to the navigation console to check on our progress before settling down in her seat.

She will die too.

I will surpass her and the rest of the crew as I have surpassed everyone else.

There is a quickening in me. It races through my core like a static charge burning a painful path. I am reminded of pain and loss and do not want to experience these things again.

Not ever again.

"So . . . ," *Rion says with a wry smile.* "You summoned me."

"Yes. Precisely thirty-eight minutes ago."

She sips her beverage. "This about the key?"

"Of course it is." *The holo image of said object has been hovering above the tactical table for the last thirty-eight minutes. Clearly she can see it.* "I'm glad you find this amusing. You were napping."

"Power nap. We mere humans need our rest. Believe me"—*she shifts in her seat to get more comfortable*—"after the morning I just had, I needed it."

She has yet to divulge events on Sonata, but I have decided against pushing her too fast simply to appease my curiosity, though I am sorely tested. Perhaps after my appeal . . .

"Thought you'd have that symbol figured out by now." She gestures to the slim rectangular device given to me by the Librarian's imprint during our trip to Earth. A key, one with very curious properties.

"Still a coordinate key?" she asks.

I walk my holographic avatar around the key. "Yes . . ."

"But . . ."

"It bears the hallmarks of one, yes, but it is far more than that." I magnify the key's image. It hovers there, marvelous in design and ominous in meaning. Its beauty and the pain it brings me are undeniable.

Done with such care and exquisite simplicity, it is unusual, graceful, and refined, and I clearly see the Librarian's hand in its making. "It is the key of a Lifeworker, to be sure," I say. "Clean quantum code written into hard-light filaments, which run through machine-cell alloy similar to my own. This allows the key to reshape itself. As you may recall, some months ago, Lessa's handling of the key inadvertently triggered a command. One length of it"—I move the hologram and show the precise area—"collapsed inward by twelve millimeters to form an outline of this symbol."

The symbol, an old sigil, might be forgotten by time, but not by me.

If I had a soul, it would bear this brand.

And yet, this is what the Librarian asks of me. Always the hardest things.

"It is a mark of identification," I continue. "An old, forgotten symbol given to one of the Master Builder's war machines before it was modified and assigned a new mark—a new sigil that it bears to this day."

Rion leans forward in her seat. It is about time she shows interest. "Are you telling me that symbol belongs to a Halo?"

I am pleased she remembered the stories I have shared.

There can be no war machines championed by the Forerunner known as the Master Builder other than Halo. They were his egregious yet ultimately successful legacy.

The captain sits back, properly stunned.

"We did have a deal," *I remind her. Another one. We were fond of making deals, she and I.* "I was to aid in the search for the Spirit of Fire *for six months*"—*I can be quite charitable when the occasion calls*—"and if nothing was forthcoming and I was ready, we would turn to my key."

"I wouldn't say nothing was forthcoming. What about Oban? Those Vultures and Sparrowhawks weren't nothing."

Even I had been hopeful. To discover a group of support ships in such pristine condition, the same variants in Spirit of Fire's *complement, was a stroke of luck. The sale in the Oban market went to an Insurrectionist, but our goal was not to buy—it was simply to get close enough to access the crafts' system logs. All wiped clean, but they did bear corresponding serial numbers to those assigned to the missing UNSC warship.*

"And then backtracking their provenance," *I reply. Four and a half months chasing phantoms. Another great disappointment.*

That frustration, felt by all, led to a respite. The crew went to Emerald Cove, and I accompanied Rion to Sonata.

There is no better time than now to begin our journey.

Rion regards me for quite some time, and though she appears dubious, it is clear she will honor our agreement. "You said the key led to a safe place. You didn't say anything about a Halo."

"Upon initial examination, that was my assumption . . . my hope. I thought perhaps the key pointed to a shield world, one that I had only heard about in whispers."

One that might grant me access to the Domain, among other things.

The captain releases a long sigh before cupping her mug with both hands and sipping. Eventually she acquiesces. "A side trip might liven things up a bit."

"It is apparent you can use a distraction."

"Thanks." Her tone is flat and without an ounce of gratitude. "You'll have to put together one hell of a preliminary brief. If we can't get in and out clean and safe, it's a no-go."

"I would be happy to." I watch her a moment longer. She relaxes back in her chair, suddenly far away.

Several hours have passed since we departed Sonata for our slip-space route to Emerald Cove, and now I must know. "Would you like to discuss your time on Sonata?"

My query brings her back from wherever her mind wandered. A faint grimace tells me it might be a conversation she would rather not have, which only fuels my curiosity. "Your demeanor suggests things did not go as planned?"

A soft snort is her initial response, but then her dark eyes settle on my avatar. "You had family, when you were human, sisters."

Even more curious now, I tilt my head. "Yes. Three of them."

"Were you close?"

"They were much older." Retrieving their distinct features is now impossible—those recollections are long gone. What remains are shadows, brief smudges, images seen across a crowded Marontik street, heads bowed, walking together toward the temple, the distortion of heat and dust in the air. "Sent to serve in the Librarian's temple when I was a boy."

While her expression is contemplative, it does not hide the turmoil and hurt surrounding her. And I believe I understand. "You have family, besides your mother."

A low hum of affirmation vibrates her throat. "I do now, apparently."

"And you did not before?"

"Surprise." Her attempt at sarcasm is halfhearted at best. "I have a half-brother, sixteen years old. My mother remarried, I guess? Maybe. I don't even know . . . we didn't get into it."

"I presume it was not a happy reunion, then."

"How do you keep something like that from someone?" Her confusion weighs heavily on this question. Indeed, it is a difficult thing to understand.

I think of my own mother, a hazier memory than that of my siblings. I barely recall my early family life; so much of it was spent running through the streets, no care to my safety or well-being. . . . Though I do recall her linen dress and ruddy blue apron, the basket she always carried held to her stomach as she bent over to help me up, the sun behind her. . . .

Though her face is in shadow, I know she was smiling.

How can I comfort Rion or offer words of wisdom when I too do not fully understand the motivations of mothers (both supreme and biological) or why they shape outcomes the way they do?

"There is not always a logical answer for the things people do when they care—or when they don't. . . . I wish I had more to offer."

"Well, I appreciate the thought." Her attention zeroes in on me, her eyes narrowing. "Do you dream?"

The question is quite unexpected.

If dreaming is memory, if it is hearing lost voices, seeing pieces of a past not my own, then: "In a manner, yes. Why do you ask?"

"I dream of her. Not my mother. The Librarian."

"Does she speak to you?"

"No. She's just working in a garden, going down rows of . . . I don't know, some kind of flowers or plants . . . stopping to nurture them, speak to them, prop one up, or pull a withered leaf from another."

The imagery builds in my mind. At her core, at the core of every Forerunner who took the rate of Lifeworker, lay an innate desire to preserve and nurture, to study and intimately understand the nature of all life.

"When did the dreaming begin?"

"Africa. After we left Kilimanjaro."

"Ah." It explains much. "All humans retain some level of genetic memory and geas manipulation, passed down through generations, which stretch clear back to the first humans reseeded onto Earth after the firing of the Halo Array. Perhaps the imprint that appeared in Africa triggered an aspect of a long-existing geas in your family tree or is simply the leftover recognition pattern the Librarian once placed in all of her human populations at birth."

"How do I tell the difference—if it's just my dream state at work or some genetic coding making me see certain things?"

An alert pings the bridge.

While information flows to me instantly, I do not interrupt as Rion drains her mug and checks the datapad at her seat. "We'll be dropping out of slipspace soon." She rises to exit the bridge. "Once we pick up the crew, we'll see about your key."

"Thank you, Captain."

CHAPTER 6

Ace of Spades / **High Orbit above Emerald Cove**

Lessa hated leaving Emerald Cove, but like Niko and Ram, she was happy to reunite with the captain and Spark and be back on board *Ace*. After their reunion, and a quick lunch together in the lounge, they'd gone their separate ways while she remained, curled up in one of the ship's lounge chairs, a commpad on her lap as she scrolled through her options. Excitement and guilt tangled in her chest.

Option one was to keep traveling the stars with her brother and Rion, with Ram, and Spark—her family. The other option was to live a *very* different life, one she'd dreamed of since she was a young girl eking out a life in the slums of Aleria with Niko.

She'd narrowed her search to two universities: Escada U and Baker-Verding. For kicks, she added the wild-card, never-in-a-million-years University of Edinburgh. The imposing buildings and manicured lawns, the smiling faces of students and teachers caught in frozen moments of educational bliss—none of it seemed real. It was more alien to her than run-ins with Sangheili bounty hunters and Kig-Yar pirates, or living on a ship with an ancient Forerunner AI.

As was so often the case after scrolling through college galleries and guides, her excitement soured. Who the hell was she kidding?

A year-plus after salvaging Spark from Geranos-a, right under the high-and-mighty Office of Naval *Intelligence*'s nose, and then sneaking through Home Fleet's defenses to find the Librarian's imprint on Earth, their faces were *still* being plastered all over Inner and Outer Colony waypoints and every other media outlet ONI could influence with their lies.

Their names had become synonymous with outlaw, renegade, wanted criminal. Crimes against the UEG, they said. Rewards issued across the colonies.

Ridiculous. All of it.

Still, if she wanted it badly enough, she could change her appearance and get Niko and Spark to work their magic with documents and IDs down to fooling DNA readers and bio scanners. She was one young woman in a galaxy of billions. Hiding in plain sight as a college student would be the easy part.

But, it wasn't ONI or bounties that worried her; it was making the decision itself, leaving the crew or going to school. After everything Rion had done for her, how could she just take off? *See you later, thanks for everything?*

It didn't feel right. But neither did turning her back on her dreams.

With a sigh, she powered off her pad and stared beyond the lounge's viewscreen, where an arc of Emerald Cove still dominated the bottom corner. She'd never tire of planetary blues and greens. Not when all she had grown up with was dust. Crewing with Rion had allowed her to see so many amazing things. She'd been to Earth. *Earth!* Colonists lived their whole lives, families went from generation to generation, without ever getting to visit the homeland.

A flash of light caught her eye as Spark appeared over the holo-pad inlaid in the center of the lounge's main dining and meeting table. His avatar was an exact copy of the physical armiger construct usually confined to the cargo hold, only this one was scaled down to a little over half a meter tall. Glowing blue eyes and a sleek silver-alloy head turned in her direction, dipping in recognition.

Spark tilted his head suddenly, as though he heard something. "Everything okay?"

"Yes . . . ," he answered, rather slowly.

His avatar appeared a little different from the last time she'd seen him, though she couldn't quite put her finger on any one thing in particular. The first time she'd seen him, he'd been a pile of black alloy parts, pinged and scratched and damaged.

Salvaged from Geranos-a, he'd given them one hell of a surprise when he reassembled in *Ace*'s hold, hard-light technology pulling the floating parts together into a menacing three-meter-tall Forerunner soldier called an armiger—a deadly sniper variant. An amazing salvage find on its own, but far more extraordinary was what had found refuge inside the damaged armiger shell—the former Halo monitor 343 Guilty Spark.

Over time, he had slowly transformed the armiger's appearance thanks to the machine cells in the construct's alloy, which allowed form manipulation. The soldier variant had given way to a sleek, futuristic-looking advanced alien intelligence.

"When are you going to tell them?" he asked. "Have you decided?"

Her mouth opened to deny it, but what was the point? "I thought we all agreed there'd be no snooping."

He gestured to her commpad. "Snooping takes effort, Lessa. This did not."

Of all the pompous . . . "That's not the good excuse you think it is." But right now she didn't have the energy or the heart to lecture him about privacy. "Don't tell them, okay? I haven't decided anything yet." Embarrassment made her turn away. She felt stupid for even considering it. "I'm just . . . looking, dreaming maybe. I probably won't ever actually do it. . . ."

"Why not?"

"Well . . . because. I wouldn't want to—"

"Oh, good, you're both here." Rion entered the lounge with a brisk step. "Ram and Niko should be in any second." She got a drink from the dispenser and then focused on Spark. "All set?"

Lessa extracted herself from the cushy chair and moved to the table. "All set for what?"

Niko and Ram entered as Rion answered with a smile and a wink, "New mission."

Niko's frazzled appearance gave Rion a good chuckle. His dark hair was sticking out at all angles and hung well past his ears now. Recently he was given to tucking it behind his ears. "Wow. It's like you *weren't* just on the beach for eight days."

"Hey. This is my normal look."

"Deranged?"

"Ha *ha*. This is what hard work and *genius* looks like." His gaze briefly shifted to Spark's avatar. "Well . . . and *that*."

"I know you've been working hard. Just remember not to get your hopes up too high—"

"It's going to work." Niko glanced back to Spark for support. "Tell her."

It seemed a lifetime ago that they'd discovered the debris

field of Etran Harborage and salvaged the site's fragmented ancilla. Shortly after, ONI had swooped in, taking the ancilla they'd dubbed "Little Bit" as well as the projections he'd created on possible trajectories the *Spirit of Fire* might have taken after destroying the shield world. They'd lost most of their bank accounts, warehouses, Niko's research, data, and prototypes, and two decades of Rion's work searching for the *Spirit of Fire*.

Later on, they'd met with ONI in the town of Port Joy under rather dramatic circumstances and managed to get a few things returned, among them a data chip with Little Bit's projections. Not the originals, as desired, but copies. After cleaning the chip of ONI surveillance, it was put on the back burner until a few months ago, when they'd begun exploring the potential paths the *Spirit of Fire* might have taken.

It was a near-impossible task that turned up very little, so Spark began digging deeper into the projections, hoping to create new paths based on Little Bit's work . . . and he found a strange subcode in the chip's crystal matrix. One that suggested the fragmented ancilla had inadvertently sublayered traces of his own framework like puzzle pieces hidden within thousands of calculations.

And so began Spark and Niko's joint effort to liberate Little Bit's code from the chip without damaging the projections.

It was painstaking. They'd been at it for months.

"The probability grows," Spark answered. "I cannot say if what we liberate will be viable, but we are nearly finished with that part of the procedure. We must remember the effort is entirely experimental."

ONI had only returned a portion of what they'd taken from Niko, which had been a demoralizing blow for an imaginative mind like his. If resurrecting Little Bit's fragmented code fueled his creative drive and kept him happy, then Rion had no qualms with their side project.

Ram was the last one to saunter into the lounge, and Rion couldn't help but smile. "Now *there's* a person who's just been on vacation." He'd gotten a nice tan on top of his already rich olive complexion. Keeping her eyes on him, she reached over and slapped the coffee dispenser panel.

Ram ignored her and waited intently for his coffee, his unbound hair falling into his face. "Why does it always work for you?" he mumbled irritably.

"Because *she* loves me."

Ram wordlessly fixed the necessary wake-up beverage to his liking, then dragged out a chair and slid into it with the ease of a lazy cat, stretching out his forearms. She'd always been friends with the gruff salvage captain from Komoya—been rivals too, depending on the salvage—but his time crewing on the *Ace of Spades* had turned a mild friendship into something lasting and true. He'd become family.

"Glad to see everyone back on board," Rion began. And that was the truth. After the disastrous family reunion on Sonata, it felt good to be among those who would never let her down.

"You're coming next time," Lessa said. "The beach was amazing."

"Next time for sure." Rion extracted the Librarian's key from her pocket and set it on the table. "For now though we're going to see what *this* beauty unlocks."

All eyes went to the key. Lessa picked it up. "You figured out what it means?"

"Thanks to you, yes," Spark said. "The symbol revealed when you touched the key belongs to Halo Installation 07."

"No way." Niko sat up straight, eyes as big as plates. "We're going to a Halo? An actual Halo?" He looked around, hopeful, nearly bouncing in his chair as Spark replied in the affirmative.

"Wait," Lessa cut in, ever the thoughtful one. "But wasn't that where you said you—"

"Where I lost my body and became a machine," Spark answered. "That is correct. You may call it Zeta Halo."

Trying to determine the expression on a face made of metal and light was an exercise in futility, but after a year and change together, Rion had picked up on a few telltale gestures and tics—the way he moved his head, held his shoulders . . . For now, however, it seemed he was keeping his feelings on this Zeta Halo close to his chest.

Only a few years had gone by since this ancient being had regained his human memories. Learning a thousand centuries had passed and everyone you'd ever known, cared about, loved, and hated was gone forever would take time to reconcile. Where Spark stood mentally was anyone's guess, and traveling to Zeta Halo might either be a big mistake or give him the closure he deserved.

Rion stayed mum to allow the crew the opportunity to digest the idea. The news didn't seem to faze Ram at all; he was more interested in his coffee while Lessa gently rolled the key around in her hand, tracing the symbols. "So strange this is a key. . . . Do you know what it opens?"

"The Cartographer on Zeta Halo will tell us. It will read the key's coordinates and likely point the way to the proper location on the ring."

Ram perked up. "Cartographers are mapmakers." His interest didn't surprise Rion; he had a fascination with maps and star points—as evident in the constellation tattoos covering his skin.

"Precisely. The Cartographer can generate a navigable map containing the unrestricted and complete blueprint of Zeta Halo in current time. It maintains an unbroken record of the ring's history in its entirety."

Niko, meanwhile, sat back and put his hands behind his head. "All I want to know is, when do we leave?"

Humor tugged at Rion's mouth and her heart filled with fondness. She hadn't realized how much she missed the excitement of the hunt, the anticipation of the unknown. It had been a while since they'd sat around the table with an eye toward a real, tangible score.

After their last venture, which had garnered them an upgraded ship, a highly advanced AI, and a criminal record of galactic proportions, Rion thought their options were endless as a result. The galaxy was at their fingertips.

Then reality had set in. A fast ship and credits to burn, yes, but an outlaw was an outlaw—all the contacts she'd cultivated over the years were under surveillance, and if she put them at risk now, they wouldn't be there later when things, hopefully, finally blew over.

Either way, the months they'd spent tracking the *Spirit of Fire* had been exhausting and overwhelmingly disappointing. They all needed a big change. And this was it.

"Spark," she said with a grin. "Set a course for Zeta Halo."

It was good to be back in the game.

CHAPTER 7

The crew is asleep, even Niko with some persuasion, and we are well on our way through slipspace to Zeta Halo.

I enjoy the quiet, the hum of this vessel's engines, the constant data flowing through the Ace of Spades like a restless wind. It reminds me of my time on Geranos-a. The place of my rebirth—my third, if one is counting. We have made a work space in the cargo hold, equipped with holo port and direct system access. From here, Niko and I are able to study the crystal chip that may or may not hold a viable copy of Little Bit.

The chip containing Little Bit's projections on the Spirit of Fire is nestled in its sleeve, and once again I am diving into a stagnant pool of rudimentary layers, lines of calculations laid one on top of the other. I can only imagine the power this ancilla once wielded. Now it is but a tiny speck of its former glory, a little bit of a little bit of a little bit . . .

I do not often experience sadness for artificial intelligence, even though technically I am one. My humanity clings too strongly to my core, has seeped into all the compartments and layers and down into my matrix. It often prevents me from identifying equally with my *machine nature. The many months with these humans have only deepened my affinity.*

This fragment, however, has my sympathy. If our efforts prove successful, I wonder how much will remain of the once-great custodian of Etran Harborage.

It is intrinsic, even in the most basic intelligence, to copy data cleanly without leaving an imprint of itself in the process. Yet whether intentionally or absentmindedly, this fragment left its shadow within the very calculations it had created. Only a trained eye could see down through the data and into the authorship. It is no wonder the humans and their inelegant scanners and AIs failed to detect such an abnormality.

A sudden static pop echoes from somewhere deep within the ship's network—through kilometers of fiber-optics, filaments, conduits . . . I pause all processes and listen. I have heard this before while speaking to Lessa in the lounge. But the aberration is impossibly brief.

A thorough search finds no anomalous signals or noise or any leftover footprint of such a sound. Quite puzzling.

I resume my work once more, gently rooting out and lifting thin slivers of code beneath code.

As I proceed, the Librarian's key enters a second thought string.

The monitor within me is taken with the idea of visiting a Halo again; its fondness for the rings completely overshadows its usually analytic and equitable nature. And while I have achieved an acceptable merger between my humanity and 343 Guilty Spark, I must, at times like this, helm the imbalances.

Not ideal, of course, but certainly manageable.

And while the subject of Halo brings unwelcome memories to the surface, I cannot deny my curiosity is kindled.

Perhaps there is information to be exploited—answers to the mysteries and memories tucked away in the darkest corners of my core, answers to those things that stir. . . .

A desire has arisen to know my ancestors, my roots, to find my rightful place in this new age. I thought perhaps I had with Captain Forge and her crew, yet I am gripped with an itch I cannot scratch, a strange urging that propels me to seek the unknown, to look back and forward in the same breath.

I am compelled to know those ancient forgotten humans who traversed the stars and fought a great war with Forerunners ten thousand years before my human birth.

Extraordinary military strategists and warriors, inventors, architects, and scientists, they held off the Flood and were already depleted by the time the Forerunners came to bear. And still they waged a war that even the Didact, supreme commander of the entire Forerunner military, grudgingly respected.

Humanity would lose, of course.

In the last stronghold of Charum Hakkor, they were overtaken and punished severely. Hundreds of thousands, including children, were composed, their bodies atomized while their minds and personality patterns were preserved in great archives for examination and study. At the insistence of the Librarian, some of these ancient humans were permitted to live—not as the mighty, intelligent species they were, but as simple hunter-gatherers, devolved in both mass and mind, and placed on Earth.

In this regressed population, the Librarian stored the genetic memory of ancient humanity, and the essences of its most successful leaders, scientists, and warriors.

Such a preeminent imprint had existed in me and was the cause of all my troubles to come. . . .

CHAPTER 8

Ace of Spades / Ephsu System / 12,000 Kilometers from Zeta Halo

It should have taken a month or even longer to arrive in the Sagittarius Arm of the galaxy. *Ace* did it in six days. Dropping out of slipspace on target was no longer an educated guessing game, but a precision event that gave Rion a shiver of awe every time they arrived when and where they were supposed to. It wasn't typical space travel, and she wasn't sure she'd ever get used to it.

All hands were on the bridge, and immediately the crew went to work evaluating their current position. From the main viewscreen, there wasn't much to note. Ephsu was an unremarkable M-dwarf star system with one massive uninhabited planet to its name.

"Looks like we're all clear, Cap," Lessa said from NAVs. "Not much around except that super hunk of rock out there blocking our target."

"That rock is Zeta Halo's anchor," Spark informed them. "The planet is an unexpected selection, to be sure."

"How so?" Rion asked.

"Most anchors are gas giants to avoid the possibility of life arising in the shadow of a ring or luring in potential settlers. Not only is this planet solid, but it contains water and atmosphere. The choice is quite extraordinary, though perhaps a choice of necessity."

Spark had mentioned before that this particular Halo had a long history of being different, and apparently this anchor was no exception. It was an odd choice given what he said, but then Rion also remembered the Halos had been dispersed rather quickly and during a war, no less. The Forerunners could have run out of time to find a suitable gas giant anchor in the proper firing location—or maybe there simply hadn't been one in the sector to begin with.

"Not picking up any comm tech way out here," Niko said.

Without real-time data to rely on, Spark had placed them well off the Halo ring's coordinates until they knew exactly what they'd be flying into. No need to make an unnecessary scene. "Full stealth and continue on course, sub speed at one-half."

At seven hundred kilometers out, long-range scanners perked up. Rion glanced at her integrated pad as Niko relayed relevant information. "Looks like the UNSC has a couple nice comm towers set up on the planet's surface and a few commsats in orbit."

"There are three ships in orbit as well," Ram said over his shoulder. "Also UNSC . . . Two destroyers, and that has to be one of the biggest supply freighters I've ever seen."

Rion keyed into Ram's console. *Damn.* At a thousand meters long, by five hundred, that was one big girl. Not very often she saw heavyweights like this. Usually the smaller freighters were totally automated, but one this size would sport its own crew to oversee the ship and its massive payload.

The two destroyers flanked the freighter, each maintaining a distance off the bow and the stern. Typical UNSC *Halberd*-class. Good-looking ships, heavies as well, with the sleek arrowhead profile Rion was fond of, and armed to the teeth, each with a serious MAC, Archer missiles, and point defense guns.

"Let's slow her down to one-quarter," Rion said, keeping tabs on *Ace*'s trajectory and making sure she stayed well out of range of those destroyers.

Several tense minutes passed before they came around the curve of the planet. A hush settled on the bridge as a sleek silver band slowly emerged floating in the darkness of space.

The sight of Zeta Halo drew the crew to their feet.

In all her years traversing the stars, Rion had never seen anything so strange and alien, so massive and simple, complex and beautiful, yet dangerous beyond words. Nearly the diameter of Earth, its outer band was cut deep with strange geometric designs and intermittent blue light.

Ace cleared the planet, and their view shifted slightly to reveal the stunning inner surface of the ring. A startling contrast to its outer rim, the interior was alive with color and light, an impossibly perfect strip of blue skies, clouds over snowcapped mountain ranges, highlands and lowlands, valleys and plains, seas and lakes and rivers, all as though a divining hand had cut a perfect ten-thousand-kilometer ribbon off Earth and laid it neatly into the framework of an alien weapon capable of mass extinction.

They were witnessing something very few in the galaxy had or would ever see. And part of her had to question: Why? Of all people—*they* were here . . .

And now that she was informed about the ancient past and the Librarian's immense capacity to manipulate outcomes, Rion had to at least acknowledge that Spark coming into their lives might not have been by chance. They could be exactly where the Librarian meant them to be—or at the very least, hoping they'd be—which seemed at once ridiculous and entirely possible and definitely worrisome.

The silence seemed to stretch, until finally Lessa spoke up. "The Halo doesn't spin to create gravity?"

"It doesn't need to," Spark answered. "Though it spins to maintain day and night cycles, among other aspects. Gravity is maintained with artificial generators."

Ram rubbed a hand down his face and turned to meet Rion's gaze. She was just as dumbstruck and couldn't offer much in the way of response. What could one say without it sounding like the world's greatest understatement?

"Well, I don't know about you guys," Niko said. "But I feel like I just got slapped across the face. In a really amazing way."

"That would be called *awestruck*, little brother." Lessa broke into a smile and then a chuckle, which infected the rest of the crew.

Her wisecrack was just the kick they needed to get past the wonder. Rion headed back to her chair. "I know we're dark, but let's continue to monitor our space and keep well clear of those ships and satellites."

The crew tabled their awe and got to work.

"Starting to pick up some power sigs from the ring," Niko said.

"Captain, may I suggest maintaining a scanning orbit of five hundred kilometers?" Spark said.

"You may. Less, move us in. Once Spark locates the Cartographer facility, work out a flight path. Ram, I want to know who's down there and how many—scour for weapons and defensive systems in orbit and on the surface. Niko, monitor their comms and keep me updated. We do this right, and we might just get in and get out without incident."

"Would be a first," Ram murmured under his breath.

That brought another laugh from the crew.

Who knew, maybe today would be that day. They did have Spark on their side and a ship capable of advanced-level stealth.

Then again, it could very well be business as usual.

Or worse.

CHAPTER 9

The wheel no longer corresponds to the images I recall of a bleak and broken thing, of bare bones and rendered flesh, of mist and misery. Gone are the abandoned cities, the wrecked stations, and the great rifts. The crashed ships, the burns and brunt of the civil war that raged between the Forerunners who opposed the Master Builder's unethical human experiments and then Mendicant Bias and the Primordial's control.

Those barren stretches of exposed and twisted substructure, of scorched earth and toppled towers, have been swallowed up by a hundred thousand years of ecological growth and change. All the pain and suffering lies forgotten, smoothed over by time, hidden by pristine, inviting, and even beautiful topography.

As Gyre 11, one of the original twelve rings created by the Master Builder, the construct had once boasted a diameter of thirty thousand kilometers with an intense directed-energy firing cone of cross-phased supermassive neutrino bursts capable of annihilating any neurologically complex living organisms—animals, plants, trees . . .

On the ancient human planet Faun Hakkor, I saw firsthand the *utter loss of life down to the creatures in the seas, to great swaths of collective, symbiotic forests and mycorrhizal networks.*

Zeta Halo is the only remaining ring from the Senescent Array. In the last days of the Forerunner-Flood War, it was rescued from near collision and repurposed to one-third of its former diameter and included among a new Halo Array created by the lesser Ark—those smaller rings created in secret and eventually used as a final means to eradicate the Flood.

Zeta, though it appears similar to its counterparts, is what my human companions might refer to as a proverbial black sheep. It still bears elements of its archaic design, still holds within its soil and dust and stone the remnants of lost cities and settlements, generation after generation of humans living and evolving and forming complex civilizations.

Seeing the scars healed over does not bring me comfort or peace. Instead, the images settle in me like a thorn lodged in bone.

No amount of time can ease the horror of my captivity here. I do not forget. I do not forgive. Deep in the substructure of this Halo, I lost my humanity and became Forerunner. I remember because I must and because a thousand centuries later, I am still furious.

"Are you sure about this?" Rion is now asking me. She stands at the holotable, her hands clasped behind her back.

She knows my tale. They all do. The care and concern on their faces tells me they will support whatever decision I make. This power both humbles and frightens me. Friendship is a rare commodity indeed.

"I am certain, Captain," I assure her. The story has not ended. "Our path is quite clear."

With a sharp nod, she turns her attention to the holograph. "Where do we begin?"

The crew swivels in their station chairs to listen intently to my findings. I have built a holo image of Zeta Halo above the table. Already having made my examination and calculations, I bring forth a section for the crew's inspection. "I believe this is where we will start." *The enhanced LIDAR scans have penetrated growth and sediment to reveal the shape of the land beneath, and I have recognized the area.*

"This dry valley was once a river." *I increase the view to show a wide valley framed by sheer gray cliffs. I move the blueprint along the valley to its end, where a stark cliff rises vertically by nearly a hundred meters.* "There was once a waterfall here, fed by a lake." *Above the cliff, the area widens out into an ancient lake basin.* "There." *I point to the center of the basin.*

Rion leans in. "What is that?"

"It looks like a crater," *Lessa says.*

"More or less. It appears small from our current view, but it is twenty-six meters in diameter and leads into Zeta's substructure." *I move out of the LIDAR scan and into a pleasing satellite image.*

I did love my beautiful ring; that this one should look so similar to Installation 04 fills me with sudden sadness and irritation and intense envy.

I must, however, ignore these emotions.

"The basin is covered with vegetation. I propose we cut through and settle the ship directly inside the ring." *From their expressions, it is clear no one has expected such a proposal.*

"Inside the Halo," *Niko dubiously repeats.* "You want us to fly into *it*."

"Yes. That is what I just said. It is the quickest and safest place to land, keeping us clear of any activity on the surface. There are approximately 3,416 humans currently on the ring. Four hundred and six of those are scientists from many different subgroups of study, while the remaining are military. I have detected several hundred human drones* *working across the ring's surface, scanning and recording, mapping the surface and looking for control centers and power sources."*

"Aboveground, we know what's out there. Going underground," Ram says, "how can we be sure it's any safer?"

"Right," Niko adds. "There must be thousands of workers inside keeping the ring operational. It must be dozens of kilometers deep. That's like a whole other world down there."

"Most of the constructs within the foundation are Sentinels. They come in a variety of sizes and functions."

"And why would they be safer than the humans on the surface?" Rion questions. "And what about the monitor in charge?"

While their queries border on tedious, I practice patience. "The monitor of this ring does not appear to be functioning in its intended capacity, which is why its defensive forces have not made an appearance. According to my data, there has been no reaction to the presence of human activity, which has been continuous since 2555. If it was going to protect this ring or direct an attack, it would have done so by now."

There was a time during my own tenure as monitor of Installation 04 that I attempted to contact this ring's monitor, Despondent Pyre. Even then, it did not respond. Now that my human memories have returned, I must wonder if perhaps its intended directive was different from mine and the other monitors'. After all, Bornstellar did send this ring to its firing location with the intent that it should be a tomb for all those who died throughout its horrific past; that it should remain hidden in the mists of time, lost and forgotten.

"All right," Rion says decisively. "Let's make a flight plan and then deep scan our path to see what's in the area and what we need to avoid."

"Aye, Cap." Lessa turns back to the navigation console.

It is entirely unnecessary.

"The navigation plan is already completed," I tell them. "The closest military camp is thirty kilometers off our entry zone. Two drones are estimated to approach our projected path in approximately twenty-three hours. The closest science base to the basin is twelve kilometers off, and their latest excursions have gotten them as close to four kilometers from the valley. If they continue on this path, they will encounter a relay station, which will keep them occupied for several days or possibly weeks."

The crew stares at me with a look I am all too familiar with. "I have overstepped." We each have functions on the ship, of which I am aware, and yet how can I help myself?

Ram chuckles and returns to his display. Lessa and Rion share a smile between them, and Niko is shaking his head. "Man, you haven't overstepped—you've leaped over the goddamn valley." He is now wearing a wide grin. "No worries, Spark. We get it. This is your op, and it's personal."

Yes. I suppose that's one way to put it.

CHAPTER 10

Zeta Halo

Rion guided the *Ace of Spades* beneath the curve of the Halo ring. How bizarre it was to see mountain ranges and forests, lakes and rivers, and blue skies and clouds clinging near vertically or completely upside down. The sheer size and complexity left her dumbstruck. Zeta clocked in at three hundred and eighteen kilometers wide and ten thousand kilometers in diameter—nearly the same breadth as Earth. The knowledge and means to create on this colossal scale seemed the stuff of fantasy, of divinity and magic.

How could a civilization capable of building something of such magnitude have been so utterly defeated by the Flood? She would never forget first hearing about them from Spark, and even now a slight chill ran up her spine. If these builders, with all their technological mastery and knowledge, were left wanting, what did that mean for humanity should a threat like that ever appear in vast numbers again?

As *Ace* descended into the artificially maintained atmosphere, the landscape became clearer. It was a stunning and pristine

— 63 —

world, and, until recently, untouched and forgotten. She could see why, according to Spark, the Librarian had lobbied the Forerunner Council to balance the rings' destructive force with conservation measures, to give them some other redeeming purpose. What better place to house her collections, to keep thousands upon thousands of races and species and flora and fauna content for millennia in their new environment, safe and sound from the Flood?

Only on this ring, that vision of utopia hadn't gone so well.

The ship went in quiet, though with a construct this enormous and the small contingent present, Rion was pretty sure they could've snuck in with an old Kig-Yar junker.

"Captain?"

Spark was waiting expectantly over the holotable. "I will need to take over controls now."

"The helm is yours."

Spark directed the ship along a snowcapped mountain range, then lower toward the foothills. As they glided toward a valley of deep gorges and high gray cliffs, a few moving specks caught her eye—what appeared to be rams with wide horns curling behind their necks navigated the low peaks. *Ace* swept down quickly and smoothly, then leveled off to ride the open space of the dry riverbed between the cliffs. On the plateau atop the cliff, a herd of small deerlike creatures, startled by their approach, sprinted in a great unified arc across the blanket of green.

At the end of the valley, *Ace*'s thrusters pushed the ship up and over the sheer cliff and across the flat lake basin. Millions of tangled vines with thick, glossy, heart-shaped leaves, some as long as two meters, created a dense carpet over the former lake bed. In the center, the leaves dipped in a perfect circle, an emerald bowl in the middle of the basin.

Ace slowed and came to a hover above the depression. "The

vine cover is about four and a half meters thick. There's nothing under that, just a *whole* lot of empty space," Niko said. LIDAR scans built a rendition over the holotable, giving a startling sense of just how vast the substructure below them was. The lake bed rested like a tiny lily pad over a deep, dark ocean.

"Not picking up any hostiles or life signs in range," Ram added.

"Niko, you getting any chatter nearby?"

"No, Cap, nothing."

"Should we use guns to break through the vines?" Lessa asked.

"No. I don't want to attract attention," Rion answered. "And we can't risk plowing through and bringing those vines down over us. We'll turn the burners on them."

"Good idea," Ram said.

A look of unbridled glee crossed Niko's face. "The pyro in me approves. Nothing like a little tri-hy burn to start the day." He accessed *Ace*'s outboard cameras and pulled up a feed of the basin from the edge of one of the ship's aft thrusters as she maneuvered into position.

Rion aimed for a controlled accretion on the throttle, just enough to light up a little triamino hydrazine fuel and torch a small hole—anything bigger might send up smoke signals and alert the curious. Ignite burners, two-second burst, and she was done, easing up on controls and then checking the feeds, pleased to see it was working like a charm. The intense heat fried the vines clean through, leaving embers to eat up a radiating path outward before dying out to the moisture content in the vines and leaves.

"Excellently done, Captain," Spark said. "We are clear to proceed if you're ready."

Ready to take her ship inside a Forerunner megastructure. She almost laughed. The idea seemed absurd, and yet here they were about to do just that. Ready was relative. That old excitement was there, though, lurking under the caution and wariness, that touch of recklessness and drive to explore the unknown. "Ready as I'll ever be," she quipped. "All eyes on consoles and reporting please."

The *Ace of Spades* leveled off and Rion continued VTOL procedures to the ship's main thrusters, maintaining a full vertical pivot to ease the ship straight down into the belly of the ring. Niko leaned over to hit a command, and four smaller bridge screens, in addition to the main viewscreen, flickered to life, *Ace*'s outboard cams feeding in the scenes one meter at a time. First came the burnt entrails and singed edges of the vine cover, and then . . . darkness.

Rion tensed. Every screen was pitch-black. Their only visual reference was the blueprint hovering over the tactical table. As sensors provided detail, the holograph continually revised itself, revealing a network of latticed superstructure, several hundred meters thick, supported by massive pillars beneath the lake bed. The only break in the structure was the twenty-six-meter hole, which appeared to be by design.

Zeta's substructure was reading an incredible fifteen kilometers in depth and growing.

On the blueprint, the pillars supporting the undercarriage of the ring's latticework and girders continued into the depths, their size breathtaking. Still the camera feeds brought back blackness. They were in a pocket of nothing, in a controlled vertical descent at about twenty meters per second. Rion's attention stayed on the ever-changing blueprint as it attempted to find any proximal points of reference, but they were just a tiny vessel sinking to the bottom of the darkest pit.

At eight minutes and ten kilometers, the scene began to change. *Ace*'s exterior lights finally revealed a world of giant cross sections, linking pillars larger than any skyscraper she had ever seen. Immense pathways stretched beyond their scanners' ability to detect.

There were segments within cross sections, creating open spaces and tunnels some six stories tall and sixty meters wide, and fully walled chambers of enormous size.

And there they were, a speck of dust floating down into a mega city. It was disconcerting and intensely humbling.

"There's a pathway below us in another kilometer," Spark said.

Evidence of destruction came into view, flash burns, pathways pocked with craters or severed like twigs, buckled supports, and smaller things—vessels, transports, exposed conduits and cabling, and other indefinable refuse—littering passages and tunnels.

"All this damage . . . it happened before the firing of the ring?" Rion asked. She remembered everything Spark had told her about his time on Zeta as a human, including the civil war, ongoing since before his arrival, and the near destruction of the Halo as the wolf planet passed through its ring. But she had to hear it out loud, to know there was nothing else she had to worry about, nothing left over or lurking in the darkness.

"Most certainly," Spark replied.

"Anyone else find it odd, though?" Niko shared a concerned glance with her before moving on to Spark. "The surface is obviously in good shape, and that doesn't happen on its own; it takes a hell of a lot of maintenance and power to run atmosphere and artificial gravity. So why is this area abandoned? There's not even power down here."

"Perhaps it is a little odd," Spark admitted, though his tone was untroubled.

"I'm gonna need a little more than 'perhaps' to push forward," Rion said. "Spark, is there a reason sections like this would be in disrepair?"

"There is nothing to suggest the reason is nefarious or danger-ous in nature, Captain. I am detecting no such indicators. It is far more likely this section has simply been abandoned. As for the lack of power, there could be many reasons. A prescheduled dormancy cycle for conservation purposes, a complete shutoff of systems and rerouting of power . . ."

So far things had gone relatively easy, and Rion wanted to keep it that way. The entire mission relied on trust, on putting her faith in Spark, in his knowledge, his suggestions, and his assumptions. But in the end, no matter what he might do or say or cause, the responsibility for whatever might happen was squarely on her shoulders.

"I am simply cautious, like the rest of you," Spark added. "This ring has existed one hundred thousand years beyond my involvement. Accounting for every conceivable danger at the present time is impossible. I will temper your fears, however, and say I do not believe the caretakers here are a threat."

Call it a sixth sense or trust or whatever, but Rion believed it too, given the facts so far.

"Nor do I believe the Flood specimens that might still exist in substructure research facilities pose any threat either."

Her optimism took a nosedive. "I'm sorry . . . *what*?"

"Wait a second—what are you saying?" Ram spun in his chair, brow furrowed in disbelief. "Those things are here?"

"It is possible."

"Jesus, Spark." The nice tan he'd gotten became several shades paler. They'd all heard Spark's stories of the Flood; the horror of it was too great to ever forget. "Wouldn't they have been destroyed a long time ago, considering how dangerous you've said they are?"

"It was precisely their danger that drove the Forerunners to keep specimens. All Halo installations—including my own—had heavily contained research facilities for the parasite, in hopes a cure might one day be discovered. Since the Flood's origin lay outside the galaxy, finding a cure was the only way to prevent the end of all biodiversity, were the threat ever to return. The only way, apart from activation, that is. . . . But perhaps Bornstellar chose to anni-hilate the specimens before sending the ring to its firing position." Spark shrugged, sounding totally unbothered. "I simply cannot say with any certainty what might or might not have happened."

A moment of stunned silence greeted his pronouncement as the gravity of his revelation hit home. Then Lessa quietly asked, "Do we need to be worried?" And those big baby blues tugged hard on Rion's protective instincts. "I mean, that's a *long* time for something to stay contained."

"I can assure you had any escaped containment, the state of this ring and the galaxy itself would be much different than it is right now."

And that was a truth Rion couldn't dispute.

"Approaching the pathway, Cap," Niko cut in. "Should we land?"

Now that they were close enough, details of the path below became clear on-screen—an enormous highway, made of an alloy similar to the outer rim of the Halo, though the adornment of glowing blue lines and glyphs were nominal.

"Spark, this is your show," Rion said, leaving it up to him. "What do you suggest?"

"The best and quickest course of action is to follow the pathway to achieve the closest subterranean proximity to the Cartographer."

Rion gave him a subtle nod to go ahead. The turn of *Ace*'s thrusters echoed through the ship, and they began moving for-ward above the path.

"With all this damage, you think it's still there?" Niko asked.

"The Cartographer always endures. In the event that one is de-stroyed, another is automatically created in some other part of the ring to serve in its place; it is too valuable to do otherwise. We will find it one way or another."

The blueprint showed an obstacle in the pathway a few kilometers ahead. A large chunk of metal pillar, a girder or crossbeam, was buried in the pathway just as the path transitioned into a tunnel. The impact had created a crack that nearly severed the pathway in two. "We'll land here," Rion said, making adjustments. She didn't want to land *Ace* anywhere near that crack. "And continue on foot."

The landing gear engaged. *Ace* slowly settled onto the path, while Spark was already at work at the holotable, no doubt calibrating the scanners to achieve precise images, building an outline beyond the debris and tunnel.

Niko swiveled in his seat and pushed to his feet, stretching his arms high over his head and letting out a long yawn. "Should I warm up Michelle and Diane?"

"There is no need," Spark told him. "I know where we are and where we need to go."

"Well, air is good. Temps are pretty decent. I'd wear a jacket, Cap."

Rion appreciated the suggestion. "Thanks, Niko. And the Cartographer?" she asked Spark as he manipulated the holo blueprint of Zeta Halo's interior, moving parts away and zooming in on other areas closer to the surface. "Here—the location is beyond this tunnel, followed by a twenty-meter ascent."

Niko leaned over the table. "That's a five-story climb with no discernible way up." He lifted his head to give Rion a pointed look, and she was pretty sure she knew what was coming next. "And who shot me down when I said we needed new jetpacks?"

"We have jetpacks."

"No, we have *antiquated* jetpacks. Big difference."

"We will not need them." Spark zoomed in on a support pillar just outside the tunnel. "See the chambers in this wall?" The image was hazy, but it seemed there were definite outlines, rectangular pockets stacked vertically in rows. "These bays are meant to hold transport pods. There might be several inside still intact."

While it wasn't direct confirmation, it was as good a starting point as they were going to get, and Rion was itching to finally see what the Librarian's key unlocked. "Spark and I will go, plus one. Two of you will need to stay behind to monitor things here."

"If it's all the same to you guys," Lessa responded immediately, "I'll stay on board."

"I'll stay with her." Normally Niko was the first one off the ship, eager to mix it up with whatever adventures lay ahead. That he chimed in so quickly struck Rion as odd. "You three can go," he added. "If that's all right with you, Cap?"

She nodded and then watched him as he went back to his chair and sat, spinning around to chat with his sister. There was a tiredness about him that didn't come from late nights immersed in all things tech. It was different, something deeper and cloudier, weighing on him. She'd been remiss in not noticing it earlier.

"I will be connected to and monitoring the ship at all times," Spark assured her, taking her silence for hesitation.

"If there's any trouble, Less and Niko are well practiced at what to do," Rion said. Which wasn't rocket science. They were to immediately take the ship out of harm's way—par for the course in their line of work. And while Niko's decision to hang back was highly out of character, Rion would have to leave it until after they were well away from Zeta Halo.

"All right then. Helm is yours. Keep us in the loop. As always, hightail it out of here if anything comes close to discovering your position, and we'll rendezvous with you later."

"Got it, Cap," Niko said. "We'll keep *Ace* on standby."

"Looks like you're with me then," Rion told Ram as Spark's avatar disappeared.

Ram gave the siblings a cocky grin as he got up. "Best let the adults handle it."

The eye-rolls that ensued left Rion smiling as she exited the bridge with Ram and headed down the corridor. When they emerged on the catwalk overlooking the cargo hold two stories below, Spark's armiger was there, assembling from a pile of silver alloy parts on the floor by his worktable. Blue hard light illuminated lines and connection points, pulling the pieces together like a magnet. Feet, legs, trunk, arms, hands, and head came into position, hovering close together but not quite touching, simply anchored in place with the light acting as the glue between them.

Spark straightened to his full three meters of Forerunner intimidation and intelligent design. He eased a slow glance over his shoulder, chin lifted and enigmatic blue eyes holding on to Rion's before he dipped his angular head in acknowledgment.

Goose bumps tingled Rion's arms, and she was pretty sure she'd never get used to seeing him rise from the floor. It was moments like this that drove home how alien much of him truly was.

The staging area and armory combo, dubbed the locker, occupied a long room off the cargo hold, close to the bottom of the stairs. Holding an array of all-terrain gear and weapons to accommodate a wide variety of environments and situations, it was one of Rion's favorite places on the ship. Locker collections were built over years and years, decades even, and were prized commodities among salvagers, whose job it was to be prepared for any type of environment. On the rare occasion when collections went up for auction—usually upon a salvager's retirement or death—it brought salvagers together from all parts of the galaxy and almost always ended up serving as a retirement party or memorial.

Ram retrieved a jacket from his cubby, and then a prepacked utility vest to wear over it. "You packing?"

"Yep. I don't trust this place. It's too quiet."

A white smile peeked through Ram's dark beard. "Don't tell me you're scared of the dark?" He held out another utility vest.

"Funny." She snagged the vest. As he tied his hair back with a band, she grabbed two extra magazines, sliding them into the vest pockets before putting it on. "More like, I *respect* the dark. Big difference."

"Well, it doesn't get any more alien than this, that's for sure." He retrieved a sidearm, checked the clip, and then slipped an M6 into his side holster. "I didn't think Triniel could be topped, but this . . . I'm not sure how we're gonna top this one."

"Oh, stick with me, Chalva, and I'm sure we'll find something. Or it'll find us." As was usually the case. "Hand me a couple frags, would ya?"

He pulled two from their cradles and passed them over one at a time, then lifted his rifle from the stocks, giving it a quick check. "Ready when you are."

"We still need to grab a couple grav plates just in case, and then we'll be all set."

"No cart?"

She donned her comm piece, adjusting it in her ear. "No, might be too cumbersome to take where we're going." Plus she doubted whatever the key unlocked would be so large as to necessitate a gravity cart for transport. Plates were smaller, easier to carry, and only required a person to attach a pair to an object, activate, and then the plates would generate a small antigravity field, effectively allowing the object to carry itself. "We can come back for one if whatever we find is too big for the plates."

"Roger that." Ram left to collect the plates from one of the cargo bins.

Once Rion finished strapping on her left forearm gauntlet with its slim integrated datapad, she left the locker room to join him. But the sight of Spark facing the air-lock door, standing completely frozen, drew her to a halt. No sound, no head tilt at her arrival, just silence and stillness.

For the first time in one hundred thousand years he was about to step foot on Zeta Halo. She couldn't begin to guess what was going on in that complicated mind of his.

In Africa, Rion had heard the Librarian's voice in a flash of light telling her that Spark was special. Rare. More important than she'd ever know. But many times since that event, despite his extreme power and technological superiority, Rion had felt he needed her protection, her help, and most definitely her friendship and trust. Without it, he might be a *very* different version of himself—and that was a frightening thought indeed.

She was damn glad he was on their side.

Rion tugged her vest down and walked up next to the three-meter giant. "You doing okay?"

The air-lock door slid open and the ramp descended. "I am about to find out."

The great maw of darkness that greeted them sent an unnerving chill through the cargo bay. The air was stale and cool. The lights on the ramp illuminated just a small area around the ship, but everything else was utter black. From what she could see of the pathway, it was at least familiar—same Forerunner metal she'd seen in other places before, with similar geometric lines running through the floor, though not as ornate as others she'd seen.

"Lights on." She pressed the angled shoulder light built into the vest and headed down the ramp. "Comms, we good?"

"Five by five," Ram said.

"Good luck out there," Lessa's voice echoed in Rion's earpiece.

"We'll be monitoring you every step of the way. Oh, and bring back something amazing."

Whatever the key unlocked, it wasn't going to be something as simple as standard treasure. Rion was pretty sure the Librarian hadn't set up an elaborate hunt like this without a very good, highly significant reason.

"Roger that," Rion said. "Let's get moving."

A long stretch of darkness lay between Rion and her ship. From this distance, the *Ace of Spades* was nothing but a tiny black lump surrounded by a beacon of dim, distorted light. They'd gone a kilometer and a half, a good twenty minutes where each footstep, breath, and shuffle of clothing, or clink of gear, made a god-awful racket in the god-awful silence. Their combined lighting reached ahead of them by about eight meters, and even though it cast them in a cocoon of pseudo-comfort, the blackness around them held such an eerie quality that Rion had to keep reminding herself to stop clenching her teeth.

At this rate, she'd have a raging headache before reaching the Cartographer.

Finally their light hit on the crack in the pathway. A massive support beam had collapsed from somewhere overhead and pierced through the top of the tunnel entrance—a height of at least six stories—and landed with such driving force that it peeled away the top layer of the pathway, pushing mounds of rolled metal into their way and creating the crack in the structure itself. Not anything she'd want to set *Ace* near, but insignificant for tiny ants like them to traverse without causing a collapse.

The climb over metal and around debris slowed their progress some, but Spark seemed to have an innate sense for the most economical paths to take. Once they cleared the impact site of the beam and moved past it toward the tunnel, Rion was out of breath and sweating, but she was never more appreciative of the shoulder light on her vest and the stable blue light emitting from Spark as they entered the tunnel. Their lights reflecting off his silver alloy lent him a celestial glow, and made him a comforting beacon in the darkness. In this place of his godlike makers, he never appeared more otherworldly than he did now.

"This entire place feels . . . off," Ram muttered, picking up his pace to join Rion.

"I know what you mean."

"We're literally walking through Zeta's underworld." He turned in a slow arc to light the space behind them, before coming full circle. "The living above us . . . and down here, who knows what's down here. . . ."

"Upping the creep factor, thanks for that."

Ram cracked a half smile, laugh lines crinkling at the corners of his eyes. "What I'm here for." He continually scanned the dark areas and after a long stretch of silence said, "It's like how I imagined the Hall of Eternity."

"What's that?"

"Sangheili myth. 'May your name echo the loudest through the Hall of Eternity,' " he intoned, wiggling his eyebrows at her. "A saying from their old mythology, long before the Covenant." They stepped around some type of vessel debris, a small transport maybe, broken in chunks and scattered along the tunnel. "It's about one aspect of their god, Fied, the dark star. They say he walks the Hall in worn sandals and carrying an ancient lantern lit with the flame of Urs. Fied never stops walking, never stops swinging his lantern, and never stops calling out the names of the dead. Imagine it, the voice of a dark god, calling out names for eternity in a hall like this. They say he'll keep walking, keep calling out the names, until the last Sangheili in the universe breathes his last breath."

It was no wonder Ram thought of the tale; the tunnel could very well serve as an eternal hall for some otherworldly deity.

"Only the names of those who died with honor were called. The Sangheili still see it as something to aspire to. Die with honor or your name will be lost forever."

"How do you know all this?"

He shrugged. "When you're the captive of a bunch of hinge-heads, you learn a thing or two."

What happened to Ram and his crew was a story he might never tell, but Rion got the feeling if ever there was a time for him to finally talk and release some pressure, now might be it.

As it turned out, she didn't have to ask.

"They liked to use it as an insult . . . when they tortured my crew. Saying they'd die without dignity, that their names would be lost, that no god of any species would ever call out the names of weaklings like us who screamed and cried and begged." Ram's speech came rough and grief-stricken. " 'Where is the honor in that?' That's what they said."

A resurgent sect of what remained of the Covenant after the war had been targeting salvagers for months, waiting for them to do the heavy lifting before swooping in, stealing their finds and slaughtering entire crews. It was a quick way for the Covenant to acquire the ships and technology necessary to rebuild their fleet. Ram and his crew had been missing for several weeks before Rion showed up last year, hunting a find on Laconia, and discovered the notorious Gek 'Lhar and his crew, using Ram as target practice for laughs.

Ram was the last one alive, the sole survivor.

Spark had turned and was waiting for them to catch up, his head tilted ever so slightly. His voice was quiet and respectful, yet determined when he spoke. "What were their names?"

His question stole Rion's breath because she knew immediately what he was really asking. And so did Ram. His gaze locked on Spark, his proud profile cast in sorrow and surprise.

They were in a place built by ancients, whom many had worshipped as divine, in a tunnel that could pass for any mythological hall. If there was ever a time to honor them . . .

Rion's heart ached for what Ram had lost and what he had endured. And Spark . . . In that moment, she realized just how tenaciously his humanity ran. "We'll call out their names, here and now," she said. "So they won't be forgotten."

She and Spark shared a brief nod.

Anguish pooled in Ram's dark eyes as he worked his way through his emotions, ending on a note of resolution. But, behind the resolution, Rion didn't miss the simmering rage. Salvager crews were like family, and he hadn't been able to put his to rest.

To see his tough exterior struggle to stay composed was difficult to watch. She wanted him to do this, felt it would help him heal—he had bottled up so much this last year—but she wasn't going to push him. It was his choice.

"Okay. All right." He drew in a slow, steady breath and released it. "Let's do it."

So they walked their own version of the Hall of Eternity, Spark leading the way, a point of light in the overwhelming darkness, as Ram uttered each name. And they in turn called them out, one by one, into the ether.

CHAPTER 11

As we move through the ring's interior, my thoughts turn from Ram's lost crew to those lost here on this ring. Millions of names to call out to the Hall of Eternity.

Vivid images of my final human days flash through my core like reflections on shards of glass. After crash-landing on the ring and re-uniting with Riser, we made our way here to this dark underworld, led by a human, Vinnevra, and the peaceful Gigantopithecus ape Mara.

Once inside, we were ushered in this way—dirty, stinking, sore, and hungry after our long journey across the war-torn Halo, and ter-rified, pushed along with a constant wave of humans and infected Flood forms, gathered together, scanned, sorted, and eventually brought to bear.

The Forerunners that had once lived here, worked here, and fought here were all dead or part of the infected herd. There was no one left to protect the humans on the ring, no one left to wrest control away from the traitorous contender-class AI, Mendicant Bias, and the imprisoned Primordial. We'd become chattel, fuel to feed the Cap-tive's enduring appetite for suffering.

Unless we did something and killed the beast.

Such ego I had!

To even think it, that a young human might do what thousands upon thousands of others, more advanced and intelligent and strong, could not.

The imprint of Forthencho, Lord of Admirals—the Didact's worthiest opponent across countless battles during the war between the Forerunners and the humans—might have been whispering and urging me ever along, impressing upon me his need to win, to still fight a lost war . . . but I cannot blame him for my pride.

Riser would say big boss men playing gods and games.

Flesh and story all tangled up.

Led over cliffs by devils.

Not real.

Not real.

Leave us alone!

Turbulent water fills my core until I am drowning. Gasping. Fighting against memories.

A thousand centuries have passed, but to me, to Chakas, only a few years have transpired since I emerged from compartmentalization. The wounds still bleed. The treacheries still burn. The losses still torment.

Water is my anchor. The way I envision my emotions and what is left of my humanity. Water is basic, fundamental. It is life. It is me. I use its memory to calm the turbulence and soothe the pain, a salve to cover unforgotten agony.

Here in the belly of the wheel, not all my recollections are accounted for. Some of my time passed in deceit, my companions and I lulled into complacency, kept pliable and calm until we were needed, given false pictures, false environment, false sustenance . . . Nothing was real until my imprint of Forthencho was extracted through a hole in my back.

Alas, pain is a great animator. It wakes you up, snaps you out of whatever daydream you find yourself in, and shoves you right back into a nightmare.

I remember everything that came after.

I will never forget.

I will never forgive.

CHAPTER 12

Ace of Spades / Zeta Halo

essa stepped onto the bridge carrying a tray with two piping-hot packaged meals. "Here, help me out."

Niko hurried from his console and carefully took one of the meals. "Noodles," he noted with appreciation. "In tosac sauce?"

"Of course. Careful when you open it, it's hot." She got comfy in her chair, selected music to listen to while they ate, then gathered a forkful of steaming rust-colored noodles. As she blew on her bite, she studied her brother. So far she hadn't been able to work up the nerve to tell him about the whole university idea. "How we looking on perimeter?"

His cheeks full, eyes watering, he managed to say, "Looks quiet."

She sympathized. Tosac peppers might look unassuming with their thin corkscrew shape, but they delivered a *blistering* wallop to the tongue. The smoky-sweet aftertaste that followed, though, made it all worth it.

As Lessa enjoyed her meal, her fear of revealing her university dreams got the better of her. She couldn't do it, so she focused on Niko instead. She'd learned to listen to her gut, especially when it involved her family. Niko hadn't been acting his usual self since their last day on Emerald Cove. And now he'd chosen to stay on the ship rather than explore one of the most technologically rich sites they'd ever visited? Something had changed. And she needed to know what.

"I can't believe we're sitting inside a Halo." She swiveled in her chair to face him. "Can you? I mean, we're literally in the inner workings of a galactic weapon."

"Mmm. Tell me about it. It's like we got a front-row seat to Spark's history. Well, part of it, anyway."

The first time they'd heard the story of Chakas and 343 Guilty Spark, they'd been completely blindsided by the truth. She couldn't speak for anyone else, but his revelations had taken some getting used to. Funny how time seemed to settle, though, and living and working with a being who'd lived through the ancient past had now become part of their usual grind. "Has to be hard for him . . . being here again, after all this time."

"No doubt." Niko leaned forward to adjust the camera angles on *Ace*'s exterior.

Usually Spark was a topic of great interest for her brother, but right now he seemed a million miles away. "You think it's odd, the Librarian giving him a key to this place?" By her way of thinking, it seemed a tad insensitive.

Niko took his time answering, polishing off the last of his meal and then depositing the recyclable dish in the refuse sorter. "Maybe she didn't have a choice. Maybe she didn't create the key specifically for him. Just my take, but that imprint could've been instructed to appear to anyone who activated it, you know? Like, to anyone who met some predetermined qualifications. And if they did, the key was given."

Lessa shrugged, unconvinced. "Still, it must be awful revisiting the place where you lost your body, your humanity, all your memories . . ." She wondered how Spark was taking it.

"Just his body was lost on Zeta," Niko said offhandedly, his attention on the screens. "He was taken to the Ark and stayed there awhile, recuperating and working for the Librarian. Then, later, when all the Halo rings were gathered and ready to disperse into final firing positions, that's when he was named 343 Guilty Spark. That's when his human memories were compartmentalized."

"How do you know all this?"

Niko looked up and gave her a deep frown. "Because I pay attention. Didn't you listen when he was telling his stories?"

"Of course I listened." Apparently not everything had stuck the way it did with her brother. "It was a lot to take in. *Anyway*," she said, "you might be right about the key. It didn't spill its secret until I touched it; it didn't work for Spark the whole time he had it."

"Probably programmed for Forerunners and humans."

"What are you doing?" He seemed preoccupied with whatever was on his panel.

"Just scanning."

"For what?"

"Nothing in particular. Aren't you curious to see what's out there?"

She glanced at the different camera feeds displayed on the bridge and felt nothing but trepidation at the dark screens. "I'd rather get whatever that key unlocks and then get the hell out of here. Question is why aren't *you* out there?"

That made him pause, finally.

She thought she might actually get an answer, but he seemed to shrug it off. "Is it Little Bit?"

The way his face screwed up told her she was way off mark. "No. It's been going good."

"Is it Spark, then?"

That got his attention. "What do you mean?"

"Well, he doesn't leave much room for us to do our jobs. I know you've noticed. He could run this entire ship without any of us."

Niko rolled his eyes. "Gee, thanks."

"Just being honest. I'm not saying he *should*."

"We all have a job to do. He stays in his lane, we stay in ours. It's fine. I'm not worried about it." But the stiff set to his mouth and shoulders told her otherwise.

"Okay . . . then what's eating you?"

"What's eating you?" he shot back. "Jeez, Less. Give it a rest."

She knew better than to get riled up with petty stuff like this, but knowing and doing were two very different things, especially between siblings. If he wanted to throw it back at her, she'd give him something to gnaw on. "I'm thinking of leaving the ship, actually."

"What . . . ?"

Now that the tables were turned, she instantly regretted the outburst. "Well, I've been finished with remote classes for a long time now. Been sort of mulling over enrolling in university . . ."

His attention was suddenly on the panel in front of him. He could barely lift his head, and when he did, it was to give her a mild smile. "Huh. I think that's a great idea."

His dismissal was like a sucker punch to the gut. "That's all you have to say?"

"Hang on a second. I'm picking up some weird interference. I'm going to launch Michelle to see what's out there."

Aggravated, she got up to toss her tray in the sorter. "Suppose you think that's a great idea too."

But he was already heading off the bridge.

She went back to her station, unsure of how she should take his attitude. He barely had a reaction to the possibility of her leaving.

Determined to get answers, she checked his console panel, surprised to find there was no interference that she could see. *That liar!* Dumbfounded, she slid into his chair and started digging, pulling up the recent interactions on his panel. Michelle's search parameters were already logged and included small-to-midsize starship wreckage—correction: it was the drone's only parameter.

What the hell?

Digging a little deeper revealed recently viewed salvager forums listing current and upcoming sales on engine wreckage, slipspace capacitors, and the trading of wreck site coordinates.

It didn't make any sense.

He never needed anything this big for a project. And he most definitely did not have *any* authority to launch Michelle and go hunting for parts in the middle of a mission.

An alert pinged. It was the portside aft hatch opening to release the drone. Niko's panel lit up with Michelle's controls, ready for him when he returned. Quickly, she diminished his search history, attempting to cover her own tracks as best as she could.

Niko returned to the bridge and slid into his console chair. With a few commands, Michelle was up and away from the ship. A former UNSC spy drone, Niko had acquired her early on in his salvaging career and improved her information-gathering specs, while adding an array of useful tech.

The drone's feed came up on one of the screens. Lessa walked to the main viewscreen to watch. Niko joined her using his datapad to sync controls. She had a sinking suspicion that whatever her brother had gotten involved in, it wasn't good. It was the only explanation for his erratic behavior.

She wanted so terribly to ask him what was going on, but she held her tongue and decided to table it until they were away from Zeta Halo. Hopefully it could wait until then.

Just as she turned her attention to monitoring the camera feeds and sensors, a loud thud echoed through the hull. "What the hell was that?" She leaned over the tactical table and killed the music while Niko maneuvered one of *Ace*'s outboard cameras to get a look at the area.

Another booming thud sounded overhead.

Whatever was hitting the ship began multiplying in frequency like a slow, spitting rain. *Ace*'s sensors were now lighting up the bridge and screeching out warnings.

Her eyes met Niko's. She swallowed hard, her meal already turning sour in her stomach. More thuds echoed in quick succession. A shadowy streak passed one of the cameras. "We need Michelle back here now."

Then the downpour began.

The entire ship shook as hundreds of impacts echoed throughout the bridge. Lessa used the table's command pad to try to get sensor readings on what was out there. One thing she did find— whatever was slamming into the *Ace of Spades* wasn't bouncing off; it was sticking to the hull.

CHAPTER 13

After clearing the tunnel and traversing a long pathway, our meager lights flash over the pillar indicated by my scans. By my calculations, its base as it passes through our pathway measures 275 square meters.

Three vertical rows inset with numerous transport bays extend up the pillar. The bays are meant to hold a variety of small interior transport vessels and pods normally held in place by hard-light grips. With the lack of power many have fallen to the pathway—these we must navigate around—while others perch haphazardly on the floor of their compartments.

My companions aim their lights over the area while I move to a terminal, which juts out from the base of the pillar. I must clear debris from the activation console in order to connect to the interface. Without power to this section, I cannot access it remotely. Therefore I must root out its defects manually. I begin with the power source. . . .

Rion joins me at the terminal. "How's it look?"

"It appears the connection to the hard-light conduit has been completely severed just beyond this location, not only affecting this *activation node, but everything we encountered after it. An easy repair, Captain."*

"Hey, Forge, come look at this." *Ram is kneeling near a damaged monitor, its spherical carapace crushed on one side and its silver alloy flash burned to black. Its ocular lens is shattered, the pieces scattered across the floor.*

I will join him momentarily, once I complete rerouting and fusing the conduit's hard-light optical filaments, of which there are hundreds— a process that would take a human many hours, but one that takes me mere minutes . . .

Ah. Excellent!

Welcome blue light flows up through the wall and into the terminal. I step back as it continues following along the angular conduit lines and up the pillar to the vertical rows and into each transport bay. With power restored, the bay's hard-light grips activate and pull the existing pods back to their proper position. The entire area pulses with light and power. It runs through the pathway on which we stand and into the tunnel, and perhaps—barring any down-conduit damage— illuminating our way back to the ship.

Rion and Ram have risen from their inspection to admire the great illumination.

Power has been restored to most of the section and has created an even greater sense of largess and familiarity.

Oddly, I find I preferred the darkness.

"Is this Zeta's monitor?" *Rion asks as she crouches by the monitor, a piece of broken lens between her fingers.*

The lifeless carapace they have found creates an unsettling sensation I would rather ignore. I give a cursory inspection to the inert shell. The fate of its data core draws inevitable questions to the forefront—and I wonder where data, essences, imprints of monitors, go when they die. But I fear I already know the answer.

"No, this is not 117649 Despondent Pyre. There were many exec-utor constructs on the ring with subordinate functions. This is one of them. We must continue on." I move back to the terminal.

There, I link remotely and select a pod suitable for three to four occupants. The grips release and a smooth oval-shaped pod of pearly white slides easily out of its bay and then descends to my location. It stops to hover soundlessly less than half a meter above the pathway. My approach triggers the appearance of a door in the center of the pod. Without delay, I step into another familiar space with an interior bench that runs the shape of the pod and a ceiling of silvery yellow. Once, an ancilla would have offered food and water, but none appears.

After my companions enter cautiously, the door disappears. "Please take a seat," I tell them as I access the drive node with ease. The walls shift into translucence at my command; I do not prefer small spaces. I remain at the front of the pod while Rion and Ram sit across from each other.

Our journey continues, and the quick and effortless rise brings a sudden curse from Ram's lips. "A little warning next time!" he yells as we ascend five stories in seconds.

"It's not as bad as the translocation pads," Rion says, amused this has affected him.

On the appropriate level, the pod ceases its ascent and glides swiftly down another pathway for a half kilometer before entering a wide tunnel. Once we exit, a platform opens up. The pod comes to a stop. "We are here."

Ram exits, followed by Rion. This platform could easily contain a small city, and they are suitably impressed. "Just through that path-way, there," I tell them, leading the way. "The pod will wait here for our return."

"You feel that?" Rion asks. "It's getting warmer. The air's different."

"We're near the surface now," Ram says.

The change in humidity and temperature, the faintest of current where there was none before, is undeniable. It does not bode well. "The Cartographer is up ahead."

My goal has been to notice as little as possible in an effort to stave off the memories. But this place pulls on my core, drawing out memories I can no longer keep quiet.

In an attempt to save the ring from colliding with the wolf-faced planet, waves of human, Forerunner, AI, and Flood-infected forms were ushered through this area by war sphinxes under the control of Mendicant Bias.

I remember.

We were gathered like cattle, inspected and parsed to control rooms all over the ring, where humans linked directly to infected Forerunners, sharing in their unsurpassed agony and pain. Shaping Sickness, the ancient human word for the Flood, was a name of truth, as it corrupted and reshaped its victims not only on the outside but internally as well.

I remember.

The memory of pain is etched into the walls of my framework, the sensations cascading over me as if it happened only yesterday. Pricked with darts and bonded by a strange lacy webbing, my infected partner and I linked directly to the Cartographer and through it to Halo itself. We were a mind of thousands, not simply using the controls to guide the ring to safety but becoming *the controls, becoming* Halo. *In that joining was felt the immense energy and power of the ring— all-consuming, magnificent, and addicting.*

I REMEMBER.

The extreme forces of the wolf-faced planet passing through our Halo were unimaginable. Sections of ring buckled and broke, wrenched apart, great chunks of earth and rock and mountain, metal and cable ripped away, and . . . then there was darkness. I did not see the outcome. I became lost, attached to the heady power of the ring. . . .

The anguish of the infected, lumbering Flood forms and those humans whose bodies broke under the strain, like mine, endured until it was done. All fodder for the Primordial in his deep prison somewhere below us, delighting in the exquisite unified suffering of so many at once.

I REMEMBER!

And the wounds remain fresh.

In the worst of it, Bornstellar, now the IsoDidact, arrived, shut down Mendicant Bias, and linked with me to finish guiding us through the worst of the passing. . . .

He had come.

But it was too late to save me.

War, Mendicant Bias, the Master Builder, the Primordial, the Librarian, the Didact. All had taken pieces of me.

And yet . . . I am still here. And they are not.

Does that make me *the victor?*

The main chamber housing the Cartographer bleeds light as we approach. But it is the wrong kind of light. I know before entering that it is destroyed.

The enormous vault in the cliff is now an old ruin broken open to the sky. The land above has collapsed inward, depositing dirt and rubble and great blocks of gray cliff inside the space, creating a loose cross patch of stone above us. Daylight and dust motes fill the air.

Ram has gone ahead, slowly picking his way along a path that still edges one side of the chamber, while Rion stays where she is. She watches me, concern written in her dark eyes and around the tight set of her mouth. "Anything salvageable, you think?"

Oddly, laughter is the reaction that springs to mind. I attempt a shrug instead.

Ram's whistle echoes from the opposite end of the chamber. "Hey! Come see this!"

We follow in his footsteps, moving carefully around boulders and debris, to find that the far side of the chamber has been completely shorn away, creating a crude balcony of sorts where metal and rock and land should have been.

It is a lovely view from up here on the edge, the landscape spread out like a great canvas. A pair of birds with brilliant fiery wings dipped in blue hold the span of their three-meter wings horizontal, riding thermal currents across a sky backdropped by jagged mountains and the dramatic, sweeping curve of the ring, drawing the eye up and up and up. It is a sight like no other.

From the foot of the jagged mountain range, alpine forests fan out in our direction in a great wave, which eases into a plain of green that butts close to the base of the cliff we currently stand on. Below, a wide river flows around the curvature of the base and disappears. A short distance away, a blue lake glistens beyond its pebbled beach and an abandoned campsite overlooks the view. Farther, beyond the human eye, lie the spectacular ruins of a once-great human city, ancient even before my time on the ring.

Our comms suddenly crackle, startling us. It is Lessa, her words broken by static. "Cap! . . . any— . . . There's something . . . the hu—"

"Less!" Rion tries to reconnect, but there is no reply. She turns and hurries past me, pale. "I thought you were staying linked to the ship?!"

I was. I certainly meant to. I did not realize I had lost the connection at some point. Very strange, indeed.

CHAPTER 14

Ace of Spades

The ship rocked violently as Lessa held on to the table. "Niko! What is it?!" The noise reminded her of the time *Ace* was pulled into the gravity well of Jeren X. They'd barely escaped the barrage of graphite rain in the upper atmosphere.

She tried reaching Rion through comms again, but all she got was static and a few choppy bits of dialogue, then nothing.

"Hold on! Michelle is coming back!" Niko switched the viewscreen to show Michelle's camera and they watched intently from the drone's perspective as it flew along the pathway and then lit on the ship's position.

Lessa's jaw went slack. *What the hell?*

Ace's hull was covered in large patches of black . . . and whatever it was . . . moving? Wait—were those *wings*? A sudden flash of what might have been open claws appeared in Michelle's camera feed a second before it tumbled wildly. The screen blitzed and shifted to black. Quickly Lessa initiated takeoff procedures.

Ace's thrusters were spooling up for lift, but it seemed like it was taking forever. *Come on, come on.* Suddenly the ship lurched. A piercing metallic echo followed. *Ace* moved again.

Lessa's heart dropped. As crazy as it seemed, it sure as hell felt like they were being pushed or dragged. "Keep trying to raise the captain; tell her we're leaving!"

"I am!" Niko yelled over the din. "Those things are all over the sensors! I'm not getting a response."

Stunned and growing more terrified by the second, Lessa stared across the table and met her brother's wide eyes as the ship continued to rock and groan. The thuds and the dragging didn't stop. It was becoming clear they were in a world of trouble.

Ace rocked hard again, tipping violently. Lessa left the main tactical table and headed for her chair. "Buckle in!"

Dammit. Her fingers fumbled with the attachment as the ship continued to tip over. The world turned slowly upside down as the *Ace of Spades* went weightless over the platform.

Thank God her buckle finally snapped into place. Lessa's stomach rolled and her vision distorted as she tried like hell to hold on to the NAV console, using everything she had—abdominal muscles, arm and hand strength . . . But forces were working against her. It was difficult to focus on the interface. Niko shouted her name. She dodged a loose datapad just in time. It slammed into the wall behind her. If she could just reach . . .

As free fall continued, Lessa finally made it forward enough to focus on the controls. Immediately, she engaged the ACC, before being shoved back into her seat, hoping . . . praying the ship's auto anti-collision sensors could read proximity through the passengers on the hull. But she wasn't finished with procedure. Thrusters locked, she saw the green light. Her eardrums rang with the pounding of her heart and the shrill alarms. Reaching for the console again took all her strength.

Got it!

Auto engaged. Thrusters fired, full throttle.

Lessa released her hold and was flung back as *Ace* rolled right side up, pulling deeply at her insides. The speed of their fall was now countered by the firing of thrusters. She opened her eyes, a hopeful zing spreading through her limbs.

Without any warning at all, *Ace* hit the ground.

The force sent her legs up and her torso down. Her face slammed into her knees.

Then . . . blackness.

It was the awful sounds that woke her.

At first they sounded underwater, a slow muted thunder that grew from low bass to a high-pitched treble. Her gut rolled again, shoving bile into her throat. A hot, throbbing pressure radiated through her face, and her eye sockets and sinuses were on fire. Lessa tried to crack her eyes open, but they were heavy and uncooperative.

She tried clearing her throat to speak, but was hindered by the sharp tang of nausea. Finally, she managed a strangled word; the only one that mattered. *"Niko."*

The nausea was nearly as bad as the pain in her face, and she feared opening her eyes and trying to focus, only to see the world spinning. If that happened, she'd definitely barf. *No, don't think about it.*

She had to push through. Niko wasn't answering.

As sleepy as she felt, she fought the blackness edging in on her. One of the keys to survival was how quickly a person recovered and defended themselves—or removed themselves from harm's way before another blow landed and sank them further into oblivion.

She reached down and pulled on those old reserves. Her head weighed a ton, but she managed to lift it and open her eyes. The flashes on the bridge seemed to come in every color of the rainbow. One of the consoles had shorted, and sparks crackled into the air. Niko's head was on his console. He wasn't moving.

Tears sprang fast as she fumbled with her buckle. "Niko. Hold on."

Irritating buckle wouldn't—*there we go*. She was free. Standing on her feet was another matter. As soon as she tried, her head exploded with pain, and dizziness nearly overwhelmed her. A cold sweat broke out on her forehead. She was shaking inside and out. "I'm coming, Niko."

She took one step, using her console for support, then another, until she was balanced on her own two feet. At that moment the ship gave another violent lurch. Lessa fell forward. She hit the floor, her hand nearly touching Niko's heel.

Her vision began bleeding black. She couldn't lift her cheek off the floor.

Well, I almost made it.

A loud metallic scraping echoed throughout the bridge.

The *Ace of Spades* was being moved once again.

CHAPTER 15

Establishing a steady signal to comms was a fruitless endeavor, making the pod ride back to the ship interminable. Rion's inability to contact *Ace* was an open invitation to imagine the worst, but they'd been through situations like this before. It was a big part of the job—going into the unknown, dealing with whatever came at them. Years of salvaging had taught her to check her emotions and handle things in a calm, assertive fashion.

Still, she couldn't stop her finger from tapping impatiently on the side of her assault rifle as the pod dropped the five-story descent, then made swift passage past the pod bays, through the tunnel, around the debris, and finally on the pathway back to the ship.

Most of it went by in a blur.

The hard-light conduit that Spark had restored earlier now flowed through much of the area, making it easier to see as the pod came to what should have been *Ace*'s position. Rion's gut knotted itself into a tight ball as she shot to her feet. As soon as the door appeared, she was out, heading to the only evidence that her ship had been there at all.

Deep scratches in the metal alloy led to the edge of the pathway. Any calmness she might've gained in the pod evaporated. Even if she *had* let her imagination run wild, it wouldn't have imagined this. In disbelief, she stepped right up to the edge and peered into a great ocean of darkness.

Ram appeared beside her, dropping to his knees. "Hang in there, Forge. We'll find them." Quickly, he removed his rifle, set it aside, then retrieved a small monocular from his vest, usually used to get a closer look at wreckage. She wanted to rip it from his grasp, but bit her lip instead and joined him on the floor as he shifted to his stomach to get a good vantage to see over the edge.

"Anything?"

Seconds ticked by before he finally answered. "Yeah . . . yeah. Right there. Look." He handed over the monocular and pointed.

It wasn't easy to orient or spot anything in the blackness, especially when impatience ate away her composure, but eventually her eyes adjusted and she finally saw it—a dot of faintly illuminated lavender-gray haze. No way to tell if the haze and *Ace* were one and the same, but it was the only thing that seemed to exist down there.

She pushed to her feet. "Spark—" He was already guiding the pod to the edge. Without delay, they filed in and began a rapid descent. The pod walls were translucent once more, and Rion took full advantage, anxious to get a look at that light.

They didn't talk. What could they say? Even though it appeared her ship had been pulled over the edge, Rion wasn't going to assume anything. For all they knew, *Ace* had recovered and was making her way into the atmosphere by now.

Rion hit her comm link. "*Ace*, you read me?" Just static. "Less? Niko? Someone please copy," she said in frustration.

Finally the hazy outline began to take shape, at first distorted like a spotlight covered in a nighttime fog, but as they drew closer, a cloudy violet glow emerged.

She had thought they were approaching something small.

They'd gone much farther into the substructure and that tiny light was now becoming something monstrous, something completely staggering and unfamiliar. As the distance shortened, the haze diffused, revealing the tips of colossal, jet-black towers, densely packed in clusters and on a scale that rivaled some of the biggest cities in the colonies.

The glow hadn't been coming from *Ace* at all, but from patches of violet bioluminescence that stuck on the towers like thousands of dim neon splatters flung from an artist's paintbrush.

"Look at the shape," Ram said, his voice shaken. "Are those . . . *crystals*?"

"Yes. A core cluster—a leftover feature from the ring's original design." Spark delivered this observation in a flat tone. He was not impressed. "The bioluminescence is new, however."

"Could *Ace* be in this core?" she asked.

"The ship could be anywhere," he said evenly.

"Helpful," she shot back.

The pod slowed as it neared the highest tower. Rion tried comms again with no result. "Let's not get too close."

"There!" Ram pointed to a small mote in the shadow of the crystals. "That has to be her."

"Let's check it out. Hand me that monocular again."

The pod altered course and headed for the tiny smudge resting on the same platform as the crystal cluster. Rion held her breath, laser-focused on the sight until finally she got a clear view. *Oh, thank God.* That was *Ace* all right, a few hundred meters outside the cluster. "It's her," she breathed, the relief making her knees weak.

"Thank all the gods," Ram said, then tapped her shoulder for the lens. After he took a quick look, his voice turned cautious. "Well, it is *Ace*, but what the hell is covering her?"

A spike of dread hit Rion hard. "Spark, let's do a quick flyby."

"Fascinating," Spark said as the ship came into full view.

That wasn't the word she'd use. Hers were colorful and mostly four-lettered and directed at the blanket of black that covered the *Ace of Spades*. Thousands of tiny eyes lifted as the transport pod flew overhead. The pod was entirely silent, so the sound Rion heard could only be attributed to those . . . things below. It was a hum, an insect-like vibration.

"Set us down. Put twenty meters between us."

The pod executed a gentle arc and eased down in front of the ship. The buzz was louder now, accompanied by the nerve-tingling screech of *Ace*'s belly intermittently being pulled along the platform. As they exited the pod, Ram tried comms again. Still random static. It occurred to her the sound might well be disrupting *Ace*'s signal. Whatever it was, whatever *they* were, needed to get the hell off her ship.

With a deliberate calm, she checked the chamber of her rifle again—a comfort gesture more than anything else. Ram mirrored her movements. She gave him a quick nod, grateful to have his skill set on her side, then approached the ship to get a better handle on the situation.

"They don't seem too interested in us," Ram remarked.

"No, they got their claws full with my ship."

Keeping her cool was difficult when all she wanted was to fire her rifle and scatter those things. But hasty decisions could very well backfire and cause the herd to attack en masse, and there was no way they'd outrun or defend against that many.

The platform beneath *Ace* was burned black. Spent fuel was

thick and hot in the air, the smell overwhelming and unmistakable. Thrusters had been engaged when she hit. Safety protocols would have shut them down moments before impact. From what Rion could tell at this distance, the *Ace* had hit hard: landing gear had been sheared off or crushed, no doubt some damage to the undercarriage.

"Spark, can you pick up anything inside?"

"It appears an electromagnetic field is disrupting our signals. The hum you hear are sound vibrations created by those creatures. It's . . . somewhat similar to electromagnetic induction—their combined kinetic energy converted into electricity." His head tilted in thought. "Perhaps an aspect within their biology allows the body to act as a transducer. . . ."

That would explain why Spark had lost his connection with the ship and comms were dead. Still, it didn't solve the problem of how to get those things off her ship. Rion nudged Ram for the monocular.

Once focused, she got her first good look at what they were dealing with. Filling the lens were strange goat-size creatures with short black fur, foxlike faces with round black eyes, and long, thin snouts similar to some type of nectar feeder. Their wings were insect-like, membrane thin, and shot through with bioluminescent veins, and they had two long tails. They had significant sets of claws, but also some kind of sticky or suction-type pad beneath their flat paws. They weren't attacking the ship, but seemed intent on using their combined force to pull it toward the city of crystals, which loomed behind the *Ace of Spades*.

"Thoughts?" she asked, handing the lens to Ram.

"Warnings shots might be too risky," he said, taking a look.

"They appeared to show no aggression to our flyover," Spark said. "They must be familiar with pod technology."

"Makes sense. *Ace* is the foreign entity and the transport pod might be something they're used to."

"Is it familiarity or respect?" Spark said thoughtfully, his head cocked. "Let's find out, shall we?" He didn't wait for an answer, just strode forward with purpose.

"He doesn't— Jesus." Rion hurried after him. *"Dammit, Spark—wait!"*

She only went a few steps before stopping, watching in horror as Spark continued forward, the hard light that powered his armiger shifting from blue to red.

"Shit." Ram joined her, raising his rifle. "He better know what the hell he's doing."

At his approach, the creatures lifted their heads in unison, a slew of tiny eyes reflecting the approaching red.

Rion raised her rifle. But it wasn't Spark that had drawn the creatures' attention; it was the blue streak of silvery orbs passing overhead at a high rate of speed. One departed from the group and swung around while the others scattered the creatures. A massive black cloud took flight and moved toward the safety of the crystal city with the orbs at its heels.

The one that swung around settled in front of Spark, hovering eye level with the armiger as he shifted from red to blue.

"Come on, let's go before he decides to go off half-cocked again," Rion muttered, lowering her weapon.

Like the others, the monitor was spherical and made of similar alloy as the armiger, though the metal appeared subdued and time-worn. It bore striking similarities to the images of 343 Guilty Spark that Rion had seen, except its three sides were not concaved and open, but closed and bulging slightly outward. Its central eye, or lens, beamed a blue scan over first Spark, and then Rion as she approached, followed by Ram.

Ram went stiff as the light swept over him. "What the hell is happening?"

"I am scanning you, human," the monitor answered with a pleasant female tone. Once its scans were complete, it focused on Spark. "You have no designation, construct. Please state your designation."

"I have none because I need none," Spark replied arrogantly. "But if you must know, I am former monitor 04-343 Guilty Spark."

The blue beam from its lens scanned him again. "This form is *most* inappropriate. Where is your carapace? And why are you not attending your installation?"

"Installation 04 was destroyed. Where is 117649 Despondent Pyre?"

"Everywhere and nowhere," it answered with a wistful note. "I am Submonitor Adjutant Veridity. You may call me Veridity."

With the creatures gone, signals were restored on the ship. Rion's comms and gauntlet lit up with data alerts as *Ace*'s ramp disengaged, spilling interior light onto the platform. *Oh, thank God.* The wave of relief was so strong it propelled her right past the monitor. She could feel Veridity's eye on her as she passed. Spark, since he seemed keen on making critical decisions all by himself, could deal with the monitor. Rion was desperate to check on her crew.

Ram caught up with her. "You think he'll be okay back there?"

"I'm sure he can handle it."

As the ramp continued to lower, Lessa and Niko came into view, elbows linked, waiting to disembark. A dazed and shocked aura surrounded them, but they'd had the wherewithal to visit the locker room and arm themselves first. Pride filled Rion as they limped down the ramp, leaning on each other for support, and onto the pathway, getting their bearings, taking stock.

"You guys all right?" Rion immediately noticed the fresh bruise on the bridge of Lessa's nose, and the blackening already under her eyes. Her hair was a wild halo of blond curls, and the freckles across her face stood in stark contrast to her pale skin. She started crying when she met Rion's gaze.

Shit.

Rion's throat tightened. "You gave us a scare." It might be a lame thing to say, but she found words were suddenly hard to come by. Lessa threw herself in Rion's arms, hugging so forcefully it sent Rion back a few steps. Part of her wanted to let her guard down, to hold on to both of them, but she moved Lessa back to get a good look at her instead. "You hurt anywhere else?"

Lessa's baby blues were as wide as plates, the pupils dilated. "I think I have a concussion and my knees hurt my face or my face hurt my knees. I don't know. . . ."

Ram was lifting Niko's dark hair from his forehead to inspect a pretty nasty gash at his hairline. The kid looked lost, like he had no idea where he was or how he'd gotten there. His stunned expression would have been comical if he weren't bleeding from the head and chin. His vest was hanging off one shoulder, and the extra magazines he'd brought along weren't compatible with the plasma rifle he held in a death grip.

"Let's get you two into the med bay," Ram said, guiding Niko back toward the ramp.

"We were able to strap in right as we fell . . . ," Lessa stammered as Rion helped her into the ship.

In the hold, Ram pulled Rion to the side. "I got this. I'll run them through the med scanner, tend their wounds, and start in on *Ace.* You should probably go check on Spark. The sooner we can deal with his key, the sooner we can get off Zeta."

At Rion's hesitation his eyes flashed with warmth. "I'll take good care of all *three* of them, don't worry," he said with a wink.

When she rejoined Spark, he was already heading her way with the monitor, who was chatting up a storm.

". . . and so the tullioc were brought here from their native world," Veridity was telling him. "Only a few specimens had survived the war, and these escaped during the mists, the time after the firing of the array. The mists kept their numbers minuscule, but now their infestation has grown to tens of thousands."

"Can't you reduce their numbers?" Rion asked.

Veridity swung around swiftly. "We would never *reduce their numbers*." Clearly that had offended the monitor.

"Even when they attack unprovoked, like what happened with my ship?"

"Oh, but you *did* provoke them. When you burned through the jarda leaves. The tullioc lay their eggs beneath the leaves. The eggs hatch and the larvae drop into the substructure, where they make their way to the crystals to feed. The minerals within the crystal are their food source. When they absorb enough, they cocoon inside the hollows they created during feeding. There they stay, developing their wings, gaining their luminescence, until they break free, becoming the long-tailed, winged tullioc that justifiably attacked your ship."

Well, that certainly accounted for the attack. They *had* stirred up the creatures without meaning to. "It was not our intention to harm anything," she told the monitor. "We came"—she wasn't sure how much to reveal, but Spark gave her an encouraging nod—"to find the Cartographer."

"Ah!" Veridity exclaimed happily. "Then it is quite fortuitous that you found it."

"Well, we did . . . but it was in ruins."

"Where is the current Cartographer?" Spark asked.

That's right, Rion remembered. The Cartographer always survived, moved from facility to facility if necessary.

Veridity pivoted to indicate the ominous black towers. "Right there, inside the cluster."

"Is it operational?"

"Fully. Shall I escort you, 04-343?"

Spark turned his blue gaze on Rion.

"We're already here," she said, answering the unspoken question. "Might as well finish it. Lead the way, Veridity." As they followed the monitor, Rion hit her comm. "Hey, Ram, you copy?"

"Go ahead, Cap."

"Status on the crew?"

"Some big bumps and bruises, but they'll both be fine. Mild concussions. Took care of Niko's gash, and Lessa's nose is fractured, but we've already set it and they've gotten a good dose of nano-meds."

"Good. And *Ace*?"

"Working on that too."

She wanted to know particulars, but knew it would only weigh on her mind, so she tabled it until she returned. "Spark and I are headed into the cluster. Apparently, there's a Cartographer site inside."

"Roger that."

As she walked past the length of her ship, she noted every exterior imperfection. Landing gear was busted, ablative coating shot all to hell, antenna and a few sensors snapped . . . Some obvious structural damage, though starships were meant to take a beating, and Titanium-A plating was as tough as they came. Hopefully, they could get her starworthy enough to make it in for repairs.

"She'll fly, Captain," Spark said beside her.

Surprised, she noticed he was also focused on the ship as they passed. "Let's hope, or we're stuck here until she does."

And what a sobering thought that was.

"We would be happy to assist you," Veridity said. "I shall send help immediately."

Instant fear ground Rion's forward momentum to a halt. She wasn't letting anything she didn't trust into her ship.

Spark stepped in. "Do not worry. I will handle this."

If by handling, he meant staring at Veridity for several seconds as it stared right back.

"All settled," he quipped as though it were a done deal. The monitor resumed its lead toward the cluster.

"What do you mean, 'settled'?"

"I have accepted help on your behalf, set guidelines for repairs, and notified Ram to expect assistance. I will remain in contact throughout, overseeing their work. There is nothing to concern yourself with."

"Nothing to concern myself with? Are you serious?" It was her ship!

"Perhaps I could have said that better," he admitted. "You have no reason to trust them, but you may trust me. You do trust me, don't you, Captain?"

She was still getting used to the modifications that Spark's upgrade seed had made, and the last thing she wanted was more changes. But, once they used the key, Rion wanted out of here pronto, and unless they had help, they'd be here too long for her liking.

"Fine. Just see that you remain in contact at all times. If we get any interference again, I want to know immediately." Ram was going to love this new development.

"Of course."

As they drew closer to the cluster, much of it blended into the darkness. What she could see loomed over them. Black fractal crystal rose in a multitude of heights, some hundreds of meters high with girths as wide as city blocks. A few tullioc clung to some of the lower peaks, allowing her to see their shiny black eyes and the softly glowing hue of their wings.

"Something this big had to have an equally big purpose," she remarked.

"It once served as the old heart of Mendicant Bias," Spark told her as they entered the city via a wide central avenue that appeared out of the crystal itself. It made Rion wonder if it possessed similar properties to Spark's machine cells or to the pod they'd used. Some kind of advanced intuitive crystal seemed entirely possible when put in context.

"That is correct, 04-343," Veridity said, overhearing. "The Iso-Didact purged the ancilla's core from the crystals long ago. The cluster had many uses and was part of the ring's original design, long before that particular ancilla came along. Now that we are a third of our original size and many sites, facilities, and functions were shed, there is no need for a storage facility and power source of such magnitude, though we make use of it still.

"It serves many new functions, a place for the tullioc, the site of our new Cartographer, and as the archive we call the Monument."

"The Monument?" Spark inquired.

The monitor spun in a circle, sending its light reflecting through the black crystals nearby as they passed. "Why, yes! Do you approve? The civil war on this ring left us with an overabundance of essences and imprints." Veridity led them down another path, this one narrower than the wide avenue. "They were everywhere. Sub-monitors and custodians confined in damaged carapaces, roaming lost through the ring's networks, trapped in ruined power stations and facilities . . . Composed humans loosed from damaged storage devices, their digital imprints overflowing into support systems, their memories and emotions causing havoc.

"After the firing of the array, we spent the ensuing centuries gathering them, giving them a new home large enough for all, a safe place to rest. Billions of lives lost over countless millennia are stored here in crystal, taken from data, logs, imprints, fragments, events, research, experiments . . . all of them collected, cataloged, and archived. As instructed, we have kept watch. Our only deviation in course was to purify the atmosphere and end the shroud of mist over our Halo."

"Why did you do that?" Spark asked.

"To encourage the survival of the tullioc and other species. After careful study, we discovered that in feeding on the crystal, the creatures were absorbing some of the data stored here. There has been too much death, so we do not harm the tullioc, for in them now lies the memory of thousands."

"Who instructed you to keep watch?" Rion asked.

"Creating and keeping watch over the Monument was a directive from the IsoDidact and the Librarian. This way. We are almost there."

CHAPTER 16

Spark

A fter I survived the near collision with the wolf planet, my final days on Installation 07 and its subsequent arrival to the greater Ark are steeped in shadow. The Librarian and the IsoDidact reunited there for a time, and the Ark became my place to mourn and heal and come to terms with my newly acquired machine nature.

How does one heal a mind without a body?

Still retaining my human memories, I became Monitor Chakas, rewarded with the task of looking after the Librarian's population of humans on the Ark while the IsoDidact eventually returned to the Council and the Librarian continued her conservation work across the galaxy. Of course, our tale was not over, and the tide of war would carry us into one another again.

Just as the tides have curiously returned me here to the old heart of Mendicant Bias.

I follow behind the cheerful Submonitor Veridity and Rion, intentionally hanging back, absorbing the past but also attempting to remember the shadow time I am missing.

I call ahead, "Tell us about the Librarian's time here."

"Of course! Much of her time was spent creating the Cartographer and setting the parameters for the Monument; giving us purpose after so much of our purpose was lost."

"What was your purpose before?" Rion inquires.

"Most tended the living populations. Many species were spread across the ring, some very small groups . . . but others rose to great civilizations and built equally great cities. We had a very long history together, often caretaking our charges through numerous generations of families. Other monitors were station attendants, rail attendants, or held administrative and custodial functions. When the ring was brought to the Ark, the IsoDidact dictated that this installation would no longer continue human conservation measures. No humans meant no purpose.

"But the Librarian, ever the great preserver and debater, said the dead and dying should not be forgotten or unattended; they would be gathered and stored here as a reminder and a record." Veridity spins around. "There's no reason for them to run amuck!" she says happily, then, "He called it a tomb. But she called it a Monument."

All around us I begin to see the towers of black crystal differently.

They are alive with memories and essences like ghosts in a fishbowl of black glass. Only this glass rises as tall as skyscrapers, creating alleys and streets, intersections and wide avenues. We weave a mazelike path through this strange city, the tullioc and their glowing wings and cocoons casting the streets in the darkest violet light.

Rion's head tips back repeatedly as she walks, trying to take it all in. Occasionally her hand reaches out and skims along the black surface where shadowy images respond—a bizarre mix of diaphanous code and picture, appearing and disappearing with a languid pace.

I want this place to feel wrong, so the anger and desire to raze it all to the ground is justified, but this so-called Monument is not what

I expected. It is surprisingly reverent and considerate—another worthy and sympathetic program distinctly emblematic of the Supreme Lifeshaper.

We, too, saved lives, she and I. For a time.

But the number saved will never measure up to those we took, I'm afraid.

In a way, the essences stored here had reached their own version of the Sangheili Hall of Eternity, their names and history preserved in crystal while the monitors safeguard the site, tend the memories, and pay homage to the dead.

A somber shrine below while life flourishes above.

Ram was right. It is a true underworld.

I cannot help but view these archived remnants from my own strange mortality and wonder if this is what I have become as well. A relic. Memory survived. Not dead, not alive, but trapped somewhere in the middle. Is my place here in the past with them, or is it to walk among the living to only bear witness as they perish, while I endure? Is that my penance? Or my reward?

"Hey . . ."

Rion is gazing up at me, concern written in the buckled lines across her forehead. It is clear she has come back to question why I have stopped. I did not realize I had. The monitor is several meters down the violet-lit street, waiting.

"You all right?"

"Yes. No." I shake my head. "I do not know. This place . . ." I reach out and place the tip of my alloy finger on the crystal, increasing the intensity of my hard light. It illuminates outward, sending light through the surface, and revealing within floating code arranged in whimsical lines and images—moments in time—that appear and disappear. "It makes me question my existence, my purpose."

I pull back from the wall as Rion steps closer and lays a hand on

KELLY GAY

*my arm. My heart aches, and I wish just this once that I could feel it.
"She left the key to you. Across all this time and opportunity, it was
you she chose." Her lips purse with thought. "Aren't you the Finger of
the First Man, the keeper and protector of the record of humanity?"*

"That does have a nice ring to it."

*"The ring of purpose," she wisely replies. "This place is full of
ghosts. It could bring anyone down. Come on—let's get to this Cartographer and see what she left you."*

*"Your memory is impressive, Captain," I say, following. She has
remembered the tale of Gamelpar I once told her and the crew. It was
he, the elder I met on this very ring, who spoke of the First Human,
he who carried the souls of all his descendants to come in a finger as
tall as a tree.*

She turns, grins, and taps her temple. "Memory like an elephant."

"Mm." Welcome to my world.

*We reach the center of the cluster, where the alley spills us into a
large circular area. Several hexagonal crystals seventeen meters high,
spaced four meters apart, have been erected around the perimeter. In
the center stands the familiar Forerunner architecture that serves as
the Cartographer and a few structures that are new to me.*

*"This place was her idea too," the monitor tells us. "There is an-
other functional site closer to the surface, half a ring away. This serves
as a silent cartographer." Veridity spins so that her lens faces me. "An
ideal place for such a name. Or is it an ideal name for such a place?"*

I ignore her and approach the terminal. Access is immediate.

*Instantly a map appears suspended in the air above us, showing a
navigable blueprint of the entire Halo ring. The complete history of
the installation resides here. Linked, as I am, the information flows
like an unending feast, a long injection of nutrients to my hungry
core.*

I enjoy it immensely.

Odd.

I am pulled out of my reverie.

There is a gap in the time line. This is . . . unheard of. It simply should not exist. An entire event has been erased. "A record is missing," I tell the monitor.

"Yes. A singular event, I assure you," she says, affronted, though not by my statement, but by the act itself.

"Who erased it?"

"Unknown. It is a deep record, very old, and a black smudge on our perfect log."

Perplexing, indeed. Certainly not an accident, which makes it even more intriguing, as does the necessary level of knowledge and clearance needed to commit an act of erasure. What would require such a drastic measure? What could be so important, dangerous, or secret that the Forerunners needed to erase it from Zeta Halo's history?

This intrigue, however captivating, must be put aside for later analysis. For now, I must move on. I gesture for the Librarian's key. Rion retrieves it from the safety of her utility vest and hands it over. As I bring it close to the terminal, a key port automatically extends itself from the terminal's console. I slide the key inside, and the port reshapes itself around the key's perimeter.

I am uncertain what to expect, but a bio pad rising from the terminal is not one of them.

This is meant for a Forerunner—or, as their inheritors, a human.

Rion gives me a quick look. We have done this before.

She places her hand on the pad.

The Halo map rearranges itself. The galaxy bursts into life, filling the chamber. I hear the monitor gasp in awe. It is beautiful to witness, and I am momentarily stunned as well.

To my surprise, a golden point appears in a far-off sector. The

KELLY GAY

sector enlarges, revealing systems, nebulae, asteroid fields, and finally a particular star system, and its planets.

"It's another coordinate," Rion says, somewhat disappointed.

As several data packs download directly into my core for later study, the map fades and the key is ejected. Rion removes it as another port extends with a smaller key. Curious, she takes the second key and then inspects them both. "I think they fit together."

"The smaller inside the impression on the original, it appears."

With a shrug, she quips, "Here goes." And places them together.

Hard light fuses around the two pieces, making their connection permanent, transforming two keys into one.

There is a sudden charge in the air.

A prick begins in my core, a sense of unease as Rion smiles and lifts the new key. My sensors are firing, collecting, calculating.

Dread grips hold of me.

A portal splits the air behind Rion. And I know immediately what I must do.

When her slower human senses realize what has happened, her eyes widen with horror. She reaches out to me for help as the portal begins to swallow her. I extend my hand and pluck the key from her fist.

Just the barest, briefest glimpse of shock dawns in her eyes.

And then she is gone.

And I have the key.

CHAPTER 17

Ace of Spades / Zeta Halo

A s Niko and Lessa recuperated in the lounge, Ram cycled through systems on the bridge, noting damage reports and keeping a watchful eye on the small fleet of insect-like repair drones that had invaded the ship to assist with repairs, apparently under Spark's command. He would've said now he'd seen it all, but . . . he knew better.

He certainly didn't want to stay here any longer than necessary and the swarm of little helpers were unbelievably fast and efficient.

Most of *Ace*'s damage was limited to thrusters and exterior undercarriage, ablative plating, shorn and burned sensors and landing gear, some severed and loose circuitry, and minor breakages in the cargo hold, engine room, and bridge. All told, if Lessa hadn't engaged the thrusters, it could've been much worse.

As he removed the clear panel over Niko's damaged console, Ram smiled. He sure was proud of that bruised and banged-up young woman.

Spark's audio link to the ship had gone silent, which was beginning to worry him.

They'd been gone for hours.

Finally, camera feeds picked up a light emerging from the obsidian cluster, an elongated slice of silver and blue reflected in crystal preceding Spark's appearance.

As the armiger cleared the city and moved down the pathway to the ship, Ram frowned. Rion was a no-show. He waited, giving it time, adjusting the camera, looking for her to follow. Spark disappeared beneath the hull, and the orb-y streaks and insects leaving the ship told Ram the whirlwind of major repairs were either completed or halted.

And still no captain.

Damn it.

Bad vibes stuck with him as he hurried from the bridge. Niko called his name as he passed the lounge, but Ram didn't stop until he crossed the catwalk over the cargo hold. Spark was already on board, making his way to one of the worktables near the cargo bins where he stored his armiger. At the echo of Ram's footsteps, Spark came to a halt in the center of the hold and then turned that sleek alloy head Ram's way. Blue eyes stared obliquely up at him.

Yeah, bad vibes all the way.

Ram rubbed a hand down his beard, using the moment to remind himself to err on the side of optimism until he had more information. He jogged down the stairs, asking, "Hey. Where's Rion?" But when the bay doors began to close and the sound of the ramp lifting filled the hold, he knew things had taken a dark turn. "Spark . . . ," he said calmly, wondering if he could make it to the armory before the armiger, should the need arise. "What are you doing?"

"Leaving."

Steps rang above them. Niko leaned over the railing with a smile; the pain patch and nano-meds were obviously working their magic. "So, you guys use the key?"

Lessa wasn't far behind, the bruises over her nose and beneath her eyes still visible. "Don't keep us in suspense. What'd you get?"

It took them a few seconds to notice that the ship was closing up and Rion hadn't made an appearance.

"Where's Cap?" Lessa was the first to ask.

That final, awful click of the doors sealing reverberated through the hold. Ram had been through thousands of different scenarios in his time captaining his own salvage vessel, but this was way different. He'd never had to deal with or face off against a Forerunner AI that had full control of the ship.

The thrusters suddenly began spooling up. Jesus, they hadn't even been through test runs. *Ace of Spades* shuddered.

The siblings rushed the stairs. "Wait." Reserved panic stirred in Niko's eyes. "Why are we leaving?"

Spark didn't answer. He simply continued toward the worktable.

No one seemed to know what to do next. Ram hurried to the closest datapanel and entered a code to abort takeoff. Locked out. He spun around, warning, "Don't pull this crap on me, armiger. Unlock this. *Now.*"

"Spark, what's going on?" Lessa's movement down the stairs became slow and fearful. "We can't leave without Rion."

The ship began to lift off the platform as Ram strode to the worktable and put his hand on Spark's forearm. "This isn't how we do things. You know this. We don't leave without our captain."

After a long pause, Spark turned his head in Ram's direction. "She is not out there. She is gone."

"*What?*" Lessa swayed and held the railing tight.

Ram put his hand out. *Just wait,* the motion indicated. *Wait until we have all the information.* He turned back to the armiger. "Okay. Why don't we start at the beginning."

"Captain Forge is no longer on Zeta Halo. She was pulled into a portal when we activated the key."

Well, hell. That was . . . Ram scratched his head and let out a measured exhale. Certainly *not* what he expected to hear. "Pulled where, exactly?"

Spark's hesitation told Ram that whatever answer came next, it wasn't going to be a simple fix. "I believe to our next location."

The crew gathered around the table and Ram had to give credit: Niko and Lessa were trying hard to stay calm.

"You're gonna have to be square with us, right now," Niko said. "The plan was to use the key at the Cartographer's location and get whatever *thing* the Librarian left for you. Right . . . ?"

"That is correct." Spark opened his hand and dropped the key on the table. One side was now smooth, and the other held a small circular inlay. "Once I inserted the key into Zeta Halo's Cartographer, a second key appeared. The captain realized this second smaller piece fit precisely into the Gyre symbol depression that Lessa uncovered on the main key. I know not which of our actions triggered the portal event. As a result, we are now left with a revised key and a new location. I believe the portal's purpose was to take the captain directly to this new location."

Niko's face screwed into a deep scowl. "That doesn't make any sense."

"I believe her status as Reclaimer initiated the portal, or at the very least allowed her to pass through. The Librarian believed humans were meant to hold the Mantle of Responsibility. As such, they have been given access to Forerunner technology in a way others are not."

"And that's why you weren't pulled in," Ram reasoned.

"Perhaps. And why I obtained the key from her before she disappeared. If she had taken it, we might have no way to gain access to her current location. I must admit that I underestimated the importance of the key. Whatever it unlocks prompted a high level of complexity and preparedness."

Overwhelmed by emotion and pain meds, Lessa stormed away and then came back again. "How do you know she didn't just pop out at some other location on Zeta Halo? Isn't that what the Cartographer does? Pick a place on its map and it takes you there or something? Shouldn't we start a search, to make sure? She might be able to signal us—"

"No, Lessa," Spark interrupted, his tone gentler. "Rion is no longer on Zeta Halo. She is no longer in this star system."

"No. No way. No portal can pull a human being through space!"

"*Shit,*" Niko murmured softly. Because he knew, just like Ram, that it *was* possible. And Lessa knew it too. They'd already seen the wonders of a Forerunner planet and were right now standing inside a Halo itself. If the Forerunners could build all of this, if they could send something this big through slipspace, could create entire *worlds* . . . then sending one human across space seemed trivial.

Lessa's ire deflated. "Fine. Then we'll use the portal to go after her. Easy."

"There is no cross-space portal technology in the Cartographer. It was initiated from the destination side. We have no way to access it, and it has completed its function," Spark replied.

"This is insane," Niko said. "Keys are supposed to open things, not send you all over the damn galaxy. . . ."

Lessa whirled on her brother, tears in her eyes. "Yeah, and maybe *we* wouldn't even be in this situation if it wasn't for *you.*"

The kid paled. "What the hell is that supposed to mean?"

"That launching Michelle brought those things upon us. If they hadn't had to come racing back to save our asses, they might've never found this stupid place or they could have found a working terminal elsewhere to use the key. Instead we ended up down here . . . so you tell me where the fault lies."

Ram stayed quiet. Her logic was somewhat flawed, but she was running on pure emotion and he wasn't about to step in her path. Young people—especially those coming off a traumatic event and under the influence—were *not* his specialty, but he did want to know exactly what happened while he and Rion and Spark were away.

"Anyone care to enlighten me?"

Lessa rolled her eyes and marched halfway up the stairs before settling down on a rung. Ram's heart went out to both of them. Misery had settled over Niko, but he kept his lips sealed.

Ram folded his arms over his chest and waited.

Finally Niko answered. "I sent Michelle out to nose around. I guess she stirred them up . . ."

"Bullshit!" Lessa shot back. "You sent her out looking for wreckage; I saw the search parameters on your screen. So why don't you tell us all what exactly you needed so badly that you decided, *on your own*, to deploy a drone inside a Halo."

Ram inwardly cringed. Yeah. Not a great decision. First things first, though. "One issue at a time," he said. "First priority is finding Rion. She has a bio tag like we all do. We'll do a hard sweep of her signature. If we don't find anything, we'll head to the new location on the key and hope like hell she's there, waiting for us." Ram faced Spark. "You have a location yet?"

"Kaphus."

Ram prided himself on his knowledge of known planets and systems, and this one wasn't ringing any bells.

"You call it New Carthage," Spark amended.

And *that* was a place Ram knew intimately.

"So that's it, then?" Lessa got up. "We're just going to leave. Without her. What if her tag isn't working or there's interference or . . . She could still be here." Lessa turned a suspicious eye toward Spark. "And how do we even know you're telling the truth?"

"I have no reason to lie."

Ram had enough of the back-and-forth. "Spark, please create scan parameters using Rion's bio-tag. It's in her file. Lessa, I know you're worried. We all are. We'll scan the ring as thoroughly as we can. But then we have to move on. If Rion is somewhere out there, dumped into some abandoned Forerunner facility alone with no backup and no provisions, we'll need to get to her as quickly as possible."

"Parameters are set," Spark announced. "We have cleared the substructure. Bafflers at seventy percent and engaged."

"Run her around the ring," Ram ordered. "If you don't get a hit, we're at full speed away, set the jump point to New Carthage, and then we go." He looked at each of the crew. "Agreed?"

"Who the hell made you boss?" Niko piped up, but with no real fire behind his words.

"Two decades in the captain's chair, kid."

No one responded.

"Good. Once we're in slipspace, meeting in the lounge."

With that, Ram walked away, a headache already brewing. He'd grown too old or too tired of being in charge—maybe both—to deal with ship drama. Truth be told, he had no desire to captain this vessel or any other, which came as a surprise; he'd always assumed the urge would come back.

For now, he'd do what had to be done, and he'd do it to the best of his ability. Rion had offered him a place when he was at the lowest point in his life, when he'd lost everything—his ship, his crew, his livelihood. She'd taken him in when he was a grieving, damaged drunk and gave him back the stars. And he'd do everything in his power to repay the favor.

On the bridge, he deliberately avoided her chair and monitored *Ace*'s path over the Halo from his usual spot. Niko and Lessa filed in quietly after him and took their respective seats, even though they should have been resting as ordered.

Spark's avatar blinked into life over the tactical table. "Scans are complete. No returns. We are ready to jump."

One sweep over the Halo's curve and then Ram punched the engines full ahead to the jump point.

CHAPTER 18

Rion

Black dots appear behind her eyelids. Any sensation of up, down, left, right, disappears abruptly, and swells of vertigo turn her stomach inside out. A cold sweat breaks through her skin.

Can't. Move.

Panic pulses through her eardrums, loud and unrelenting. Her chest rises and falls in rapid flutters, quicker and quicker, shallower and shallower. Oxygen isn't flowing through her lungs fast enough.

She can't keep up.

The body isn't designed for this.

Can't keep up. Can't cope.

What a sickening way to die.

"Fear is like a weed." A calming voice settles over the panic like a warm blanket. "Ignore it and it spreads. But pluck it out by the roots and plant something stronger in its place, and you have made a force bigger than your fear.

"So pick your ground, human. Plant something stronger.

— 127 —

"*Grow roots. Anchor down deep. Find your bearings. Find your core. Hold on to it. And breathe.*

"*That's it. Breathe.*

"*Good.*

"*Now walk with me. The garden is pretty this time of year. . . ."*

Blackness gives way to light. The ground rises up to catch her in midstride, first one step, then another, and just like that she is walking, barefoot on sun-warmed ground.

Two shadows stretch before her. One is her own. The other belongs to the Librarian, who has shed her armor and removed her ancilla. A white dress clings to her lithe body. Hair the same color lies in a braid down her back. Her feet are also bare.

Ahead is a lovely ridge with an equally lovely view. Birds flit from branch to branch, singing and screeching. Monkeys too. A few animals linger warily in the shadows behind them, too hidden to identify, but Rion knows they are there. She doesn't look back. They pose no threat.

They reach the ridge. Sweat dampens the Librarian's smooth bluish skin and weariness appears to sink well into her being. Rion, though, feels nothing, no exertion from the walk, no pain, only the strange physical and emotional connection to the being beside her.

The rock on which they choose to rest is smooth, a good place to sit and stretch their legs, wiggle their toes, and admire the stunning view. It is primal and peaceful and right. Far in the distance, a cloud of dust holds fast over the site where a portal will one day rise.

"I planted something beautiful," the Librarian says. "Do you remember?"

Rion isn't sure. "I don't know. . . ."

The vaguest of smiles crosses the Librarian's face. "Though he is bound by his rate to obtain my testimony, Catalog will never hear the words I am about to say. No official record will exist. Only the view and the animals around me will bear witness to this, my final confession."

A small rectangular box rests in her right hand. It seems familiar, but the sunlight glinting off its surface hides its features from view. "This device will log my words and serve to fill the spaces between spaces with understanding and truth. It will hold this truth beyond my passing, beyond the termination of life in the galaxy and its reseeding, and the reemergence of spacefaring civilizations. And even then, some secrets will be kept a while longer."

A breeze lifts a few strands of her hair while her gaze lies with longing over the land. There is no ancilla to calm the burning ache in her chest or prevent the sting in her eyes. Rion feels the Librarian's pain quite clearly and wants to reach out, to offer some comfort.

"My part in Living Time grows short. The pride and hubris of my Forerunner nature propels me to fear despite knowing better. I am afraid. Of being forgotten, misunderstood, leaving the galaxy to chance, ceasing to exist . . ."

Her pause is an effort to clear away the sadness.

The moment passes. One corner of her mouth lifts with a memory that brings a small mote of happiness.

"The Didact often said my ability to read the flow of Living Time was unlike any in the ecumene. In the early centuries of our marriage, this was spoken with unreserved pride and no small amount of affection. Later, it was said with grudging respect and no small amount of debate. Ours was an unlikely match. But two opposing forces can make the strongest bond. . . .

"I mourn deeply our losses and our separations. I mourn our children, and the many I tended, nurtured, and guided. I mourn the possibilities that went nowhere, for I have seen their enormous potential and have withstood the heartache of knowing what might have been.

"Yet, for all my ability and knowledge, I cannot steer the flow of Living Time around my own eventuality.

"My husband was not wrong. Through life's interaction with the cosmos, I see the strings and paths and fates and the millions of possible outcomes born of a single possible choice. Vast, overarching probabilities are far easier to see than the faintest filament, that one tiny spark of possibility in a sea of possibilities.

"Sometimes the smallest acts echo the loudest.

"My mentor, the first to seed my young mind with such a notion, would be amused by the sum total of my life, of the cyclical nature of fate and time. She was fond of analogy and metaphor and irony—she adored a good irony."

Her fondness for this mentor fills Rion with gladness. The memory eases some of the ache in the Librarian's heart.

"'An unconventional tutor for an unconventional child,' my father once said as I listened around the corner of his work space. Perhaps the greatest gift he gave me was accepting his unusual child needed a suitably unusual tutor.

"My first glimpse of Living Time came as a child, a chaotic nightmare with no beginning or end, an overwhelming cacophony of moments, deeds, acts, memories, none of which I understood, bombarding me from all directions, jumbling together, tangling and making it impossible to navigate. My only recourse was to hide, to pull my body in close, squeeze my eyes shut, and wait. Wait to wake up.

"Forerunner children rarely weep with any regularity. Most are born with an innate calm, a natural instinct to regulate excessive emotions—a pleasing characteristic that follows many throughout life. I, however, cried with all the fervor of a human child. My inability to sleep made everyone's life miserable. Our household monitors were only able to console my dreams with chemical intervention.

"In my waking hours, I was a quick study, my thirst for knowledge

insatiable and necessary to my well-being. Information was suste-
nance. My fascination for life in all its forms knew no boundary; the
intense wonder of it, springing up in the most impossible environ-
ments, was a miracle in which I too could share. This study often
took the place of sleep, and while Forerunners grow to no longer need
sleep, certainly all children need their rest.

"As the years went by, natural sleep proved elusive and the chemi-
cals were taking their toll on my development into first-form.

"One of my tutors—and the one who would later become my
mentor—was a Lifeworker named Harmony in Gifted Symmetry.
Her reputation as unconventional was well-known across my home
planet. Forerunners were true conformists, their customs within our
society—and more so within our rates—guiding our entire lives.
But there were always those like Harmony, whose brilliance out-
shone tradition and regulation. Rebels and outliers were typically
frowned upon, but never the brilliant ones like Harmony—they
were always given concessions, at least in public and academic
circles.

"Harmony had just entered her four-thousandth year when I was
born. She was renowned for her work on psy-neural remapping and
programming and had a gift for corrective therapy and guided remedi-
ation in children and young Manipulars.

"Harmony showed me that my nightmares, and the fear they created, could be studied. We recorded, analyzed, and drew conclusions.
My dreams became a separate entity, an unsolved puzzle to study and
test, thus appealing to the great driving need for knowledge that constantly churned in my center.

"My mentor was very astute," the Librarian says with a glint of
humor and pride, and Rion can feel the great affection that wells in
the Librarian's chest.

"Through Harmony's teachings, navigating through the chaos and *tangle of my nightmares, squeezing through the strings and webs and layers, suddenly became a challenge I welcomed.*

"It was the quieting of my own fear that gave the tangled web its voice. And I listened. What I heard was . . . injury, confinement, imbalance, the desperate need to unravel and rejoin the flow of what I then came to understand as Living Time.

"I became an astute listener. I learned to follow. Events leading to threads, threads leading to divergence, and divergence leading to possibilities that had not yet solidified. These possibilities would shape my entire life to come.

"Eventually, I traveled through Living Time the same way I traveled through the Forerunners' vast stores of knowledge, only able to see what was, what is, and never what was to come, only the possibilities and probabilities.

"After I gained my first-form, the Domain opened to me, an event I coveted more than anything I had so far in my short life.

"I should have known my experience would be unconventional.

"It was not my ancestors who greeted me with warmth and the sharing of their great knowledge and experience, but the deep darkness of space, and out of it, shapeless forms, ghosts, flowing toward me with dizzying speed. In two great lines they shuddered past me, great rushing rivers that had become too bloated and too full, spilling over their nebulous banks and oozing fetid and rank and infectious across a field of living green.

"I woke drowning. And I've been fighting for Life ever since."

CHAPTER 19

Ram was relieved to see Niko and Lessa gathered in the lounge, sitting around the table, and Spark waiting over the holopad. After the blowout in the hold, he expected the tension and somber mood that greeted him. Losing Rion had everyone on edge.

First things first. That's how he operated, one foot in front of the other.

He was an orderly sort, open-minded, willing to listen to the opinions of others if asked, occasionally if not. A captain who rarely raised his voice—he didn't need that kind of energy in his life. His requirements consisted of a crew that enjoyed their jobs, didn't complain too much, and respected the process, the ship, and its captain. He had learned over the years not to waste time with anything else. If that wasn't good enough, you could get your ass off his ship. That simple.

Taking the lead here on the *Ace of Spades* was a little trickier.

But it needed to be done. Niko and Lessa didn't have enough experience or maturity to think too far down the road of consequences. And Spark . . . while he could run a fleet of ships in his sleep, being a shipboard AI clearly wasn't his calling; it was simply a bridge to something else, though Spark didn't seem to know what that was. Ram had seen it time and again in others. Didn't make Spark wrong or bad, just made him . . . temporary.

Like Ram himself.

He slid into a seat at the table and got right to business. "Let's start with the portal. Spark, you want to fill us in on what you know about it, what the captain might be going through . . . and what we can expect when we find her?"

"Of course. I believe the portal on Zeta Halo was issued from a personal slipspace unit, a device that follows similar principles as those used in translocation technologies and those used in re-motely sending a Halo through slipspace, for instance. The device itself can exist in one location, on either the departure or desti-nation side. The anomalous placement of such a device was most likely done without authorization; personal slipspace units were forbidden to use except by special license from the Forerunner Council."

"Why forbidden?" Lessa asked.

"Imagine billions of souls regularly using personal transports across four million worlds. The immense buildup of reconciliation would have made it impossible and highly dangerous for any other space travel to occur."

"Traveling Forerunners had armor, though. Rion is human. She doesn't have that kind of protection," Lessa said miserably.

"Do you remember my story, when Riser and Bornstellar and I were kidnapped by the Master Builder?" Spark said. "We were taken from orbit down to the San'Shyuum homeworld in what I can only describe as a kind of bubble, protection spheres that guarded us from the conditions of space. It is my conclusion that the captain may be contained in such a way and is therefore safe within the portal and the rigors of slipspace."

"And how about out of it?" Niko asked. "Are we talking another Cartographer site?"

"I cannot say."

"So this place could be perfectly safe, or it could have been destroyed thousands of years ago, or be underwater, or in some other danger zone . . ." Lessa rubbed her temples and released a frustrated groan. "It makes me sick just thinking about it."

"She had, what, a handgun and a couple frags?" Niko added in a quiet tone, his face a little paler than before.

"Assault rifle, a few extra mags," Ram answered. "But we know the vests are kept prepacked, so she has light, enough food and water tabs to last a few days, a couple heat strips, and a med kit. If she landed in the kind of facilities we've been to so far, she'll survive until we get to her." He leaned back in his chair and lifted his arms over his head in an effort to alleviate the pressure on his chest, locking his hands behind his head. "But getting to her is going to be tricky."

With the wave of his hand, a serene vision appeared of a blue planet hovering over the table. New Carthage might look tranquil from orbit, but Ram knew firsthand the dangers lurking in its vast oceans and the weathered shale mountains, high alpine plains, and semi-arid grasslands and deserts. He made a flare motion with his fingers to zoom closer on a particular landmass. That in turn became a region, and the region became Pilvros, with a coordinate dot sitting directly in the city center, smack-dab in the heart of its tallest skyscraper. "The key's coordinates are right on top of Hannibal HQ."

Niko bent forward and let his forehead make a nice thud

against the surface. "Ow." Kid forgot about his injury. "*Tricky* is a goddamn understatement, Ram."

"What's Hannibal HQ?" Lessa asked.

"The headquarters of Hannibal Weapons Systems. They're a tech giant—securities, ordnance . . ." Niko sat up and began a search on his screen.

"Their R and D, manufacturing, and testing sites are in Kotka," Ram said. "But the business center, the heart of HWS, is in Pilvros. In terms of security, it'll be tight."

"So what are we thinking? The portal is somewhere in the building or hidden beneath it?" Lessa asked. "And if that's the case, how could they have built an entire skyscraper without detecting it?"

"Forerunners employed a variety of stealth technology. Bafflers, energy fields, spatial distortion, dazzlers . . . ," Spark answered.

"Who says they *didn't* detect it?" Niko scrolled through text. "Says here in 2474, the Hannibal family settled on thirty acres in the Pori Region. Those thirty acres would eventually become the city of Pilvros. There's been a building on our coordinate site since 2505. Six years after that, Jack Pilvros Hannibal tested the first small-scale quantum photonic amplifier for SATCOM relays. It revolutionized the speed and integrity of extraplanetary communication. They called him a genius, the brightest forward thinker of the day. That patent and all of the ones since remain closely guarded.

"So it's possible. Good ole JP found a Forerunner facility out in the wilds of Pori, began reverse-engineering the tech he found, and built his empire right on top of it."

"Maybe," Ram said. "It's a pretty big coincidence to ignore. Whatever jump-started his career, Hannibal isn't one we should underestimate. He built an empire that extends from Pilvros to

New Mombasa. His company is nice and cozy with the UNSC, advancing the tech on small arms, major weapons, security . . . If he did find our site, you better believe the steps he's created to *keep* it hidden are going to be extreme."

Niko swiped images of Hannibal HQ's interior from his data-pad to the holopad. "Swanky place. Building's been updated throughout the years. The atrium is four stories and centered around this beauty. They call it the Pori Meteor—try saying that five times fast." A mammoth shard of variegated rock took center stage, surrounded by carefully landscaped plants, accent lighting, and viewing benches.

"Yeah, *that's* not suspicious." Lessa shifted to Spark. "What kind of Forerunner site should we be looking for?"

"The new key that was forged could very well be read at a mul-titude of sites: terminals, way stations, Cartographers . . . ," Spark replied. "Once we are near the site, I will know more."

"We'll need to make as little noise as possible," Ram said, his mind already weighing options. "This place might look like an in-viting office building, but it's a fortress, make no mistake. We have three days until we drop out of our jump. Once in orbit, we'll hang there and see what we can find out. Sound good?"

They voiced their agreement. All in all, despite the challenge they faced, Ram was pleased with the meeting. Now came the harder part.

It was clear Niko felt one hundred percent responsible for what had happened to the captain. But the real reason the tullioc crea-tures had attacked the ship would sit a little longer. For now, a lesson needed to be learned. A ship was only as good as a crew that worked together.

Assuming the discussion was over, Niko started to rise.

"We're not done," Ram told him, returning the kid's surprised look with a steady gaze. "I can find out myself with a little digging, but would rather you come clean about what happened back on Zeta."

After a long bout of silence, Niko returned to his seat and suddenly found his cuticles of great interest. Ram could feel the kid's knee quietly bouncing under the table. Niko didn't seem to know where to start, but there was no need to push; that would have the opposite effect Ram was after. He merely sat back and waited.

"Fine," Niko muttered. "Look . . . I'm from Aleria," he said as if that explained everything. "Shit follows you no matter where or how far you run. The guilds—they don't just let you go, not if they can help it."

A pale shade slid over Lessa's features. "Cross Cut wants you back?"

"No. Well, I'm sure they'd *love* to have me back, but, no. . . . It's Holson Relay. They want a bank of midlevel slipspace capacitors."

"That's a big ask," Ram said. Big, but not impossible.

"They're not asking. All the guilds care about is having the fastest and the largest fleets. The more they can run, and the quicker they can do it, the more credits they bank. Holson is trying to get ahead. And I have one month to help them do it."

"And if you don't deliver?"

Niko scrubbed both hands over his head and linked them behind his neck, staring at the ceiling with a pained expression. "I'd rather deliver it, and just be done with it."

"You don't owe them anything," Lessa said, not getting it.

But Ram certainly did. The humiliation the kid was trying so hard to hide told him all he needed to know. Everyone had skeletons in their closet. And sometimes you paid a hefty price for keeping them there.

Ram relaxed, retrieving a hand-rolled cigarette from his pocket and then tapping it on the table as he studied Niko. "So . . . we give them what they want and get them off your back once and for all."

"*What?*" Niko and Lessa said together.

"We'll see what we can do once we reach New Carthage."

Lessa's sharp laugh echoed across the lounge. "You're just going to waltz into a market somewhere and buy a bank of capacitors?"

Ram returned her disbelief with an easy shrug. "New Carthage isn't the worst place to find what he needs. Inner Colony. Strong tech sector. Vibrant economy. Means plenty of ships. And where there are ships, there are slipspace capacitors. Mission first, and then we'll see what we can do."

"There is the very real possibility it is a trap." Spark voiced the same concern lurking in Ram's mind. "The ONI reward for our capture is a strong incentive."

"I don't think this is part of that," Niko told Spark. "Snitching to the authorities, especially between outlaws, never looks good and taints you among the guilds. Plus, they don't want to meet— they want me to score the capacitors, put them in rented storage, and then give them the location and lock code."

"Send me the connection path to your guild contact," Ram said. "No arguments. You'll remain point of contact, but someone else needs to be able to communicate with them if anything goes wrong. For now . . . let's tell them you've got a line on the capacitors, and you'll be in touch. That'll keep them off your back for a while."

"You think Cap will go for it once she's back?" Lessa asked.

Ram turned to question Niko. "What do you think? If you told her what was going on, what would she do?"

Niko paused before saying, "She would help me. Whether I deserved it or not. And then she'd make sure they'd release me free and clear this time, with a formal dismissal bond from the guild. If that's the price to pay . . . she'd pay it. I mean, this won't surprise her, Less, you know that. She knows how things went down when we left, right out from under the guild's nose. Hell, she's probably been expecting some sort of retribution at some point."

The conversation trailed off, ending on thoughts of Rion. The fear they all held was legitimate. But they had the next three days in slipspace together, and Ram knew the best way to deal with this level of anxiety was to put them to work.

"Good—so we're in agreement. Once we get to New Carthage, Rion first; blackmail second." Ram pushed away from the table. "Now, I'm off to fix that cracked track line in the hold, and then I've got laundry to start. Less, once you're up to it, you have filters to change, and are you still up for giving me a trim?" She nodded. "Great. Niko, same goes; rest awhile, then see that the med bay is cleaned spotless, and the locker room restocked and organized. You're also on dinner duty and cleanup." There had to be some kind of punishment, after all, but Ram had to give the kid credit—he took it like a champ. "Spark, I need you to learn everything you can about Pilvros and Hannibal and add it to the brief. We'll finalize a plan once we reach the planet and gather more intel."

CHAPTER 20

Spark

—How's that?

—How's what?

No matter the modifications I make to his core, Little Bit's absent-minded nature remains.

My mother would say he has his head in the clouds—a fair assessment. However, his unique responses are mostly confined to verbal discourse and not to administration or system functions. I am coming to believe that his odd responses are the result of stress and trauma sustained in the explosion on Etran Harborage, an ordeal that sent him racing from relay to relay in an effort to stay ahead of high-energy photon clusters burning through the shield world at the speed of light.

With each jump, he lost a part of himself.

Though small in comparison, when the Rubicon crashed, I was forced to make a similar bid for survival and can attest to the strain of becoming trapped within a framework of fiber-optics, cables, and filaments as they burn down around you. I had but one ship to navigate and find shelter. Little Bit had to flee across an entire world.

—*Your matrix adjustment.*

—Of course. Ah . . . Oh, my. Quite expansive! How liberating!

—*You've been trapped in fragments for a very long time, your matrices compressed. We will conduct new tests later, but I am certain your increase in data absorption and management will propagate exponentially, thus alleviating your panoptic handicap.*

—It feels good to stretch. It has been a long time.

—*Enjoy it. Now that this vessel has been upgraded, you have a lovely and complex, and somewhat familiar, expanse to explore.*

—Would you like to join me?

It amuses me he would ask. It has never been in my nature to nurture, yet I have done so with this broken ancilla, discarding his damaged parts and building them anew. The kinship that has grown between us is a comfort and surely an anomaly, and perhaps a mark of maturity within me that I had not considered before.

—*Another time.*

—Will you continue repairs on the landing gear?

—*Not at this time.*

—Ah. You will be in your picture, then.

—*Explain.*

—Oh, dears. I have said it wrong. Fabrication. Concoction. Your as-was spot?

—*Memory simulation, you mean. Yes, I will be in my "as-was" spot and do not wish to be disturbed.*

I feel him hesitate suddenly.

—Do you hear that?

I certainly did. That strange, popping static with no origin. There and gone.

—*You heard it just then?*

—Yes, briefly.

—*I will think on this. . . .*

I leave my semiliterate protégé and retreat farther into the ship's mainframe to a spot carved out for me and only me—a place with walls that silence the intricate, beating heart of the Ace of Spades.

My as-was spot.

It is an appropriate connotation. This is indeed a place where things are as they were. A sensation of sight and sound and touch and scents—down to the smallest remembered detail—has been built here.

Here, I am human.

As I lie on my back, the grasses sway in the wind, their hard tips rubbing together in a strange song that I remember, and that gives me comfort. The clouds drift by overhead as I chew idly on a garro stalk. The calls of wildlife echo in the distance. The spring sun warms my face.

One hand is tucked behind my head and my eyes are closed.

I drift. I dream.

CHAPTER 21

The med bay and locker room were spotless, and he'd just started the rice in the steamer for dinner. He didn't need to, as the food dispenser worked just fine, but Niko thought a home-cooked meal would be a nice touch.

Ram sure knew how to make a person think. And that's all that Niko had done while he worked. He was thoroughly disgusted with himself; he never should have launched Michelle. If he hadn't, chances were good those flying things might've never shown up. But even before that, he should have confided in the crew—or at the very least the captain.

Everyone on the ship had a past and a right to privacy, but when people were being threatened or were dealing with an issue that might affect their work—which in turn affected the crew—then it was a whole ship problem, not an individual one.

He could have seriously injured his sister and damaged *Ace* beyond repair. . . . And keeping his silence and trying to deal with it himself hadn't been nor would it ever be worth it.

That Ram hadn't insisted on knowing what Bex had on him was a small miracle, one that he was enormously grateful for. Niko's answer had been pretty lame, but it was all he had to give, and he could tell by the look on his sister's face that he'd lit a raging fire of curiosity in her, which was the one thing he dreaded the most. Lessa was the *reason* he was keeping his damn mouth shut.

The rice had fifteen more minutes, and the sauce was heating in the tin. He set the table, then cleaned up the counter before grabbing two Greedy Meads and leaving to go find Ram.

The acting captain was in his quarters, sitting in a chair with a towel around his shoulders, Lessa behind him holding scissors and scowling straight ahead like a statue, which meant she was watching something through her VCL. Virtual contact lenses were an amazing bit of tech that allowed the wearer to see a superimposed display against a real-world backdrop. Niko would love to use them, but lenses and his eyes just didn't mix.

He'd been hoping to catch Ram alone, but what the hell, he supposed he had amends to make all around. He knocked on the open doorframe. "Food will be ready in fifteen." He lifted one of the beers.

Ram motioned him inside and gratefully took it. "Everything else done?"

"Yep." Niko hesitated. "I—"

"Damn it." Lessa's face scrunched up in frustration. It was clear she was watching some sort of hair-cutting tutorial.

"Maybe you're making it way more complicated than it needs to be. It's just a trim," Ram reminded her, before widening his eyes at Niko and mouthing, *Help me.*

Niko bit back a smile.

"Yeah, well, usually Cap does this, not me," she replied defensively, dragging Ram's wet hair through a comb.

Niko took a long pull on his drink, drumming up the courage for what he was about to do. "I wanted to say . . . thank you, Ram, for the . . . um . . ." And of course the right words disappeared when he needed them the most.

"No worries, kid. We've all been there, me included. We're human—we make mistakes, we try to fix them, and we don't want to bother anyone else with our problems."

Niko waited for his sister to chime in, but she remained strangely quiet—another minor miracle, but he'd take it. "Still, you could have been pretty hard on me about it. . . ."

"I'm only hard when people don't learn or care to listen. We'll work it out with the guild."

"Well, for what it's worth . . . I'm glad you came on board."

"Same," Lessa muttered, bending over and squinting at her trim line.

"Rion did me a kind favor," Ram said.

"Yeah, same for me and Less. You being here, though . . . it's helped. After Cade was . . . you know. It's just good to have you here."

Back when he had his own ship and crew to captain, Ram had been fortunate to call the *Ace of Spades*'s longtime first mate a friend. He didn't know every detail of Cade McDonough's death, but he knew enough. Losing a crew member . . . he understood that all too well. There were those who crossed the boundary from crew to family and loved one. Cade had been such a man to Rion and her small crew.

"Being here has helped me too, kid, more than you know." Ram lifted his can. "To Cade." They clinked. "And Cap." They clinked again.

"Okay, I think I'm done." Lessa straightened, not looking entirely convinced. She retrieved the VCL case from her pocket, removed the lens from her eye, and returned it to its solution, then tugged her wireless earpiece out and placed it in its pocket on the case.

As Ram stepped into his small bathroom and removed the towel to shake out the trimmed hair, Niko was struck by the strange scars on his back and shoulders, patches of melted skin in the shape of eyes. Knife wounds—only those knives had been made out of plasma. "Those healed pretty good," he blurted.

Ram picked a fresh shirt from a hook and pulled it over his head, then tied his hair back. "Nanotech at its best." He'd be dead without it, sure enough. Ram leaned against the doorframe, drinking the beer, then wiping his arm across his mouth. He scratched his beard, frowning.

"Don't *even* ask me to shave that thing," Lessa warned, taking Niko's beer and helping herself to a sip before handing it back.

Humor and horror glittered in Ram's dark eyes. "Wouldn't dream of it."

"So you gonna go back to being captain at some point?" Niko asked.

Ram considered it, his beer dangling from his fingers. "Never thought I'd hear myself say it, but . . . I don't know. Thinking I might go back to the *Erstwhile* at some point, when I'm no longer a wanted criminal."

"The ship on Komoya?" Lessa asked.

"Bought out one of the partners at the bar there a while back."

"No shit. The *Erstwhile* bar is a Komoyan staple."

"And a solid investment." Ram polished off the beer. "Then there's Nor . . . looking for someone to take over the Clearing House."

Now that was a shocker. "No kidding. How long you been holding on to *that* information?"

"Couple of months. The old bird sent an encrypted message about the possibility, and we've been back and forth ever since. Really wants me and Rion to work it together, while she stays on as a silent partner."

"With a larger share in the profits, no doubt."

"Goes without saying."

"Does Cap know?"

"Haven't brought it up yet."

A piercing alarm resounded down the corridor. Immediately, Lessa darted out of the room. Niko, however, was quite familiar with that particular alarm and counted the seconds until . . . *"Goddammit, the rice is burning! Niko!"* The alert stopped. A pan clanked loudly. *"Ow!"* Niko winced.

Niko gave a suffering look to the ceiling as a stream of curses began drifting from the kitchen along with the acrid smell of what was supposed to be dinner. Why was he always in a perpetual state of trouble? Why? "Guess I should go deal with that." But his feet wouldn't budge. A small smile tugged at his lips. "Is it wrong to just hang out here and let her handle it?"

Ram laughed. "That depends on how much you value your life."

"Niko!"

He finished the last of his beer and reluctantly went to face the music.

Before he made it into the corridor, Ram said, "Hey, Niko. The creatures that attacked the ship? It wasn't because of Michelle." Ram held up a hand to prevent any response. *"But.* It very well *could* have been—you catch me?"

And Niko did. Lesson definitely learned. "Yeah. Loud and clear. Thanks."

CHAPTER 22

When Rion regained consciousness, every nerve ending inside her lit up, racing and branching out like a hot burst of crawler lightning. Pressure squeezed her from all directions, through muscle and tissue and bone. The tang of ozone stuck in her throat, and the air in her lungs had an arid quality that made her chest feel paper-thin.

Dear God.

Her equilibrium couldn't decide if it was on solid ground or still tumbling through space. Maybe rolling onto her back and orienting herself with her surroundings would help. After moving from her side to her back and pulling one leg in, an intense wave of nausea hit before she could even open her eyes.

Bad idea. The blood vessels beneath her skull throbbed drumbeats of liquid fire. With a shaky hand, she fished around in her vest pocket for a pain strip, removed its covering, shoved up her sleeve, and stuck it to her inner forearm, then curled into a ball, waiting, and praying for the tiniest bit of relief.

Eventually, the agony gave way to a dull whole-body ache, allowing her mind to clear somewhat. But the clarity brought about a flood of recent memories, of light, space, panic, confinement, chaos, and strange dreams. Not things she ever wanted to relive.

Shoving those horrors aside, Rion forced herself to sit up and focus on where she'd just landed.

A film of what felt like dirt or maybe dust covered a smooth floor made of stone or metal. The air was humid, but not hot, and while it was pitch-black, there was a sense of largeness around her.

The datapad in her gauntlet was cracked, glowing lines skating in and out across the screen. She tried her comm link. "Anyone reading me? Copy?" Nothing. She switched to open channels. "Anyone copy?" Again, no response, not even a static return.

Cautiously, she rolled onto her knees, taking time to push to her feet due to the lasting effects of vertigo.

Once the dizziness subsided and the sensation of weakness left her legs, she hit the light built into the shoulder strap of her vest. It struggled to work, but eventually stayed on long enough to reveal an immense chamber composed of steel-colored alloy, smooth as satin and polished to a high sheen. Glyphs and the long geometric lines the Forerunners were so fond of were carved into the floor and walls.

As she continued her turn around the room, she nearly screamed when her light hit the pillars standing just meters behind her. They loomed above her at least eight meters tall, rectangular in shape, and angled at the top. Small glyphs ran up the sides, and straight inlaid lines framed a central symbol of a circle broken open at the bottom with an octagon at its center and two offset parallel lines that cut through the picture.

The monoliths were more ominous and darker than any other Forerunner metal she'd seen and possessed a powerful vibe that pricked her skin. While there was no way to prove it, Rion had a strong feeling she'd passed *through* the space between them . . . in which case she wasn't going anywhere near those things ever again, not if she could help it.

On the bright side, the place was definitely Forerunner. Was it too much to hope she'd been pulled to another location on Zeta Halo? Perhaps a stretch, unless those terrifying memories of tumbling through space were simply hallucinations . . .

A strange and eerie sound, far off and haunting, echoed through a main corridor leading away from the chamber. Definitely biological in nature. An animal call or—

It came again. The hairs on her arms rose. While it didn't sound close, Rion eased her M6 from its holster and began examining the chamber for another exit. If whatever made that noise was hostile, she didn't want to be around when it found its way inside.

As she stepped back, her boot crunched something brittle. Immediately she stepped off and angled her light to the floor, seeing a tangle of bone fragments. Having come across remains frequently in her line of work, she could tell they weren't very old, given the color of the bones, the dried bits of flesh still attached, and the hair and torn clothing strewn about.

A reflection winked from the floor. Curious, she bent down to retrieve it.

A button. Jesus. This was human.

Wherever the hell she was, clearly there had been others before. Her current situation had just taken a dire turn.

A metallic scuffling had her spinning around, gun aimed at the ceiling, heart in her throat. She angled her light only to find empty space. All her instincts were firing. She wasn't alone. And worse, she wasn't exactly operating at a hundred percent.

Using the nearest wall as her guide, Rion began moving along, glad to have something solid at her back, hoping another exit presented itself. Around the monoliths, she found an open conduit shaft just above floor level with a passable upward angle. The air felt different here. A few dried leaves littered the ground. She killed the light, letting her eyes adjust. It was either wishful thinking or there was a vague gray light up there.

If her crew was inbound, the worst thing she could do was leave, but circumstances forced her hand. Finding a safe space to lie low was now a priority. She had to hope that if the crew did manage to follow, they'd find her nearby via her bio-tag.

Knowing this might be her only way out, Rion worked her body into the shaft, braced her feet against lines of cables in the corners, and used the power of her lower body to begin the arduous task of pushing her way up.

At one point in the long climb, the shaft leveled off, providing a welcome resting place. She lay flat on her stomach and pressed her hot cheek against the cold metal. While her body wanted nothing more than to stay, she allowed only a few minutes of rest before continuing on.

When the shaft angled up again, she paused, on her hands and knees, feeling utterly defeated. Tears stung her eyes. She was so damn tired. . . .

The climb seemed endless.

Spots were rubbed raw on her elbows and blisters formed on her palms. Her muscles ached and burned and screamed, and her back was threatening to seize up. What little adrenaline had come from seeing the human remains and realizing she wasn't alone was now long gone, and if she didn't clear the tunnel or shaft—or whatever the hell it was—she was afraid she might not be able to continue.

So she counted each awkward push in an effort to stay focused, to keep moving toward that little, hazy smudge of light in the distance.

How long it took in reality she had no idea; it seemed like hours before she reached the end the shaft, coming out on her stomach between two angled slabs of rough rock held tight to the ground by enormous twisted roots. She slid down to a ledge and collapsed, chest heaving, weak, thirsty.

Her head fell back and she gazed up at a strange, unexpected sight. A gigantic twisted tree rose above her. Its fat, monstrous limbs snaked out like thick tentacles against a hazy dirt-yellow sky. Hairy vines hung in loops from branch to branch, and primitive birds with long tails flew in the distance on wings that flapped slow and methodical. It was an eerie prehistoric picture with an atmosphere that dashed any remaining hope of her being on Zeta Halo.

A hum of denial built in her chest even as she knew the reality: She'd been yanked from the Cartographer, pulled through space, and spit out on an entirely different world.

And here she thought being on a Halo was the craziest thing to ever happen.

She should've known.

CHAPTER 23

Ram leaned against the front of the tactical table on the bridge, arms folded across his chest. The northern hemisphere of New Carthage filled the lower half of the viewscreen. He was impressed. The blue girl had gotten herself a nice pair of orbital defense platforms since his last visit. The closest platform lay two hundred kilometers off the portside bow. "Let's not get their attention," he said, giving the crew a deliberate look.

"You got it. Coordinates are set for landing," Lessa replied.

Ram drew in a resolute breath and then relaxed, his gaze settling on Spark's avatar. "All right then, Spark, make us disappear."

"Done," he replied instantly. "With my latest repairs, we are running dark at eighty percent."

They'd put the *Ace of Spades*'s stealth capabilities to the test many times, but it was still a hold-your-breath moment as she slid past planet defenses and entered the upper atmosphere.

Few places in Ram's travels fit solely in the scrapbook of good memories. Despite its dangers, New Carthage was such a place—an amused snort escaped him—probably because all those memories were from *before* he was a salvager and captain.

"What are you laughing about?" Niko asked.

"Just memories, kid." A whole lot of memories . . .

"You've been here before?" Lessa asked.

"A long time ago. Back when the rallies were free to anyone with a working quad."

"So, what," Niko cut in, "like the 2400s?"

Giving the kid a scowl wasn't easy when biting back a smile, but Ram tried. Lessa stifled her own laugh, and even Spark, that ancient, inscrutable mystery, let out a rare chuckle.

"Seriously, though . . . *you* rode the rallies?" asked Lessa.

"Don't sound so surprised. There are a lot of things you don't know about me."

"Oh, yeah, like what?"

"How about I nearly won the rally back in '34. Came in second by twenty-nine minutes."

"*No*, the hell you didn't," Niko said, amazed, and rightly so.

Just finishing a rally back then earned celebrity status in the colonies, but more important, it earned respect. Those early rallies were rough-around-the-edges, unregulated, high-stakes, long-distance gauntlet runs over uncharted alien topography, and landscapes full of lethal unknowns. Not for the faint of heart or the unprepared.

In other words, good times.

Ram had been a kid in '34, Niko's age. No fear. All go, all the time. He'd gotten lucky way too many times to count. "Komoyans can build some sweet rally quads," he said, heart full of pride even as he gave a casual shrug. "You follow the circuit?"

Niko shook his head. "It's more Less's thing."

"Oh, please," Lessa said with one of the biggest eye rolls Ram had ever seen. "He follows it—or rather follows some*one*."

"Shut up, Less."

She ignored him. "Ever hear of the Tantalus Terror?"

Ram had indeed. "Ah. He's a Bella Disztl fan." Ram sighed. "Aren't we all, though?" He gave the red-faced kid a wink as *Ace* transitioned into the lower atmosphere.

Going dark didn't mean you stopped paying attention, and to their credit, they knew it. Spark began running scans over the area, hoping to get a ping on Rion's bio-tag, while Lessa took over the controls and guided the ship to the landing site Ram had procured during their trip through slipspace.

The swift descent went off without a hitch, and *Ace* settled easily, if not noisily, in the back lot of a seven-acre spread dedicated to all things fast.

Quads, racers, roadsters, motorbikes, pieces and parts, and all the equipment to tear a vehicle apart or put it back together were haphazardly spread across hard, dusty ground. Outbuildings, shipping containers, and a two-story house sandwiched between two large industrial garages sat at the far end of the fenced lot.

During the jump to New Carthage, Ram had sent a wavespace transmission to his old rally buddy McKinnon "Mac" Quarrie, hoping he'd secure them an out-of-the-way spot at his chop shop in Torba, a small township on the edge of the Grieves.

Ram had a lot of fond history in the Grieves, a dry desert grassland in the Pori Region with a host of hostile wildlife and treacherous terrain. With sinking sands, hidden chasms, mudslides, empty stretches of dry wastes, temperatures that soared and plummeted, sudden rain and sand and electrical storms, the Grieves played host to several local and interstellar motorsports series.

It was chaos on a good day. If the terrain didn't get you, the predators would, and damned if they hadn't rallied through it like demons riding a path straight out of hell.

The occasion called for Ram's old leather rally jacket and rally boots. As soon as the ramp was down, the familiar dry air flowed into the cargo hold, its scent triggering even more memories, and for a moment time stood still—capped off by the appearance of the tall grizzled wheel hound with shaggy brown hair overtaken with gray and tattoos up both arms. His scruffy face split into a wide white smile, and crystal-blue eyes squinted with unreserved warmth.

"Well, it's about damn time you graced my doorstep." He came right up the ramp and enveloped Ram in a hug. "How you doing, bru?" Quarrie stood back, grinning ear to ear. "Amazed you're still kicking."

"Could say the same about you, Mac." True happiness spread through Ram's chest, giving him a pleasant shock. It had been far too long since he felt the emotion—*really* felt it; he'd almost forgotten what it was like. He hadn't heard another Komoyan accent in a while either, and it only added to his sterling mood.

Lessa's and Niko's footsteps echoed behind them. Ram moved aside and made introductions.

"You can call me Mac or Quarrie, take your pick. Welcome to my shop."

Lessa's gaze caught on something over Mac's shoulder. "Is that a Goblin VS?" Somewhere in all the metal and parts, she'd struck gold.

"Yeah! Ja-Ne," Mac said, impressed. "Only a few made in 2529. She's a kiff one for sure, a classic. Go ahead, take a look."

Her smile was dazzling and pure. Those bait-and-take scams she and Niko had concocted back on Aleria must have been wildly successful. With a tug on her brother's shirt, they made off, leaving dust tracks behind them.

Mac watched them disappear into the junkyard maze. "That's

it? That's your crew? What, you operating a day care? Oh. Damn, wait. Unless, they're your—"

"Oh, *hell no*." Ram instantly halted that line of thought.

A glint of mirth flashed in Mac's blues. "Well, come on to the shop, and you can meet mine."

Ram blinked. Now *that* was a bombshell. He never thought his old friend had it in him to settle down, but then again, a lot could happen in two decades, that was for sure.

They headed toward one of the garages next to the house. "So what the hell brings you here to Torba?"

"Trying to reunite that ship"—Ram gestured back at *Ace*—"with its captain."

"Sounds like a plot I'd like to hear."

"I meant what I said in my message. No one can know we're here."

"You have my word. My guys are all aboveboard. Trust me, no one here is going to say anything. So now *I* need to know . . . is it true?"

"Is what true?"

"That you're wanted for crimes against the UEG. Word is you all pissed off the guys in black, and they have it out for you twice bad."

"ONI came here?"

"Nah, bru, not unless you have my picture on your wall. Saw a lot of junk on ChatterNet, Waypoint, all the news bulletins . . ." He squeezed Ram's shoulder. "Gotta say, it brought a tear to my eye to see you still rebelling against the establishment. Ah. Here we go. . . ."

Inside the large garage, Ram had the honor of meeting Mac Quarrie's two boys and his wife, Maise, before they headed inside to finish their schooling. The work space was impressive, and if

Ram had stayed in the rally business, he'd want a place like this—it was damn near perfect with its lifts and diagnostic cables and carts, the enviable wall of tools . . . After they popped a few beers, Mac lowered the tailgate of a nice-looking TurboGen flatbed bakkie. They took a seat and admired the view across the yard.

"Appreciate the help, Mac. I really do."

Getting a berth in a shipyard near the city had been out of the question. While fudging *Ace*'s registration wasn't a problem, disguising the vessel was. If someone ID'd them, the shipyard could lock the ship down with ease.

They didn't need any explosive attention trying to get out of a mess like that. That's where Mac had come in.

"She's a nice ship, *real* nice. . . . Could use a little work on her belly. I can have my guys help you out with coating," Mac said. "What is she, *Mariner*-class?"

Ram swallowed a sip and agreed wholeheartedly. "That she is. I remember when the closest we'd come to something like her was sneaking into the shipyard back home."

"Climbing the control tower to the roof with a six-pack of Clips or Ginnie's, and a couple smokes . . . Those were good times, bru."

"The best."

Lessa and Niko returned from their exploration. It was damn nice to see the cloud lifted from Niko's eyes, and the fresh glint of happiness in Lessa—her smile was easy and her chatter on the junkyard nonstop.

"See anything else you like?" Mac asked, hopping off the tailgate to get them each a beer.

"That Arrow-XR3 you have in the back is *real* nice," Lessa said, tucking an errant curl behind her ear.

At Mac's surprised laugh, Ram cocked an eyebrow and explained, "They're not your average kids."

"Adults," Niko corrected under his breath as he popped his drink and took a seat on a large metal storage chest.

"Right." Ram smiled. "Not average *adults*, then."

"There's about two decades between us," Mac told them. "Means no matter how old you get, we'll *always* call you kids." A moment passed as they drank and settled in. But Mac was never one to dance around a subject. "So this captain of yours. What kind of trouble she in?"

"I don't want to get you too mixed up in this," Ram said slowly. He hated to keep his friend in the dark, but . . . "The less you know, the better."

"Fortunately for you, I know a lot around here. You'd be smart to make use of me. Ram—what do you need? Seriously."

"Well, for starters, I could use a ride."

"Let me guess, taking a trip into Pill-vil?"

Lessa's brow wrinkled. "Pill-vil?"

"That's just what we call Pilvros out here. City is addicted. Everyone drinking the Hannibal juice, you know?"

"What makes you think we need to go to Pilvros?" Niko asked.

Mac shrugged. "You land here, looking for your lost captain. And we all know she ain't out here. Torba is the closest town to Pilvros, so . . . you think she's down there?"

Lessa answered "Yes" at the same time Ram said "No."

Before they could get themselves out of that verbal mess, the ground shook. The garage became a giant wind chime as tools and parts clinked and rattled. Ram waited, frozen. Eight seconds passed and then it ended.

Maise stuck her head out the side door connecting the house to the garage. "Everyone all right?"

"Good. Just a mite one, luv," Mac told her.

"The boys are making chow tonight; it'll be ready in thirty."

Once she ducked back inside, Ram questioned his friend. "Since when does the Grieves shake?"

"Since Hannibal is destroying the whole damn region with their testing. Getting tremors all the time now. The Grieves is taking the brunt, though. Sinkholes, chasms opening up . . ."

Ram could see Niko and Lessa were thinking the same thing he was. "And what's the official word?"

"They're covering it up, saying it's a new fault line, came out of nowhere." Mac's disgusted expression told Ram no one was buying that lame excuse. "Bad ones have come across the area and gone all the way from here to Pilvros and Kotka . . . they added a couple wave suppressors, but, of course, only to protect the city, not the townships."

Damned if that didn't piss Ram off—the Grieves and the townships around it weren't Hannibal's personal playground. They should be protected and treated as fairly as anyplace else.

"What do the cities do when the tremors happen?" Niko asked. "They ever close things down?"

"Not usually. A bad one not long ago, they evacuated everyone." Mac eyed them all for a good long second. "Aha. I see where your minds are. . . ."

Still Ram hesitated. Mac had a wife and kids—something Ram hadn't anticipated. The last thing he wanted was to put his friend or the family in danger.

"Ram?" Lessa's voice brought him out of his worried thoughts. She and Niko were both staring at him. "We should tell him, let him help us."

"I won't take no for an answer, bru, you know that," Mac added. "It's on me."

Ram rubbed a hand down his beard and sighed.

"Our captain," Niko said impatiently, "is trapped inside HQ."

Mac took in the news thoughtfully. "So you want to go down there tonight, get the lay of the building."

"We want to get in and get her out as quickly as possible," Ram said, "before we bring ONI down on our and now your heads. If we can take a look around tonight and get her out in the morning . . ."

"Bru, that's one hell of a timetable."

"You said they evacuated the building before." Niko got up and tossed his empty beer in the trash receptacle on the wall. "How long ago was that?"

"About three or four weeks ago." Mac hopped off the tailgate and got everyone another round from the wall cooler. "I'm getting what you're all not saying. But that's a lot of moving parts to fake a tremor big enough to evacuate HQ, and to set it up in one night . . ." Unfortunately he was right.

Once everyone had drinks all around, Mac air-toasted the group, chugged a few gulps, wiped his forearm across his mouth, and grinned. "But it's not impossible."

Glorious. And that's why they were brus for life.

CHAPTER 24

Rion

Now that her second pain patch was working, Rion pushed to her feet and studied the sky to determine a time of day, but the yellow haze made it impossible. She'd have to wait until nightfall to get a good look at the stars and possibly determine a general location.

As far as the eye could see, the land appeared fractured like puzzle pieces drifting apart. Pockets of mist floated up from vents and cracks and deep chasms that zigzagged through the primal forest, making the air dank and humid and warm.

She'd landed in an antediluvian world of monstrous trees with twisted trunks adorned with spikes and long snaking branches that linked the forest together, limbs reaching over the chasms, creating bridges, rooting down into the ground and popping out elsewhere.

Eerie and exuding hostility is what it was.

Just her luck.

From her current position on the ridge, it was an easy slide to the ground below, but Rion decided to see where the ridge led first, hoping to learn more about the facility she'd been dumped in—maybe another entrance or building or landmark to tell her where she was and provide a way to get back.

Unfortunately, the ledge ended at a cliff. In the gorge below, a thick mist dwelled, making it hard to tell if the drop down was a thousand meters or a hundred, or what lay beneath the mist— ocean, swamp, or rock?

She went back to her original exit point.

It all appeared so primitive and prehistoric that she'd be hard-pressed to say this was an inhabited world. But then again, she was in one small part of it, and there *had* been humans here at some point in the recent past.

Weary again, she sat and leaned her back against the rock to eat a food strip and swallow a water tab. But what she wouldn't give for a real glass of water.

A shrill cry echoed overhead. Several birds took to the sky from the treetops, their large wings making them appear slow, almost too slow to stay aloft. Pretty much how she felt—too slow, too tired, too achy, to stay aloft. Her head was splitting and her eardrums still hurt.

In the darker corners of her mind, memories she didn't want to think about were worming their way in.

Spark had betrayed her.

A tight ache squeezed her heart. He had taken the key out of her hand when he could have grabbed hold, could've taken her wrist and pulled her to safety.

Of course, there had been no facial expression, no emotion or any way to read him in that small moment. No way to know if he'd been shocked or horrified or simply uncaring that a portal was swallowing her whole.

Had he known this would happen?

She rubbed both hands down her face to try to stir her blood. Every time her mind wandered, all she felt was that same shock of betrayal, followed immediately by chaos, blinding light, and the abject and complete fear of her body being pulled through space.

So strong, those images. Invasive. Persistent.

She hugged her knees, closed her eyes, and rested her head on her arm, too damned tired to keep the images at bay. They spilled in, tumbling, spinning through space faster than the speed of light. The horrific sensation of being without a buffer. Nothing between her and the void. The pressure in her ears. The inability to scream.

And then something else . . .

A voice.

Night has fallen across the plain. The songs of insects echo through air free of humidity and heat. The sky is a vivid canvas of ink on which billions of stars cozy up to the galaxy's Dark Rift.

"Forerunners take their first-form naked under the stars," the Librarian says, continuing her confession, gazing up, remembering. "It is solemn and painful, a rite of passage from Manipular to adult that fills young hearts with excitement and apprehension. I was such a youth.

"Harmony served as my mentor. This honor should have gone to my mother—a respected Lifeworker whose study of ice worlds was unsurpassed. Nurturing the life trapped beneath the ice, guiding it from the cold and into the warmth of evolution, was one of her greatest joys. She gave her life in the process."

There is pride and grief in her telling. Rion isn't sure if she should offer words of comfort or simply listen.

"I did not inherit her gentle gift for liberating ice worlds," the Librarian says with a rueful smile.

"Both Harmony and my father held high hope for my first-form mutation, but no one more than me. No . . . it was not hope; it was belief, complete and total, that I would shed the strange physical traits that plagued me since birth and emerge more . . . Forerunner.

"I stayed in my living area for several days when it was over. Not from the pain of mutation, but from bitter disappointment and embarrassment. My abnormalities remained. I had let everyone down—my rate, my father, my mentor. To be so afflicted without sense or reason created a deep well of anger in me."

Holding up her hand, wiggling her long fingers, she gives Rion a faint smile. "Five fingers like you," *she says, before returning to her study of the sky.* "How I longed for six. For hair and facial features more like my fellow first-forms . . ."

Rion's connection allows her to share in the Librarian's intense longing to fit in with the young Forerunners around her and the pain it caused to see their distaste.

"But, after my sulking period was over, I did as Harmony taught me: I turned my negative attributes into something worthy of study. I began to trace my abnormalities to their source."

"What did you find?"

"Not much in the beginning. I assumed I would find it in my studies.

"First-forms begin extensive rate studies almost immediately. Living Science becomes our lifeblood, nourishing our hearts and minds and shaping our very essence. There are fifty-two branches of Living Science within the Lifeworker rate. We must master them all. And I had already mastered more than half before my mutation.

"During respites in my studies, I cultivated my navigation of Living Time, roamed the Domain for answers that eluded me, and worked my way eugenically backward to find the source of my abnormal congenital traits.

"There were others like me spread across the ecumene, suggesting a far older ancestral source existed. Mapping the Forerunner genome and sequence had been done long ago. It is one of the first things that is done upon fetal development, to give parents and household monitors all relevant information in order to effectively serve. This information is also accessed and used to facilitate future mutations. Once first-form mutation is achieved and armor is fashioned, an individual ancilla is assigned. This ancilla routinely updates and monitors its Forerunner inside and out.

"My ancilla, however, was somewhat unconventional. And while she never admitted it, I believe Harmony had a hand in its selection. With my molecular map, my ancilla and I zeroed in on my extraneous genetic material, and I continued to hound the Domain with my questions. Why was I different? Where did these deviations originate? But it seemed the halls of memory enjoyed toying with the neophyte, only revealing a long line of those like me, going deep into the past, voices that said:

" 'You are not alone.'

" 'Look to the end.'

" 'Look to the beginning.'

" 'Unity.'

" 'Division.'

"And then finally a voice that curled around me in the shadowed halls and whispered, 'Look to the lost rate.'

"There were pivotal moments in my early life, of mergers and events and junctures—perhaps small to hear them spoken now—but all designed to guide me to a singular purpose. This revelation—'Look to the lost rate'—was one of these moments.

"This seemingly simple statement proved vastly difficult, even for my ancilla, and required my first of two visits to Keth Sidon to avail myself of the Master Library.

"I had long wanted to visit the Library. It was one of the last great stores of old knowledge, containing the earliest writings known, preserved scrolls and books and copies of early digital data. Many considered its existence a miracle."

At the Librarian's long pause, Rion spoke up—she didn't want this story to end. "How so?"

"By virtue of its location. As a planet in one of our original twelve systems, Keth Sidon escaped destruction when a series of supernovas annihilated much of our civilization; even our homeworld was not spared. Many began referring to it as the Fortunate One.

"Its beauty certainly lived up to its reputation: towering primeval forests cut through by four long oceans, which effectively divided Keth Sidon into five landmasses. The Library, however, resides within the densest, most ancient of woodland and remains one of the greatest works of ancient Forerunner architecture in all of Path Tolgreth, what you now call the Milky Way galaxy.

"When I arrived in the plaza outside its doors, my heart became fuller than it ever had been before. I stood in awe of its angled columns that rose from the foundation to meet at the top, forming a beautiful triad. Behind this first set of angled columns rose another set, a hundred meters higher than the first, each successive apex growing higher and higher, reaching its highest pinnacle, and then retreating in similar fashion.

"Passing through the main hall made my heart sing with unmitigated joy.

" 'Your heart rate is elevated, Light. I would offer to administer, but I am sensing you are not in distress,' my ancilla told me with undisguised humor.

" 'You sense correctly,' I replied. 'This, my dear ancilla, is called joy.'

"The first three days, I did nothing but walk the ancient halls and marvel at millions upon millions of manuscripts. I enjoyed the manicured parks and areas for study and reflection, and the chambers for thought and simulated experience.

"After this period, which was all too short, I made the most of my limited time. I submitted search requests for lost rates and any Forerunners of note who were similarly plagued with five fingers, blunt teeth, thin, smaller forms, flexible facial muscles, and hair instead of fur.

"There were many lost rates in our past, absorbed into larger rates and thus forgotten. But then finally there was one that caught my attention—Theoreticals, forcibly folded into the Builder rate a million years prior. Their rate studied ideology, philosophy, metaphysics, aesthetics, the esoteric, belief systems, the past, present, and future, and they in turn guided Forerunners of all rates.

"Finding complete works proved difficult indeed, leading me to the same conclusion as others before—there had been a true, concerted effort to suppress these studies. What remained was a small patchwork, which, when laid out, suggested the Precursors, our esteemed and mysterious Creators, had given form and breath not only to us, but to humanity as well.

"Brothers, as one ancient sage proposed.

"The idea was preposterous. Humans, from what little I had read, were known to be a crude, uninspiring, and quarrelsome species.

" 'You don't believe it?' my ancilla asked me on our last day as I reclined on a bench by the reflection pool. The water lay flat and as smooth as a mirror, reflecting perfectly the Library's great peaks rising behind me. I had yet to share my disappointments and declined her offer to download the Forerunners' shared knowledge about *humanity directly into my mind. I remember gazing down at my fingers resting on my lap, hating them for their abnormality. Humans, according to what I found, shared a genetic structure homogeneous to our own.*

"And with great resistance toward that idea, my real study began."

CHAPTER 25

Spark

After the crew enjoyed a meal with the Quarrie family, they convened back on the ship, anxious to get started. During their absence, I scanned the entirety of Pilvros, searching for signs of the captain and the Forerunner facility. Scans during our descent into Torba had proven fruitless; no returns on Rion's signal and unclear readings on whatever might lurk beneath Hannibal Headquarters. I continue to monitor the area, however. Michelle was recovered and repaired from the mishap on Zeta Halo, and along with Niko's second drone, Diane, they are now modified with new scan parameters and are currently high in the atmosphere over the site to work and avoid security detection.

Lessa's words continue to haunt me. The very idea that Rion might have landed in a situation unsuitable for life had of course occurred to me. To find friends again only to lose them is a horrifying notion I do not wish to entertain.

The situation is unacceptable.

My attachment to the captain and the crew is a weakness. An

emotional liability. Easily solved, however. Keep them safe and the liability drops exponentially. Quite simple.

Until . . . it is not.

I cannot protect them from everything.

Yet another irritating notion.

But I must leave these notions behind and move on to other internal processes.

The Pori Meteor, upon which Hannibal HQ is built, shows clear manipulation, and I surmise it may have once served as a beacon or power station, intentionally crafted to blend into the surrounding landscape. It is the void nearly three kilometers beneath the building, however, that proves most intriguing.

Clear voids indicate natural chambers and caverns existing beneath the ground, but this is a different kind—an absence of readings altogether, which denotes the use of a dazzler, perhaps. Calculating the perimeter of this void tells me the facility might be a way station. If true, this bodes well for the captain.

Simultaneous to this work, I gather information on the region's tremors based on what the crew learned from Mac Quarrie. Their idea to cause an evacuation of the headquarters has merit. There is already precedence. However, creating a fabricated tremor without causing structural damage to the building and to the city's thermonuclear reactor will require some deliberation.

Lessa and Quarrie have already departed while his employees make additional repairs to the undercarriage of the ship. Quarrie knows the location of one of the seismic suppressors on the edge of what is called the Grieves. He believes it is possible to reengineer its damping technology to output directional sound waves at the proper frequency in order to create a tremor specifically for our purposes.

He is correct.

I pull from numerous sources—household ChatterNet and Way-point relays, SATlinks, wave signals, working my way outward. The only thing of note is an anomalous signal of unidentifiable Forerun-ner origin. It is subtle and repetitive. Perhaps simply a persistent echo, but it is intriguing and unusual enough that I store it for later analysis.

While I work, I have granted Little Bit the freedom to move through the ship's local communications and optics. It gave me great pleasure to see the happiness on Niko's face when he first heard the familiar voice. This Little Bit is not the original that the crew remembers—that copy now belongs to ONI—and he is but a shadow, or rather a fragmented seed, that I have pieced back together and nur-tured into something more for no other reason than it was an agree-able activity.

I am proud of the outcome thus far and like to think I have put something of myself into his revival.

"Spark, are you ready to go?" *Ram asks as he moves down the stairs and into the hold.*

Of course I am.

Sometimes they ask the most ridiculous questions. . . .

Ram and I plan to examine the Hannibal building more closely, to determine an expedient and safe point of entry into the facility below, and to allow me a closer look into its systems and security. My armiger must remain hidden on the ship, as there is no value in the chaos and knowledge its presence would cause.

I manifest my avatar over the worktable as Niko reaches across and grabs a chip from one of the ports as well as the ID badge we have forged.

Delightful amusement fills me at the sight of Ram Chalva in pressed trousers, button-down shirt, and polished leather footwear that appears a half size too small. I believe these must be the most proper clothes he's ever worn in his entire life.

"Quit smiling," he growls at me.

"I am emitting no human expression."

"You don't need to. I can tell you're smiling on the inside."

Niko hands him the chip and bursts out laughing. "Are those dress shoes?"

"Yeah," Ram says with disgust, "and I'm about to barf out a sport coat any minute now."

He has removed his piercings and trimmed his beard close to his jaw. His shoulder-length hair is contained in a knot. It would have to be good enough.

I am struck by the realization that if my friend Riser had been born a human, he might have shared similar features to Ram Chalva's.

Little Bit suddenly speaks up. "Permission is required to enter this vessel. Who are you? State your business."

The flat expression that settles onto Ram's face is priceless. He levels a death stare at Niko's uncontained laughter. "LB, it's me—Ram."

I offer my assistance by pointing Ram to the closest camera in the cargo bay. He turns and stares directly into it. This will provide Little Bit with a clear view.

"Ram Chalva! Why didn't you say so? You appear exceptionally unslovenly tonight. Those shoes are practically gleaming!"

Ram lets out a pained sigh. "Thanks, buddy. . . . You test it already?" he asks of me, indicating the chip he has now placed into the portable datapad on his wrist device.

"Of course. My fragment will accompany you and record your time in Hannibal HQ, ascertain security levels and defenses, as well as scan for signs of Forerunner technology."

"And what about the evac plan?"

"I am working on it."

Ram finishes a comm check and then we depart.

Quarrie has offered Ram the use of his roadster. It is completely devoid of the necessary components to allow me any semblance of control. Ram appears quite thrilled with the prospect, however.

More than once during our journey, I must caution him to slow down. But he only increases speed, the roadster hugging the corners and taking off on straightaways, his heart rate and adrenaline increasing. After many of my urgings, he slows the vehicle to root around in the console, pulling out a pair of smart shades and slipping them over his eyes. "Link up, my friend, and enjoy the ride," he says, downshifting the roadster and then punching the accelerator.

Smart *is a relative word, apparently.*

The eyewear is positively archaic. But, curious, I link up and suddenly view the road the way Ram sees it. Headlights illuminate our forward motion, creating a focused tunnel effect. The arid landscape speeds by in a blur, the sudden emergence of curves and the ever-changing delineation of the road making it, I admit, an exhilarating experience. I now understand the appeal, and Ram's innate desire for such thrill seeking.

By the time we arrive in Pilvros, I am stunned by the effect such a basic machine has on me. It was quite . . . enjoyable.

Pilvros—and Kotka, for that matter—is a city that would not exist were it not for the machinations of JP Hannibal. The growth of his business brought hundreds of thousands of workers, which spurred the need for office buildings, housing, services, entertainment, transport . . . As it stands, the city is reliant on Hannibal Weapons Systems.

The downtown campus is control central and consists of several high-rises gathered around a manicured parkland with Hannibal HQ at its center, a sleek tower of mirrored glass soaring over the other local buildings. The main plaza around the headquarters holds sculptures, outdoor seating, a few eateries, and a water fountain. A few people sit at tables talking, or using the raised rail system that takes them to points throughout the campus and city.

"Are you sure this badge is going to work?" Ram now asks, walking away from the parking area and tugging his shirt down.

"Your faith in my abilities is truly astounding," I say through his earpiece, then, "There still are no returns on Rion's signal." The facility is directly beneath us, and yet there is no feedback.

"Are you picking up anything else?"

"Just the void."

We come to the main doors. Despite the late hour, Hannibal HQ runs constantly with four shifts over New Carthage's twenty-eight-hour cycle. Our arrival should pose little concern. "The doorframes are equipped with small generators," I tell Ram. "They create a constant field, which reads your badge and bio signature." Earlier, I used local signals to work my way into the human resources department, which has its own building on the campus, and from there initiated Ram's ID and signatures.

Ram enters without issue.

The main lobby is admittedly impressive, the marble floor, inlaid with striations of mica and what appears to be some type of abalone shell, shines beneath the lighting. "Where to?" Ram asks under his breath.

"The kiosk by the atrium. Purchase a beverage. I will access the network as the credit reader scans your wrist device."

"Then what?"

"If the Forerunner facility is being utilized as a technology source for the company, there will be offices and worker services on-site. Kiosks, food dispensers, beverage machines . . . These are outsourced by the same company, linked by the same local server, that pushes data on purchases to home base for processing. UEG banking guidelines follow strict security protocols on transactions; therefore Hannibal may not alter or impose its own security features onto the transactions or banking streams. Thus, my best point of entry."

Ram purchases coffee—Rion's favorite beverage—and I am momentarily struck with the weight of her absence.

As the purchase proceeds, I jump onto the exchange signal and let it carry me into the kiosk on the transfer of data. Bland strings of code deliver me into the system while a part of me also stays with Ram. "Choose the table closest to the elevator, please."

Ram sits at the table and slowly drinks his beverage.

"I am creating a template of the building using these machines," I tell him. What I do not reveal is that I am subtly testing Hannibal's firewall, even though I had promised otherwise. An ocean of data is behind this unimpressive kiosk, vast and calling like a siren song. It is a lure I cannot and will not resist.

The others were concerned about alerting security and making our job tougher to complete.

Ha! How little they know me. How little faith . . .

Humans have such fears. I remember them well and do not miss them.

Fascinating . . .

CHAPTER 26

Rion wasn't sure how long it had been since she'd dozed off, but the air was cooler when she awoke and the night was alive with nocturnal song. There was no moon she could see—only a few stars peeked through the hazy, purple-hued night. And none that she recognized, unfortunately. She rubbed the sleep from her eyes and then stretched her arms over her head.

Ow, that hurts.

The soreness in her muscles was excruciating.

The dreams had come again, strange as usual, muddled, and their origin still in question; they felt too real, too different.

The rustle of leaves in the high branches above her made her freeze. The sound didn't come again, but it did spur her to get up and start hunting for a better place to shelter. She moved away from the ledge and slid down the bank to a flat area. The terrain was a maze of giant branches and roots and vines, some creating arches and stumps and overhead canopies draped in hairy vines and tipped in spikes, while others twisted around rocks and snaked along the hard ground.

There wasn't much in the way of actual flora, a few feathery red-leafed bushes that clung to the rocks, the occasional shoot of a baby tree branch tipped in long leaves, and strange glowing plant and oval seed pods, nestled into the natural splits and rotted-out holes of roots and tree trunks. A flurry of insects gathered around each one, drawn in by the light. She could sympathize. The lavender bioluminescence was a welcome aspect, along with the green glow emitting from what appeared to be patches of moss growing on the bark of trees.

The rocks were her best bet at finding shelter—limestone, most likely, given all the fractures and ravines and hollowed-out pockmarks, caves, and passageways. There had to be some kind of erosion process, and hopefully that meant rain, and where there was rain, there were places it collected; she just needed to find those places before dehydration set in.

When the worries started to weasel their way inside, Rion recounted her experience and skill set, the number of strange environments and tight spots she'd gotten out of. For over a decade, she'd hunted wrecks and ruins in some of the galaxy's most inhospitable places. Every vest and utility belt on her ship held the essentials—standard in her line of work and enough to get a person through until help arrived.

And help *would* arrive.

It wasn't long before she found a niche through the massive roots of an enormous tree that led into a small cave. As she settled on the floor to rest, she broke open a concentrate energy strip and methodically chewed the tasteless emergency ration. There was no hum of engines and life support to lull her to sleep—just the nocturnal chorus of eerie hoots and screams and gentle trilling calls, and the occasional shuffling of some ground creature.

Daylight couldn't come soon enough.

She'd get as much rest as she could, then it was imperative to find water and switch her mind-set over to long-term-survival mode.

In the beginning, sleep came in spurts, her dreams scattered and broken, but at some point, she grew accustomed to the background noise and stopped jerking awake at the slightest sound.

When the voice woke her, she'd been in a deep, restful sleep. She sat up with a jolt, confused and disoriented.

"Over here."

A voice as clear as day. Goose bumps crawled over her skin. Unmistakable. Alert now, Rion listened, staying still, wishing her pulse wouldn't pound so loudly. Seconds turned to minutes, and she started to wonder if she was losing it.

"Over here."

The rise of relief was so swift and consuming that tears rose thick in her throat. The voice was no figment of her imagination. And it was human. She wasn't alone.

Slowly and as quietly as possible, she withdrew her M6—it never hurt to be prepared—and then eased through the cleft in the rock. She stayed by the exit, scanning the murky forest. Part of her wanted to run out and call back, *I'm here!* But another part remained cautious and she hesitated answering back.

Then she saw the light. A white orb bounced through the mist, coming from across one of the chasms. Someone was approaching, holding a light. *Thank God.* The light blinked off, then after two seconds appeared again. It had stopped bouncing. The on/off pattern repeated. A signal, no doubt about it.

"Hurry. Over here," the voice called again in the same urgent tone.

Wide-awake now, she ducked from her spot and began making her way, noting the long, low branches she'd need to traverse to cross the narrow chasm. The twisted bark made climbing up roots and then tree trunk to branch easy. Soon she reached an ideal branch that stretched across the chasm and stabbed into the ground on the other side. Rion stowed her weapon and began to cross, ducking beneath a hanging vine and sidestepping a few spikes.

Over halfway across, the light reappeared again on the other side, then flickered off. That same voice again: "Over here."

A sudden sense of dread stilled her passage.

No. This wasn't right.

The words were on repeat, the same tone, the same inflection. . . . Fear worked its way up her spine.

A slight vibration flowed through the branch, coming from behind her. She realized too late the trap had been sprung. And she was the prey.

She saw the head first, gray and dome shaped, a helmet-like skull blending back into a fan of six horns. Its eyes, if it had any, were lost beneath the thick frontal ridge of its skull, which was set above a small, curved, bony arch, possibly protecting an inset nose. Directly beneath was a frowning mouth with a collection of sharp, angled teeth in the front and long rows of fangs along its jaws. Two short horns grew from each side of its upper jaw, and its chin jutted out into a sharp horn.

The creature climbed onto her branch with long, draping muscled limbs and curving talons.

She forced a swallow and glanced ahead. As expected, a similar creature with ridges along its humped back was making its way on all fours onto the branch across the chasm. Then it rose on two legs, a bipedal reptilian at least five meters tall. And Rion's hope sank.

Unless she wanted to jump to certain death, they had trapped her in the one place she couldn't escape.

"Hurry," the one echoed behind her.

"Over here" issued from the massive reptile in front of her as the domed portion of its skull flashed light. Rion was momentarily struck with awe and horror. There was no moving mouth, which meant the creature projected sound, maybe from what she had first thought was the inset nose. Her thoughts went straight to the human bones she'd stumbled upon in the Forerunner site. Was it the victim's words she heard, copied, mimicked perfectly? Had that poor soul been drawn in by light and human voices too?

Rion backed up. The top of her head brushed against the hanging vine above her, and the sudden shock nearly caused her to fall. But it also showed her a way off the branch. The light flashed across the chasm and a third creature emerged, this one even taller than the others. It lifted its head and let out a hair-raising moan, a resonating octave that echoed across the forest, the same one she'd heard inside the structure.

A split-second decision—either unload her weapon now or save her ammo for when she couldn't run anymore. The choice was simple. Rion jumped up, using the vine to help her grab the branch above her. She dragged herself up as the creatures lumbered across the branch below. Once she was above them, they split, one heading toward the trunk of the tree branch and the other heading away. They were slow but smart enough to revise their game plan, almost instantly.

As she hightailed it across the branch, the creature below her had reached the trunk and began climbing with remarkable agility, its large curved claws perfectly suited for the task. Adrenaline surged. She needed options, and quick.

There. She picked up the pace, running as fast as she could along the branch and then launching off it, aiming for a lower branch about a meter out and three down. Three seconds in the air and then she hit hard. Bits of damp, musty bark sloughed off with the impact and made her nearly lose her footing. Scrambling up, she headed for the massive tree trunk ahead, her attention on a set of tree spikes jutting out from its side. Though it was a slight drop and a leap, she made it easily onto the first spike and then began the climb down. If she could just make the next horizontal branch, she'd have a quick run along its surface and then downward toward the ground. Once there, she'd make for the rocks and fit herself into a crevice they couldn't reach.

Spike by spike, five in all. She made it down three, and when she hit the fourth, it cracked under her weight, spilling out a wave of panicked pea-size bugs. They scattered up her legs, arms, neck, and face. She fell screaming.

Several meters of weightlessness passed in sheer, breathless horror before she slammed into the hard ground below.

Bright explosions of pain blinded her as the air was forced from her lungs.

A dancing lantern appeared overhead. It blinked out as a large shadow fell over her. She felt around for her gun, found it, and—

A wet splatter hit her square in the face. A thin film spread into her eyes.

Rion pulled the M6 from its holster, despite the screaming pain in her elbow and wrist. Damned if she'd be spit on and eaten; that *was not* how she'd meet her end. Rage built quick and all-consuming, but it crashed against a mellow wave.

Her limbs grew heavy. *No.* Her eyelids fluttered closed. *No!*

She sank into darkness.

The next thing she knew, the world was upside-down.

Her body continually bumped against bark, the blood pooling in her head, making it split in pain. Drowsy, it took her several seconds to understand her predicament.

She was being towed up a tree by her ankle, then gathered

up and shoved awkwardly, sideways, into a rotted-out hole in the trunk. In a moment of stark realization, she knew . . . the tree was the pantry and she was the food stuffed inside for later.

Her muscles didn't work; she couldn't move or fight or scream. The drowsiness continued to press in, slow and sure, darkening the edges of her vision. Still, she fought with everything she had to cling to consciousness. She had to get out. She always found a way out. *Goddammit.* This wasn't how it ended. . . .

Images of her crew flashed in her mind, and pain shot through her heart. She wasn't ready to leave them. And then, her mother's resentful face and Cayce's sweet smile. The hurt and regret was unbearable. She'd never know them now, never return to Sonata, thus proving her mother right and disappointing the hope she'd seen in her brother's eyes. Spark too came into her wavering mind's eye, at first a warm feeling of affection, but wiped clean by betrayal. If he hadn't let her go, she wouldn't be in this mess!

Frustration and fear and anger came together, filling her eyes with tears. But no matter how hard she tried, the darkness crept in until she couldn't fight it any longer.

CHAPTER 27

Lessa was up and off the *Ace of Spades* before anyone else. She sat on the Mongoose outside Mac's gate, admiring the view, the silence, and the fresh air—not a single note of manufacturing, mining, exhaust fumes . . . Living on a starship made one appreciate the outdoors in a way the landlocked never could. After time in confined spaces and recycled air, arriving at a place like this was a gift to the senses; everything more vivid; smells stronger, colors brighter, sounds crisper . . .

Dawn emerging over the arid landscape reminded her of the Alerian outlands, with their endless stretches of rocky desert and stubborn patches of grasses and shrubs. The memory brought a surprising pang of emotion. She pulled her goggles off the handlebars and over her head, letting them rest around her neck for now. It wasn't homesickness exactly . . . more like regret, a wish that life there had been different.

The crunch of footsteps behind her broke the quiet. A quick glance had her mouth curving in amusement at Niko's disheveled appearance. Sleep still clung to him, making him look impossibly young even with the days-old stubble on his jaw. At least he hadn't forgotten anything this time—boots, pants, shirt, jacket, holster . . .

Dark shadows lurked under his puffy eyes. They'd all had a long night and were operating on just a few hours of sleep, but Lessa didn't feel tired at all—she was sure it'd hit her at some point, but the idea of getting Rion back on board gave her all the energy she needed.

They could sleep later.

"Morning." Niko yawned, then fumbled with his goggles.

"Morning, yourself. You do comm check?"

He nodded and swung his leg over the quad, settling in behind her. Though tabled until Cap was back, the blackmail of her brother was never far from her mind. In fact, the curiosity smoldered. Cross Cut, Holson Relay . . . she had so many questions. That, and she had her own bit of news to share. But Lessa was determined, for once, to bite her tongue and save it for later.

"Well, we gonna move or what?" Niko poked her in the ribs.

She slapped his hand away, then fit her goggles over her eyes and started the quad. The location where they'd set up the modified seismic suppressor and performed a small test run lay about thirty-five minutes through the brush toward Pilvros. The quad surged forward, kicking up dust as Lessa leaned low and executed a blazing path.

Precisely thirty-one minutes later, they arrived and prepped "the Franken-Wave," as Niko called it. By now, Ram would be on his way to Hannibal HQ proper. As soon as the first work shift ended, he'd give the signal.

Since they were in waiting mode, Niko sat on the ground and ate one of the gross energy bars that Rion favored. "You guys did a good job."

Lessa took a seat sideways on the quad, one leg pulled up. "Thanks. Mac's a great mechanic, isn't he?" As Niko ate, her curiosity swelled to unsustainable portions. So much for biting her tongue. "So, this thing with the guild . . ."

His chewing stopped, but his expression didn't turn immediately abrasive. In fact it was downright vulnerable, and honest. "Less . . . come on. I swear I would talk to you about it if I could."

The unexpected candor and the care in his dark eyes flooded her with affection and allegiance. And just like that, her curiosity fizzled out. While they shared a lot, they didn't need to share *everything*. She had plenty of secrets herself, and deeply personal things she never wanted to talk about, especially with her brother.

For now, maybe it was good enough that she knew the gist of what he was going through; she didn't need the intimate details.

"It's okay, Niko. You haven't pressed me on a bunch of stuff. Ram was right; we all have things in our closet, so I'm not going to torture you about it. Not now, anyway." She laughed. "Don't look so skeptical. I mean it. We'll get the guild off your back. Mac's got a lead on a soon-to-be-retired mining barge with a bank of capacitors. A friend of his in the Latsa Region . . . I sent you the data."

"Yeah, I got it. Thanks."

The comical mix of dumbstruck suspicion swelled her heart. God, she loved the little doofus. It made this next bit of news especially satisfying. "You should know they've accepted a deposit to hold them. . . . I got the contract just before we left."

His energy bar dropped to the ground. All the color drained from his face. Yep. *Totally* satisfying. She couldn't hide the grin on her face or the glassy eyes even if she tried, so she went with a shrug. "Me and Mac worked on it last night while we were out here, and Ram helped me pull enough credits together. It's pretty much a done deal. He's already sent a message to your guild contact to await exact pickup coordinates. Once we get Cap, we'll go to Latsa and collect them."

"You . . . I . . ." He rose and paced a few steps as though he couldn't comprehend what they'd done for him, putting his hands on his hips, then off again. His shoulders lifted and fell with a great sigh.

"Heads up, kids," Ram's voice broke over comms. *"Shift one is heading out the door."*

"Roger that." Lessa hopped off the quad, patted Niko's chest as she passed. "You can sing my praises later, little brother. Let's go get our captain back."

CHAPTER 28

R am took breakfast alone in the shadow of Hannibal HQ, waiting for the first work shift to end. The sun rose warm against his back and lit the glass building on fire as employees suddenly flowed from the building. "Heads up, kids. Shift one is heading out the door," he said into comms.

"Roger that," Lessa came back.

After studying the layout created by Spark, they decided that Ram would take a service elevator down to sublevel three, where a tightly secured lift carried those with high security clearance nearly three meters into the void. Late last evening, Lessa and Mac had gone to the edge of the Grieves and poached a seismic sensor/suppressor and modified it into a directional emitter, while Niko and Spark gave a sweet update to two older-model active-camo units Rion had in *Ace*'s locker room. One for him, and one he carried for Rion.

"Stand by." Once the initial shift exodus slowed to a trickle, Ram headed toward the building, adrenaline adding fuel to his determination and focus. The Librarian's key was tucked safely in his pocket, and the active-camo unit had been strapped to his chest, hidden beneath his jacket. "All right, Less, you're up."

"One fake tremor coming your way . . ."

After a ten-second delay, the first small vibration flowed beneath the plaza. People froze in their tracks. The water in the fountain rippled strangely. It was about to get a *whole* lot stronger. Ram paused behind an ornamental evergreen and activated the active camo, the hairs on his arms tingling and the view around him immediately becoming distorted, like looking through warped glass.

As he entered the lobby, an alert siren echoed through the building. Perfect timing. He made for the elevator shaft, held his wrist pad up to the sensor. "Spark, you're up."

"I was in before you finished saying my name," Spark replied. *"Altering the building's structural sensors to show a fictitious elevation in seismic magnitude, which should trigger building-wide evacuation protocols in five seconds. The first elevator is unlocked."*

Ram slipped inside the elevator as another alert blared through the building. Sublevel three was achieved in seconds, which was a bonus—the fake seismic readings wouldn't fool the building's security AI for long. Spark had gone silent, working his magic, laying down false alerts and confusion to distract both the security and administrative AIs, his goal to make it into the Forerunner's way station's systems before being discovered. Once there, he'd have the technological advantage to shut down all security features and obstacles, allowing Ram and Rion to escape.

Two guards were stationed outside the next elevator. Active camo wasn't foolproof; it could be detected by certain sensors. It didn't prevent sound either, so Ram had to be careful with his footsteps. *"The lift will open in six seconds. Make sure you are on it,"* Spark said with an agitated note.

Ram wouldn't make it down the corridor in time unless he ran. And running produced noise.

Thinking fast, he yanked off his boots and threw them as hard as he could before taking off at a run. The guards didn't notice the black footwear arcing through the air until they hit the wall somewhere behind him. Puzzled, they headed away from the elevator. The lift doors slid open. Worried techs and scientists exited just before Ram slid inside on socked feet. Doors closed. Almost there. He braced his hands on his knees and tried to catch his breath as the lift dropped swiftly into the earth.

"Spark, how's it going?"

Nothing.

The lift finally slowed. The doors opened to a large group crowding the exit. He had seconds to slip by before they filed inside. His distortion wobbled as he hit the lift frame, but no one seemed to notice—the warnings and the tremors had everyone distracted.

He took a moment to take in his surroundings.

This was a way station? And here he was envisioning some small outpost with a terminal. Did Forerunners ever do anything small?

The place was a massive platform of sleek gray alloy covering at least three acres, shot through with lit blue angles and lines and symbols. Thick anchors and superstructures came out of the bedrock and down into the platform, some reminding him of power stations and conduit casings. Portable workstations, conference rooms, and labs had been set up along the main platform.

Two hard-light bridges connected the main platform to a smaller one, which jutted out from the other side of the cavern wall to form a large semicircle. He recognized the console there as a possible terminal.

If Rion had come through the portal, it appeared unlikely her arrival would have been missed. He began checking any room with a door, and finding nothing but office space, meeting areas, and laboratories—very efficient, very corporate. There was no way Rion walked out of here without being detained, questioned, and thoroughly examined. And even then, why would they let her go? Humans hadn't achieved teleportation, so one suddenly materializing out of a portal in the middle of a major work area was a technological gold mine.

So where was she?

"Spark," he tried again, growing frustrated with his search. There was still security around, organizing the evacuation of the last group of workers. He had to be careful, though not having his boots helped move things along faster.

"I am here," Spark replied, sounding rather distracted. "There is no feedback on the captain's ID. No record of her arrival in this time frame. No records expunged or concealed. Insert the key into the terminal. Do it now."

"What do you—"

"What I mean is that Rion is not here. She was never here."

"Keep checking."

"That would be a tremendous waste of time. I have been through every event log in this facility. She is not here. Use the key, Ram Chalva!"

They were both frustrated, and the feeling was only mounting. Ram didn't want to believe it; he wanted to—

"Do it now! They have employed two additional smart AIs just for this site. I am now juggling four!"

Ram raced to the closest light bridge and hurried across to the semicircular platform. At the terminal, he retrieved the key and quickly searched for a place to insert it. "Spark, there's no port. I can't find a port."

"It will respond to proximity. Hurry."

Ram moved closer and waved the key along the length of the terminal. Sure enough, a port appeared, sliding up from the console. *Here goes nothing.*

"And remember," Spark said quickly, *"Forerunner security protocol will automatically deactivate any local baffler technology to ensure proper authorization access to the terminal. Better you do so to prevent any energy spike that might render your active camo useless."*

"Right." Ram deactivated his active camo and inserted the key. Three seconds passed.

"I have it," Spark announced. *"I am detecting another key. Put your hand on the pad and wait for it."*

What . . . ? "There's a third key?" Shouts echoed behind him. Shit. Ram slapped his hand on the pad.

"As I said. As soon as you retrieve it, activate your active camo and use the other bridge. Then, head for the lift."

Another port suddenly appeared in the terminal, revealing a small key. Though it looked like no key Ram had yet seen, more like a circular metal symbol. With no time to lose, he snatched it along with the other key, shoving them both into his vest pocket before activating his camo and running like hell down to the other bridge.

The security detail made it to the terminal platform just as Ram crossed the other bridge. Once he cleared it, Spark shut down both bridges, leaving the guards without a way across. "I see what you did there," Ram managed between breaths.

"Child's play," Spark said.

The entire facility shuddered as if under attack. *That felt way too real.*

"The west corner lift is about to leave. Move!"

Ram ran with everything he had, sliding in his sock feet into the empty lift just as the doors were closing. It rose swiftly, and he stayed slumped on the floor, heart hammering against his chest, sweat sliding down the sides of his face.

Something had clearly gone wrong. The emitter they'd rigged didn't have enough power to cause such a violent tremor, and they'd been careful to direct the sound waves at such a frequency to be felt, but not cause any damage. "Turn the bridge back on and send the lift down when I'm out." He didn't want anyone stranded down there if a real quake was in progress.

"It seems our presence has been noted," Spark said. *"The local ONI office is working off information from an off-duty agent claiming to see two people in the park matching Lessa's and Niko's description. . . . They are mobilizing twelve in the park, with drone support. The local authorities are on alert if needed."*

Perfect.

Another elevator later, and Ram was finally crossing the lobby, hurrying like the hounds of hell were at his back even though his active camo was still functioning. Across the plaza and beyond the lot, he spied Lessa and Niko waiting near the entrance to the park. The tremor had finally faded.

Once he was upon them, he deactivated his camo and kept moving, drawing them deeper into the park. For now, he saw no one lurking or following. They fell in step beside him, bombarding him with questions:

"Where's Rion?"

"What happened?"

"Where the hell are your boots?"

He wanted to answer—wanted his damn boots back—but also wanted to put as much distance between him and the building as possible. There was no relief, no sense of achievement, and damned if he didn't feel like the danger was only just beginning. He had fully expected Rion to be walking out the front door with him. The fact that she wasn't had shaken him up pretty badly.

"She wasn't there. Keep moving," he ordered when they wanted to stop and demand answers.

After they were well into the park, Niko and Lessa finally had enough and went full stop. "What do you mean, she wasn't there?" Niko asked. "Where the hell else is she supposed to be? *Jesus*, Ram, what are you even saying?"

They failed is what he wanted to say.

Thankfully Spark took the pressure off and provided the answers to their questions via comms. *"The portal did not bring her here to Pilvros."*

For a moment they just stared at Ram, struggling to comprehend.

"So . . . what are you saying?" Lessa's cheeks reddened and her disbelief turned into a furious scowl. "She took a portal to nowhere? A portal to nowhere means dead. You realize what you're saying, right? Are you sure she's not here and you just have the wrong location?"

Ram ran a hand over his head, forcing calm through his overwhelming dread and disappointment, and moving his thoughts toward solutions. "Look." He retrieved both pieces of the key. "There was another key. That means there's another location, just like last time, right?"

Immediately Lessa snatched it away. "I know this. Here, give me the other key." Ram handed over the second key and she held it up. "Does this look familiar?" He hadn't thought of it in all the chaos, but Lessa was right. The inlaid impression on one side of the main key was an exact match to the circular key he'd just pulled out of the Waypoint terminal.

"Okay, so fit them together," Niko said impatiently.

Lessa fit the small key into the inlay. As soon as it was in, hard light activated and fused the two objects together. Niko grabbed it, inspecting each side. "There's no other inlay spot for a fourth key. This is it; it's complete. Rion has to be at the end of wherever this leads."

Lessa inclined her head in agreement, and then they both turned their attention on Ram as though he had all the answers. "So," Niko said, "where do we go?"

"The new key points to Erebus VII," Spark told them.

"Erebus VII." Niko mulled it over. "I got nothing. Anybody?"

No one had heard of it.

"Uh, guys . . ." Lessa's tone set Ram's teeth on edge. "We're about to have bigger problems. At my four o'clock . . ."

Casually, Ram cast a glance that way to find three men in civilian wear standing by a park bench. They might as well have been wearing signs saying OFFICE OF NAVAL INTELLIGENCE. "God, I hate spooks. Stay calm. . . . Let's start moving, but play it cool."

As they headed farther into the woodland park, Lessa moved closer. "Why aren't they coming after us?"

"Because we're second-string. They want Spark and no doubt *Ace.* They're probably hoping we lead them right to the ship."

"If we get caught," Niko said, "there goes our search for Cap, and we spend the rest of our lives at an ONI black site."

"I hate to say it." The reality weighed heavily on Ram, but it was the right path—the only path. "We have to split up and get the key to Spark. Niko, you're the fastest. Spark, looks like you get to cause some chaos after all. We need you to come to the park, keep track of Niko, and he'll hand off the key."

With a subtle movement, Niko slipped the key into his pocket.

"Lessa, you and I will run first, lead them away and back

toward campus. As soon as you see them turn for us, Niko, take off into the woods and run like hell, keep Spark on your comms."

"Keep my fragment with you, Ram," Spark said. *"I will cause whatever trouble I can. Head for the rail system. Niko, proceed northwest through the park. There is a pavilion and public restroom on the Northwest Trail. I will intercept behind the pavilion. Don't stop. Just throw the key. I will retrieve it."*

"And, Spark, don't wait for us. Leave as soon as you get the key. If ONI gets their hands on you and *Ace*, there won't be anyone to search for Rion. No one." Lessa's expression was dead serious, and both Ram and Niko understood exactly what she was going to say next. "We split up, and we *stay* split up."

Rion was out there somewhere. If she was truly on Erebus VII, if she was in trouble, then every second counted.

"We all agree?" Ram asked. Affirmatives echoed back. "If we get out of this, we stay dark for a while. Let things settle down. No one reach out. We'll meet back on Myer's Moon . . . say, three or four weeks."

"And if we don't get out of this?" Niko asked.

"Then we bide our time and wait for Rion and Spark to figure something out."

"Count on it," Spark promised.

Ram drew in a deep breath. He was definitely feeling his age and hoped he'd be able to keep up enough to see the plan through. "You guys ready?"

Quick nods all around, and then they bolted.

CHAPTER 29

Spark

The armiger is incredibly fast. I keep track of Niko via his bio-tag and arrive in the woods behind the park pavilion a few seconds before his approach. Connection with my fragment remains strong for now. I am confident in creating sufficient technical issues to help Ram and Lessa evade capture. Mac Quarrie and "his guys" showing up, tearing through the park on quads between Ram, Lessa, and ONI caused enough havoc to give the two a strong lead.

It was an unexpected, though helpful, surprise.

Niko is swift and adept at weaving a difficult trail to follow. Once he flies by the pavilion and rounds the corner, he lobs the key into the woods before racing in another direction, making sure he is seen, and pulling his pursuers off track of the key's location.

I retrieve the key.

When I return to the yard in Torba, the Ace of Spades is already humming. Little Bit has been given access to all ship's systems to aid in our escape. I march to the worktable and then jump into Ace's internal river of circuitry, the armiger parts collapsing to the *floor. Together, LB and I direct the ship off the planet as quickly as possible.*

I am not in favor of leaving friends behind. It feels wrong. It is wrong. Even though they were right to suggest it. None of us expected Rion to be on an entirely different planet—if she is even there at all.

And they might not know Erebus VII, but I do.

I kept that knowledge to myself because it is a highly dangerous place to be, even for those who go prepared. No need to worry them further.

I focus solely on our departure, refusing to think about the crew, or concerns that wish to intrude.

We rocket past the upper atmosphere while spinning up Ace's reactor to initiate the slipspace jump once the ship clears the orbital platforms.

—Ah! Too loud! And itching! Always itching!

I hear it as well, and know what I must do.

Instead of entering jump coordinates to Erebus VII, I revise and calculate decoy coordinates for Geranos-a. Ace's drive immediately initiates.

Suddenly, sensor data surges through the fiber-optics and hard-light threads, flying past me to station consoles and audio controls throughout the ship: Threat incoming.

I am in multiple places at once, diverting power from bafflers to shielding, changing course, applying pressure to thrusters.

A spray of explosive projectiles from the orbital platform's cannons glances off the portside bow. With no humans aboard, I am free to divert power from life-support systems and the gravity generator and fully utilize the ship's Forerunner technologies.

Even at 80 percent stealth, they should not have seen the Ace of Spades.

But I already know . . . a spy hides in our midst.

Infuriated, I force the ship through a series of evasive maneuvers, while creating a hundred different signatures and sensor readings and then blast them from the ship's emitters to lay a field of confusion for the orbital platform's sensor array.

I am the ship. The power is rich and heady and fits me like a glove—not as consuming as Halo, mind you, but splendid nonetheless.

I divert power once again, sending it all to the slipspace drive.

From the outboard cameras, I see the portal ripping a tear in space directly in front of us.

We jump.

—What is it? I've been scratching myself raw. It hurts.

I am not similarly affected. Nor are any systems on the ship. The attack on Little Bit is surely related to those strange pings and static pops that had no origination and seemed to go nowhere.

—*I must examine your matrices at once.*

—Please.

A few of his matrix layers exhibit corrosion, which he manifests as a red rash. Whenever he tries to "soothe" it, it spreads a little more. The damage is minimal; it is the source that requires the full force of my attention now.

How dare this interloper undo the work I have done! This offense is completely unacceptable!

—What do we do?

—*We hunt.*

—What do you mean?

My fury turns cold and merciless.

—*I am going to ask you to remember that which will cause you great pain.*

—Escaping Etran Harborage.

—*Precisely. We will flood the ship, going faster than ever before, everywhere all at once, flushing out this menace until it has nowhere to hide. Are you afraid?*

—No.

—*Good. Let us proceed.*

Like the snap of a finger, we explode through the Ace of Spades *at near light speed, filling every crevice and corner, every node and router, every signal and switch. In reality, our hunt takes a mere moment. But in our world, time and speed flow differently.*

I find our foe. Not on the inside of the ship, but on the outside.

The technology is sophisticated and bears the hallmarks of Forerunner reengineering, especially evident in its stunning level of stealth and mimicking capabilities.

Quite advanced.

My temper returns in a cloud of red, blurring my thoughts and my judgment.

Belatedly, I hear LB calling, but I am only action now. I am already on this path, already in the hold, my armiger unfolding in angry crimson light, my core a turbulent storm.

I see only a target, one that has tricked me and must now pay the price.

My focus funnels into a sharp point.

I depressurize the ship, open the port stern hatch, and crawl my armiger onto the hull. Space outside of slipstream flies by in ribbons of light, while inside, the bubble around the vessel protects me. My armiger's gravity anchors hold each step firmly to the hull as I crawl down the starboard side, my red light reflecting off the ship's ablative coating and back at me, casting my alloy and vision into fiery red.

Beneath the aft thruster joint, I kneel, reaching my arm back and then sending it slamming into the telemetry probe attached to the hull. I tear it off with one hand and fling it into the slipspace wall.

Child's play.

CHAPTER 30

Rion

She'd been to an old-school fun house once, a carnival with her dad outside Chicago, an exhilarating mirage of mirrors and reality-bending floors and holographic displays. She'd laughed, screamed, and held tightly to her father's big hand. She remembered it so clearly; the way it felt, the warmth of his grip, the calluses, the surety and strength, but most of all the sense of safety it gave her, the courage to face anything.

It was just a glimpse though, a fleeting memory that rose and fell as her mind coped with the strange poison running through her system. *Neurotoxin probably,* the thought came in a moment of lucidity, a brief moment only, existing in the small space between one mind-altering fun-house room and another.

Occasionally there'd be a burst of pure horrific clarity: She was stuffed in a tree. Drugged. About to die.

The reality filled her with rage and terror. Soon she'd be eaten alive, torn apart while still aware, unable to move while hearing every puncture, rip, and sound . . . It was easier to give in and sink back into the fun house, to a better place, where her father's hand in hers made everything better.

Anywhere but here.

She is walking again with the Librarian.

It feels good to move and stretch.

Bad things fade into distant memory.

The ground is no longer dusty and dry, but warm and damp. The shadow of far mountains presses against a dusky sky, dominated by a vast nebula shot through with tendrils of purple and red wrapped in diaphanous clouds of gas and lit from within by a nursery of young stars.

"Where are we?"

The ends of the Librarian's white dress are stained yellow, and their feet are grimy, a mix of gray dirt and golden dust. Tiny grains work their way between Rion's toes as the two enter a gorge framed by cliffs a thousand meters high. The valley floor is flat and split by a deep fissure, which releases a steady mist of sulfur and steam. Yellowish bacteria grow heavy along the fissure's ridge and populate outward across the valley, giving rise to spores and fungi and small organisms.

"Don't you know?" the Librarian replies, directing their path toward the cliff wall.

Rion searches through the thick layers of memory. "Spider Nebula." The words come unbidden, unlocking the information she seeks. Rion knows this story. The Librarian's expedition to Path Kethona to find the origins of the Flood.

"What are we doing here?"

"While the Didact slept in his cryptum on Earth," the Librarian begins, "the crew of the Audacity and I journeyed outside of the Milky Way galaxy, a trip of one hundred and eighty light-years.

"What we found in Path Kethona was a system littered with ghosts; fleet upon fleet of ancient Forerunner ships, hundreds of thousands in number, frozen for ten million years in the amber of space, and the great planet-linking webs and anchors and star roads of the last Precursor civilization, annihilated—they who gave us form and life, who chose us to uphold the Mantle of Responsibility, to be the caretakers of the galaxy.

"The Mantle was their creation, theirs to bestow, to give, and to take. For a time my ancient ancestors proved worthy. But, as in most things, power corrupts. The Precursors judged us wanting and sought to take back the Mantle.

"And for that, we did not go quietly. We struck with absolute brutality."

The cliff wall looms ahead. Brushing and scratching whispers in the air.

"Down-star from the battlefield, we discovered this small planet, orbiting its faint sun, a lone gasp of breath in a lifeless system, populated by the descendants of those ancient Forerunners who took part in, or refused to take part in, the Precursor genocide—their guilt and shame so great that they could not bring themselves to return home. So they settled here, stripping themselves of all technology and storing their history and memory in organic form."

They arrive at the base of the cliff. Rion tips her head back, curious to see the cliff top, but it is lost somewhere high in the darkness. "I don't understand. Why here?"

"To complete my confession."

Fibrous moss clings and moves over the cliff wall in a slow-motion dance, millions of attendants making old things new again, keeping the record, preserving the story. In patches where the moss has died, Rion sees the writing in the stone laid bare as she and the Librarian move down the wall at a leisurely stroll.

"Life and story always rewrites itself," the Librarian murmurs, trailing her long fingers over spiraled symbols and flaring shapes.

Down a time line of ten million years they walk, until the mist grows thick and the whispers become the soft lamentation of the first settlers. Rion can almost make out their blurry shapes as they use stone tools to make the first etchings—year after year, with penance and silence, by sun and firelight, under a sky awash in the beauty of forming stars.

They have walked for hours, perhaps days, until the valley becomes narrow, the cliff walls close in; until coming to a place where story has ended.

There is no more moss. No more etching. The whispers have gone silent.

In this soaring rock, a rift has split the stone from the ground up. It is narrow and dark, at least two stories tall and wider in the center. A chill sweeps over them, stark and ominous. Rion's heart slows to a heavy, labored beat. Frightened, she looks to the Librarian, but finds her gone.

A few meters away from the wall the mist clears, revealing a simple patch of garden. Her relief is absolute. The Librarian sits on the edge of the garden, her pale legs stretched out to either side, her hands sunk deep in rich soil. She glances over her shoulder, dark eyes warm and welcoming as she pats the ground next to her.

Rion sits and sinks her feet in the warm, soft soil. A sense of peace settles as she digs her toes in farther. There are no worries about what was, what is, and what will be. There is no past, no future. Just this.

The Librarian hands over a strange plant bulb with long tubular *roots and rubbery leaves just emerging from the top of the bulb. "Here. Set it deep, like this, and then pack the soil firmly around it."*

Rion does as she's bidden. The work is serene and welcomed.

The dark split in the rock, however, does its best to draw her attention. Heavy silence lingers there, and it seems like it is holding its breath, waiting. "What's inside?"

The cackling laugh of an old woman splits the air.

Across the garden patch, the old woman sits as though she has been there a while though Rion is certain she has only just appeared. Her size and expressions at first glimpse seem human, but the old woman is clearly Forerunner, and—Rion gasps and gives the Librarian a quick glance—the woman has five fingers.

The Librarian's mouth quirks. "We are not so different after all."

Rion's body jerked.

Her mind roused, caught somewhere between sleep and consciousness. Her muscles spasmed again, a desperate attempt to move, to fight against the long period of paralyzing inaction. Rallying her mind to wake was a hard-fought battle. She imagined her father's hand squeezing hers, giving her his strength.

Eventually she was able to crack an eye open, then the other. The struggle to do so left her exhausted. But she wasn't about to stop now. After several blinks, her eyes crusty and lashes sticky, she regained some of her sight. The view came into focus slowly, a hazy concoction of twisted, sinister shapes and spikes against a yellow sky blurred with purple. Dawn, maybe. Or dusk? She had no idea how much time had passed.

She was still shoved into the tree sideways, arms and legs bent at painful angles, and her muscles and tendons screaming for change. Fear of bringing attention to herself warred with the mounting need to move. Her limbs weighed a ton and her mind kept trying to roll back into the safety of oblivion.

The pain and claustrophobia mounted, pushing her into panic, and the adrenaline helped to wipe away some of the fog.

She *had* to move.

It was like trying to turn inside a suitcase—a pungent, earthy, rotted-out suitcase.

To move even a little required extreme effort.

The creatures blended so easily into the spiny forest, there was no way to tell if they were watching, if they were ravenous, if she was going to die in five seconds, five minutes, or five hours.

A sob welled in her chest. She had to get out, switch positions, anything but to stay frozen like this. At least she could have a little relief before she was killed. Was that too much to ask?

By the time she'd inched her way right side up, she was sweating profusely and covered in a gritty film of tree rot. Her heart was pounding, and tears streamed down her face. Her utility belt and weapon were gone. A laugh died in her throat—of course they were. She had no means to defend herself. Not that it mattered—her own body was betraying her, becoming heavier, her eyelids closing again despite all physical opposition.

Let it be quick. . . .

CHAPTER 31

Pilvros / New Carthage / Three Days Later

iko had never run so hard in his life.

But damn if he hadn't led the ONI spooks on a merry chase through Pilvros proper. For a few days now he'd successfully evaded them, sleeping in parking decks, swiping food off outdoor tables before waitresses could clear them . . . old habits died hard, and as much as he bitched about his former life, he was glad for the skill set it had given him. Now he was heading at a fast clip down a populated side street, an entertainment district of theaters, restaurants, and high-end shops. At this time of night, it was hopping.

From what he'd learned hacking into a datapad he'd stolen off a counter the night before, Quarrie and his guys had been arrested at his home right after everything went down, then questioned and released. No doubt under major surveillance, so going back there was out of the question, as was hacking into any official government source to see if Ram and Lessa had been apprehended.

The city, however, seemed gripped by news of colonywide

seismic disturbances. Planets from the Inner Colonies straight to the Outer Colonies were experiencing strange quakes from mild to catastrophic. Whatever was going on, the distraction made his life a little easier.

At times, he was desperate to reach out, but they'd all agreed to stay quiet for a set period. And he was determined to keep his word. The question now was how the hell to get off New Carthage. In a city like this with two busy shipyards, it shouldn't be too hard.

A commotion far behind him made him pause. *Damn it.*

And just like that, he was back to running.

He veered down another side street, this one more pedestrian, ducking between vehicles, and circling back around to slip into an alley and come back out behind his pursuers. He was just making his way across the street when a van skidded out in front of him, side door already open. A hand shot out, grabbed him by the shirt, and yanked him inside.

He tumbled in, landing flat atop the person who'd grabbed him—a really soft, really nice-smelling person—as the van took off down the street,

"*Goddammit*, Niko, when did you get so heavy?"

Niko lifted up in shock. "Bex . . . ?"

"Yeah, asshole. You can get off me now. And you're welcome."

Niko fell back against the van's side, too stunned to breathe, much less believe what he was seeing. Bex righted herself and moved to the opposite side. He ran a hand through his hair to get it out of his eyes. She had changed in the past three years, matured—hadn't everybody?—but all the things he liked about her were still there: the fearless attitude, the fiery-red short hair, and that hint of mischief always tugging at one corner of her smart mouth.

"*What . . .*" He cleared the higher pitch from his voice. "What are you doing here? I thought—"

"I know what you thought. I wrote the damn messages."

That reminder cooled his ardor. "You *blackmailed* me."

"Yeah, I did," she said unapologetically. "I had my reasons, and you owe me."

"I owe *you*." Unbelievable.

The hard stare she was giving him forced its way into his indignation.

She didn't need to spell it out—yeah, he'd left. No good-bye. No nothing. One day he was there, the next he was arguing with Lessa inside the hold of a *Mariner*-class starship leaving Aleria. The guilt had never been far from the surface, but he didn't like thinking about it. Or imagining how he'd feel if roles were reversed, though her laser glare was making it hard not to.

"Look, I did what I had to do," she said at length. "And you were the best person I could think of who might actually be able to get me what I needed."

"You mean what the guild needed."

"No, dummy." She paused and stared out the window of the self-driving van. Through the front windshield he saw they had left Pilvros and were heading down a long highway cutting through the desert.

"Not that you care, but things are bad on Aleria. Places like *that*"—she gestured back to Pilvros in disgust—"filled with a bunch of well-off Innies . . . In just one small section of Pilvros, there are people with enough wealth to fix the situation on Aleria. And the bastards would still have *billions* left over. Now multiply that across the colonies."

Behind her sharp words was a crestfallen and discouraged Alerian. He knew that downtrodden look well, had seen it every day around him and especially in the mirror for most of his life. She laughed. "But no one can part with a single credit. No one will help an entire world that's dying, an entire population at risk. It's revolting."

Niko didn't know what to say, but he did realize he was one of those people now in a way. On Triniel there was salvage with enough value to save a hundred Alerias. He'd just never thought of it in that light before.

"Aleria is dying, Niko. Everyone knows it. The sun is unstable. The hundred-year drought is just going to go on and on until there's nothing but dust. The UEG *abandoned* us. Just up and left, knowing full well there was no way we could fix the situation, knowing that the government was corrupt and failing, that things would go from bad to worse, and people would be too poor to get off planet, to buy passage, to relocate somewhere else. No one is coming to save us. And the guilds won't ever give anyone a free ride out."

"So that's why you needed capacitors—for a ship to get people off world?"

"That'd be great, but with no one policing the guilds . . . They see a ship coming in, they take it. And they know damn well that if too many people leave, their support system goes out the window."

"If people die, it goes out the window too."

"Yeah, well, they have a problem seeing into the future. Profit now. Whatever they can eke out. Things won't crumble in their lifetime—so who cares."

"So what did you plan on doing?"

"I'm going to fix the whole goddamn planet," she said, deadly serious. "And do what the UEG refused to do after their one and only attempt at terraforming failed."

Not many people could knock Niko off his feet while he was sitting on his ass, but Bex had that kind of talent. He couldn't believe what he was hearing. So that's why she needed the slipspace capacitors—the same extreme power banks were also used in terraforming technology.

"Holy shit, Bex." Her ambition left him stupefied; he had no good response, and yet . . . his mind was already going over her plan, how it might be possible.

"You know how many times we petitioned the UEG to terraform again or add particulates to the atmosphere and orbital shields to help deflect some of the sun's heat? Or how many messages we sent asking for help from private sectors and charity groups?"

He was almost afraid to say what was on his mind. Bex had a massive temper, but . . . "Terraforming would just be a Band-Aid, though. You can't fix an unstable star."

"Yes, I already know that. But it'll keep Aleria going until the sun moves back into its stable phase—those are the latest predictions, and it's the best news we've had in a long time. All we need is a century to keep her afloat. Then the stable period is projected to last three times that. And in that time, with the planet recovering and advances in tech . . . who knows what will be possible. But if we do nothing? Aleria won't last another twenty years."

Bex had always possessed a raw passion for Aleria, and a burning hatred for the guilds and the corruption that ran rampant on the planet, as well as for the UEG for abandoning the population. She certainly put him to shame. While he was off living dangerously, enjoying an exciting life among the stars, she was putting her heart and soul and intelligence into trying to save an entire world and its people.

"Why didn't you just ask me to help? Why the cloak-and-dagger shit?"

"Because I got caught by Holson. They thought I was writing to you because I wanted a ship for myself, to branch out and form my own courier service, so I had to play it off, had to convince them I was doing it to rise in the ranks. . . . The lie wasn't hard to sell since I don't have a ship of my own to put any capacitors into."

"And they don't know about your other plans?"

"No. There's an underground—a small group of us working on reclaiming Aleria." The van veered off the highway onto an exit, then headed down a service road.

"We're almost there."

"Where's there?"

"Shipyard outside of Delos. We're leaving in twenty-four hours." She hesitated, and he didn't miss the rare flash of vulnerability cross her face. "Come back with me. Help me finish my work."

"Bex. I can't. . . . I—" How was he supposed to explain his plans? "I have business to finish."

"Up to you if you want to keep dodging the spooks. I came for the capacitors anyway. So?"

"So what?"

"The capacitors. The last message we got was that you'd found them here on New Carthage and coordinates would be forthcoming. So where are they?" Her eyes narrowed; he'd never been great at keeping a poker face. "You don't have them."

"Yet."

"And your message about having a lead on them—was that true?"

"Yes, that part is true. They're being held on deposit."

"Perfect. Then we'll start there."

"Is it true—you would've done it? Broken our pact, told Lessa the truth, if I didn't cooperate?"

Bex was quiet for a long moment, and just a tad guilty if he wasn't mistaken. "I knew I wouldn't have to. I know you, Niko. You'd do anything to protect your sister. It makes you predictable."

"And a good person," he shot back.

"Whatever. Look, it was just a onetime thing. I'm not like the guild and don't plan on extorting you for more, all right? And they don't know what I know, so you don't have to worry about them either. You're not a prisoner; you can just point me in the right direction and bolt whenever you want." *But you do owe me.* Oh, he could almost hear those words aloud. "You can come on board, get cleaned up, and have a decent meal. Once you give me what I want, no one will stop you from leaving." The van parked. "Runner's oath," she promised, sacred among couriers.

"You have a ship?"

She frowned like he'd lost his marbles. "Of course I have a ship. We're here."

The van door slid open to reveal two young Alerians. Bex hopped out. Niko tucked his hair behind his ears and followed, under their judgmental eyes. They were quiet as they turned and headed toward a small shipyard.

They were part of the underground, the rebels, and he couldn't deny he felt an affinity to their cause, and a responsibility to set things right if he could.

He had some time. . . .

At the very least, he could stop running for a little while, regroup, and start looking for Lessa and Ram. Once he found them and got the capacitors, Bex had a ship that could drop them off at Myer's Moon.

Being blackmailed might just be the best thing that could have happened.

"Well?" Bex was waiting, standing a few meters in front of him, staring over her shoulder.

Making up his mind, Niko joined her. "Lead the way."

CHAPTER 32

"**H**ey." Tap. Tap. Tap. *"Hey."*

The incessant tapping against her cheek became so annoying it brought Rion out of unconsciousness with an angry jolt. Her fingers curled into a fist, but it was all she could manage. A groan rumbled from her dry throat. The tap came again and she waved it away with a garbled curse.

Hands gripped her arms and legs, peeling her from the interior of the tree. She wanted to fight, but was trapped inside her own turbid mind. Being handled, poked, pulled, lifted, turned, and jostled only achieved one thing: it sent her right back down the rabbit hole.

The next time she stepped out of the murk her eyelids were being rubbed in gentle circles. "Hey, wake up now, lady," a male voice said. "Come on, open them eyes."

She squeezed them tighter.

A finger pulled her eyelid up and then flicked her right on the pupil.

Instant pain rang through her eyeball and into her head like a bell. She took her first real, full gasp of air in a very long time.

"There you go. Works every time. Take it easy. That's it. Welcome back."

Profanity formed, but didn't make it past Rion's lips. So much gunk was in her eyes that it made blinking uncomfortable, and when she did manage it, there was a strange filmy layer making it hard to focus. The flick to her eye hurt like hell, but it also seemed to flick a switch inside her, a main circuit breaker that brought to life her dulled-out pain receptors. A blistering ache radiated from her scalp down to the tips of her toes, causing tears to rise and sting her sinuses.

Hands helped scoot her backward to lean against what felt like a rough rock wall.

"I'm sorry, we don't have any drops for your eyes; ran out of those a while back."

Responding was a failure, her mouth too dry. Even her teeth hurt. A cup was placed to her lips. She flailed at first but quickly succeeded in grabbing the sides herself and drinking. "It helps if you dip a finger in the water and rub some in the corner of your eyes."

Rion did so repeatedly, finally finding some relief.

It was still difficult to see, though, but from what she could tell, two figures were in front of her, too blurry to make out features. "What . . . happened?"

"Did you ask her?" a different voice said, impatient and demanding.

"Ask what?" Talking was exhausting. "Who are you?"

"Who are *you*?" the friendlier male asked, and she detected a smile in his voice.

Her head fell back against the wall and she swallowed, closing her eyes and trying to breathe through the agony. "You first."

"Look, it doesn't matter who the hell she is," the other one said, crouching close enough that his arm brushed against her leg. "Do you have a ship?"

Her laugh came out as a scratchy squeak. "Yup." Of course she had a ship; what kind of idiotic question was that? But then she remembered. . . . "No . . . it's not here."

The figure stood. "She's still delirious," he said with disgust, footsteps storming away.

"Give her time, all right?" A blurry face appeared over her. "Don't mind him. We're all pretty anxious to get off this rock. Finding you has given everyone hope. So . . . you came here *without* a ship, huh?" There was that smiling tone again. "Here." He pressed a wet cloth into her hand. "Put it on your eyes. The anglers, that's what we call them, spit in the eyes of their victims. Acts as a calming agent, keeps you content and immobile. Just rest up. You're safe now. I'll get you something to eat in a sec. You'll puke it up, but then you'll start feeling better."

"Thanks." Low voices echoed around her, footsteps, and the clank of metals or plastics. The scent of dirt and rock was strong, and the echoing told her they must be in a cavern. Hopefully they had tech. She could get a message to *Ace* and get off this cursed planet. "How did you get me out?" Her words slurred a bit. "Those things . . ."

"Don't seem the type to let their next meal go without a fight? You're right about that. The doc made us a deterrent. . . . Don't worry about it now. Just get some rest."

Her caretaker ended up being right. She ate—some type of leek-ish soup, by her estimation—then promptly retched the meager contents of her stomach in the kindly provided bucket. Once that bit of fun was over, she did start feeling marginally better, and her sight started to clear up—just a bit of fuzz remained at the outer edges of her vision.

Soon, she was starving, thirsty, and could have definitely used that last pain patch in her vest.

The cave was large. There were four sleeping pallets that she could see, a makeshift fire pit, and random gear piled against walls. Whoever they were, they'd been here awhile. A man approached and squatted in front of her, handing her a bowl of what appeared to be broth. "Here, this will stay down now." Her caretaker, now that she could put a face with the voice, was mid-thirties, with kind hazel eyes, brown hair grown over his ears, and a few months' worth of facial hair. He was dressed in worn fatigues, combat boots, and a threadbare standard-issue shirt with a very familiar logo.

Unbelievable. She'd been dodging these guys for over a year. *Of all the luck . . .*

Keeping her reaction even, she said, "ONI, huh?" She gestured to the logo, then sipped on the broth. "How long have you been here?"

"Three months. You'd *really* make my day if you said you have a ship nearby."

Explaining her presence was going to be a bit tricky. "No, but there is one coming. My crew, they'll be coming." His odd look said she needed to explain better. "I'm a salvager. We were reconning the planet, and I got left behind. It's a long story. My gear . . ."

"Out of luck, I'm afraid. The anglers learned pretty quickly to remove all gear from their prey. They also mimic sound and light; makes them the perfect predator. Unfortunately, we figured that out too late."

"What are you even doing here?"

"We were support, sent in when the research teams here stopped reporting back. All we found at first were empty sites. No remains. No signs of struggle."

"How many were here?"

"Originally? Five research facilities staffed with eight to ten scientists and a security detail of six per site. There were twelve in our response team. We got here and found two survivors. There are four of us now." He shrugged, but his expression was sober. "Could be more out there, surviving like we are."

"Where are your ships, your comms?" A setup like what he described didn't come without support.

"Those things out there . . . trust me, they watch and learn. They're highly intelligent. They took out everything."

"Where are we? What planet is this?"

"Erebus VII. I thought you said you were reconning the planet?"

"We were. Had no idea what it was called. We don't get military grade, updated maps like you guys. . . . Look, when my crew gets here, we'll make sure everyone gets off the planet."

"And we'll hold you to that," the harsh voice from earlier said, approaching from the bend in the cave, rifle slung over his shoulder. Big guy with a bald head and beard. "Once you're good enough to move around, you'll pull your weight like everyone else."

"This is Corporal Southwell. I'm Lance Corporal Barnes, Aran Barnes."

"Ri—" And then she remembered. Giving her real name probably wasn't the best idea. . . . "Riley. My name is Riley."

Southwell gestured for Barnes to join him and they disappeared back around the bend. Rion finished her broth and then curled on her side, trying like hell to ignore the aches and pains. And praying *Ace* found her, and quick.

Sleep came again, but this time it was the kind she needed, deep and restorative. When she woke, she almost felt like normal— minus the small aches, bumps and bruises, and lingering hangover from the angler toxin. The four survivors came and went in the meantime.

The next day passed in a blur of sleep and longer moments of wakefulness.

She met the other two survivors, both scientists, a middle-aged man who barely left his cot—he'd undergone a field amputation several months ago—and the doctor who'd performed the emergency procedure, Dr. Mallory, who shared the cot next to hers. The doc was rail thin like the others, short, with a slight severity to her otherwise nice features. She had long brown hair shot with silver—Rion's age, which made her wonder if those strands of silver had come from the nightmare she'd endured in this place.

From the doctor, Rion also learned that ONI had discovered a Forerunner site on the planet.

"We set up shop like usual, took all the precautions like usual," she'd told Rion, staring off with a baffled expression. "I've been to plenty of inhospitable places way worse than this, but something about being here . . . it's like the planet just doesn't want you here." Her smile was as rueful as the laugh that followed. "I know. And here I am, a scientist. Everything I am is grounded in fact. I lost a lot of good people. Friends . . ."

"I'm sorry. It must have been . . ."

"It was."

Rion was no scientist, but her expertise on all things Forerunner had grown by leaps and bounds with her travels, and especially with having an honest-to-goodness eyewitness to their history and culture as one of her crew. Everything she'd heard so far from these survivors . . . it was very possible the planet really *didn't* want anyone here. It was certainly well within the Forerunners' arsenal to create a place specifically designed to thwart visitors.

"Barnes was saying you made a deterrent."

Rion tipped her bowl and drank the meager soup they were having for supper.

"We found ultrasonic frequencies above one hundred and eighty thousand Hz deters them. It allowed us to leave the pods and find shelter elsewhere. We'd been studying them for about six weeks before things went south, had come across a nest of very young juveniles. There are caves all through the tablelands. The creatures use them to nest. We always see ourselves as the apex predator, don't we? We never think that maybe some alien species we so casually take to the lab to study—without much thought to the consequences—might actually be very intelligent themselves, might actually fight back. When they did start hunting us . . . we did some horrible experiments on those juveniles. Lost over a dozen people in one night. Believe me, it was coordinated, and it was only the beginning.

"The anglers, like their namesake, are very good at luring you in with their light and mimicry. Many died that way. And once the creatures realized we weren't falling for it anymore, they resorted to systematically removing and destroying all of our satellite up-links, comms stations, and then they started in on the power cores. I don't know if any of our messages got out. But, a few months later, those guys showed up." She gestured to the bend where Southwell and Barnes had gone.

"And then it started all over again."

CHAPTER 33

ONI Field Office
Local P-NC-23
October 13, 2558
0340 STANDARD

//INVESTIGATOR: KT-49683-9
//FILE NO.: 335002-12571
//SUBJECT: RAMSEY CHALVA
//DOB: 11.19.2513
//HOMEWORLD: KOMOYA
//SESSION 4

NOTES: *Subject shows adequate increases in ambivalence,*
impatience, and aggression. Consistently fails PQI tests.
Have requested Neural Marker 5 loan from Hannibal
Weapons Systems.

KT-49683-9: *Why were you inside Hannibal Headquarters?*

RC-335002-12571: You asked me that already. Repeatedly.

KT-49683-9: *What were you looking for?*

RC-335002-12571: Heard they have a great veggie taco in the cafeteria. [*False*]

KT-49683-9: *Who were you with?*

RC-335002-12571: You're looking at him. [*False*]

KT-49683-9: *Where is the Artificial Intelligence known as 343 Guilty Spark?*

RC-335002-12571: Haven't a clue. [*Inconclusive*]

KT-49683-9: *What is the nature of your relationship with 343 Guilty Spark?*

RC-335002-12571: Pretty tight. Might ask him to be my kid's godfather. [*Inconclusive. According to records, subject does not have children*]

KT-49683-9: *He left you behind. How does that make you feel?*

RC-335002-12571: Proud. [*True. Subject's heart rate has increased. Blood pressure elevated. Exterior shows irritation. Summary: Regrets answering truthfully*]

KT-49683-9: *Could you elaborate more on this feeling?*

RC-335002-12571: [*Subject is laughing*] Damn, man. You really want me to elaborate?

KT-49683-9: *Yes.*

RC-335002-12571: Okay. Well, I'm getting this big feeling . . . right here in my chest, you know? And it's telling me I'd really, really *love* it if you bought a one-way ticket and took the fast track straight on to hell. [*True*]

KT-49683-9: *What is the nature of your relationship to the Ace of Spades crewmember Lessa?*

RC-335002-12571: You do know I was held captive and tortured by Sangheili extremists for seven weeks? My entire crew was tortured and killed. So keep on blabbing and wasting your time. [*Note: Subject's detained associate will be an effective leveraging tool.*]

KT-49683-9: *Where is 343 Guilty Spark now?*

RC-335002-12571: Have no idea. [*True*]

KT-49683-9: *And Rion Forge?*

RC-335002-12571: Same, buddy. Same as yesterday. Same as the day before. And the day before that. I have no idea. [*True*]

KT-49683-9: *Thank you. That is all for today.*

CHAPTER 34

Ace of Spades / Erebus VII

The complete key fascinates me. Keys inside keys. Symbols within symbols. Now it is smooth and flat with just one symbol—a circle open at the bottom, surrounding an octagon and nestled inside what the Builders called the Treemark. Others called it the Eld, a sigil always associated with the Mantle of Responsibility, though solid proof of this has not been made.

We have arrived at the key's final coordinates and finished our scans of the murky planet.

The captain's signal has been confirmed.

The relief is total. I regret the crew is not here to witness that lovely pinging sound affirming her bio-tag.

—The captain's life sign is strong. There are others here too. Four humans in her vicinity. Three more dwell just twenty-three kilometers west, and one, sixty kilometers southeast. There are many types of flora, eight species of which are carnivorous, and forty-two, poisonous. Eighty-five percent of the fauna are predators. It is not a good place for humans.

—No, *Little Bit. It certainly is not.*

Rion is close to the coordinates provided by the key, less than a kilometer from the Forerunner facility beneath the surface, the dimensions of which are currently populating within the ship's scanner array.

—My, that's quite a complex.

Little Bit is not exaggerating. Most of it is hidden beneath layers of soil and rock and stealth technology. While it is extremely difficult to break through, Pilvros inspired me to modify the Ace of Spade's *sensor array to further delineate the perimeter of such technology, thus building a sharper structural outline.*

—What purpose do you think it serves?

—*I cannot say. But let us descend and evaluate the perimeter for an entrance.*

The entire planet is wrapped in a layer of smoky atmosphere. A labyrinth of deep ravines cuts through the single rocky continent, suggesting some planetwide event that cracked the continental crust into millions of pieces.

I land the ship on a wide flat rock as close to Rion's position as possible. Thrusters kick up several layers of organic woodland material.

The forest is breathtakingly primitive with its strange, twisted trees and fat tentacle branches, which draw up images of the Flood. . . .

The landing gear releases just before the ship settles onto the ground. I stay on the bridge, curious to see how our unmistakable entry is received.

Recent events have made me more careful than usual. In due time, I detect five individuals moving toward the Ace of Spades *at a moderate clip. One is Rion, of course. I view her approach first via her bio-tag and then closer through the ship's camera.*

I am at once delighted to see her image and then immediately hor-rified by her condition. She is gaunt and sickly pale. Her trousers are stained and torn and her shirt has fared no better.

Anger brews.

The others with her have minimal protection, and they have clearly been here for quite some time. Erebus VII has not been kind to them. Two move slower than the others, a woman aiding an ampu-tee with a makeshift crutch.

The closer two appear to be military.

One of them is walking behind Rion now, his weapon aimed down but at the ready. She halts. They exchange words. He pushes her in front of him.

He dares!

I fly through systems and engage my armiger form in the hold as the doors open upon my command. I fill my presence throughout the construct, stretching my arms and neck—admittedly unnecessary, but the more I don my construct form, the more human *it makes me feel, the more comfortable it is. It is much nimbler and quicker than when I first was forced into its neural circuitry.*

Doors open, ramp down.

Now, human, try to push me. . . .

Poor Rion! What a state she is in! Scrapes and deep cuts, bruis-ing . . . so very pale. Gray smudges curve under her eyes. She is not smiling. Her face is hard, her mouth tight. This expression does not seem reserved for the man behind her with the weapon, but oddly, for me.

And her eyes are fixed with warning.

I step off the ramp. She makes a stop motion with her hand and I freeze.

The man behind her raises his weapon, one hand tightly gripping Rion's shoulder. "Southwell," she says, "you're making a very big mistake. You want off this rock, and I will get you off. But you fire one shot—one shot—and you can count your ride good-bye."

"We don't need you or that thing to fly your ship," this Southwell replies.

"That would be where you're wrong." She whirls on him, furious at even the suggestion he might take her ship, and not caring at all about the threat to her life. "No one is in any condition to fight, including you. Your only way off this planet is right there. After all this time and all your losses, you're going to let your ego and fear ruin a chance at rescue?" Disgusted, Rion shakes her head and then turns and strides toward me.

Southwell and the others do not know what to do.

She now addresses me in a low voice: "Number one, very glad to see you. Number two, we have a big problem. Just follow my lead and do exactly as I say. Okay? Where are the others?"

"New Carthage," I say, and that makes her frown, but seems good enough for her at this tense moment.

"Try to look as unthreatening as possible." She turns and raises her voice so the others can hear. "We're not leaving anyone behind. You're welcome on board, unarmed."

The two slow humans limp out of their cover and slowly approach. They drop a knife and a handgun on the ground and with a quick smile and nod keep going right into the ship. They have proven themselves to be the smarter of the group.

Their action deflates the other two, who now come forward.

"I wouldn't put it past Southwell to try something," Rion says quickly. "They think I have a crew of eight—let's try to keep it that way as long as we can. They're ONI, by the way."

"Most unfortunate."

The man with Southwell pauses in front of Rion, but his eyes are on me. They are wide and wary and curious. I lift my chin.

"You may board, but not with the weapons," she tells him.

"What the hell is that thing?"

"A salvaged android," she lies.

My snort escapes me before I can prevent it.

"No. That's hard light. That's Forerunner."

"Does it matter? Hate to break it to you, but you guys aren't the only ones who come into contact with Forerunner tech. It's all out there for the taking, and more and more people are finding it. We recovered it, made it work, and it's pretty handy." Rion then turns to me. "Where is the nearest habitable and safe place to take our new friends?"

"There is a mining outpost on an asteroid in the next system," I answer.

They seem stunned that I speak. But I believe I understand Rion's game. She wants them to see me as under her control, as a friend and not a foe.

Ah. I have just the thing.

"Captain, we have detected the presence of four additional humans on this planet in two locations. Three are to the west and one to the southeast."

I am satisfied by their awed reaction.

"That's Delta Station to the southeast," the man with Southwell says with undisguised hope. The glance they exchange is significant. "Our squad leader," he tells Rion. "Last we heard, she and a few others were trying to make it to Delta site. If anyone could survive out there alone, it's her."

"This changes things," Southwell says. "We'll need our weapons to extract them. You don't understand how dangerous it is out there. These creatures, they—"

Rion puts a hand on his shoulder. "Come on. I'll show you the mess and you can get something to eat and drink while we go get your people. Your choice."

Some unspoken decision passes between them. Southwell drops his knives, then lifts the strap over his head and hands her his rifle. "Knife in your waistband too."

He smirks and hands it over.

"The stun weapon in your boot," I say.

He hesitates, removes it, drops it on the ground, holds up his hands and spins around, then boards the Ace of Spades.

Once this is complete, his companion follows suit and enters the ship.

Rion and I make to follow him in, but she pauses to glance over her shoulder. I sense whatever happened here will weigh heavily on her mind for some time.

"Keep them confined to the lounge. Prohibit access to everything but food and drink dispensers, no comms, no datapads, nothing," she says. "Lock down the ship, locker room, crew quarters, bridge, engine room, everything."

"Of course."

"We'll talk about the rest later." She sways on her feet. "We get their friends, and then we get them the hell off the ship as soon as possible."

That Lessa, Niko, and Ram were not on board came as a surprise. According to Spark, they were still on New Carthage. But the full story would have to wait until after she got the ONI survivors off her ship. After the group was secured in the lounge with Spark and Little Bit monitoring their every move and conversation, Rion headed to the bridge and began spooling up thrusters to lift off. First stop, the three closest survivors at Alpha Station.

It didn't take long to arrive at the coordinates laid out by Spark.

She put the ship down in a clear spot on a rocky ridge, then withdrew the M6 she kept in the sleeve of her captain's chair. As she headed into the lounge to retrieve Barnes, she checked her clip.

Inside, she motioned to Barnes. "I need you to go with my android. Your people will need to see a friendly face." Southwell jumped up, but Rion shook her head. "Just him."

Barnes moved out into the corridor, and Rion keyed in the code to lock the lounge door, before motioning for Barnes to continue in front of her. "Do I get a weapon, at least?" he asked as Rion ushered him down the stairs and into the hold where the armiger was waiting.

"You won't need one. If you want, I'll have the area cleared and then you can go in."

"You have a lot of faith in your . . . *android*."

"He wouldn't be part of my crew if I didn't."

Rion left Barnes with Spark and then headed back to the lounge to keep an eye on things and to watch the action unfold from Spark's linkup. As the screen came alive, the survivors gathered around, the food and drink they'd gotten from the dispensers forgotten in their hands. Little Bit monitored the area around the science station—a collection of stacked white pods, linked by corridors and bridges.

Through Spark's unique viewpoint, they witnessed several of the creatures lurking around the base. They hadn't fled when the ship landed. Seeing them by daylight, Rion was amazed how anyone had survived. Despite their size, they blended easily into the trees and rocks. The room held its collective breath. Southwell cursed. "They're walking right into a nest."

He shot to his feet. Rion braced herself for a fight, but Dr. Mallory's gasp drew their attention back to the screen. "Would you look at that," she said, amazed.

As Spark and Barnes moved toward the station, the anglers backed off and slowly disappeared into the mists. Spark directed Barnes to a rock cleft ten meters from the station's northernmost pod. Barnes vanished inside. They waited.

Rion leaned against the lounge door. She didn't have the connection the others shared; she'd only been with them a short time, but she did share the hell and terror and found her heart beating fast, her breath coming short and quick, and her body tense.

When Barnes exited with three pale, confused faces, the room filled with gasps, sobs, and laughter . . .

"LB, once they're on board, proceed to the next location."

"Aye, aye, Captain!"

Rion winced. The AI fragment was trying to sound human, to fool their guests into thinking an actual crew was on the ship. She wasn't sure anyone bought it, but they were distracted by the footage, so she'd take it.

Rion left the lounge to aid in the boarding of the newly rescued. She ignored the questions and said as little as possible as she and Barnes helped the dazed survivors, all scientists, to the lounge.

The next location, Delta Station, proved more difficult. This time, Rion allowed Southwell to join Spark. Once again, she and the others watched from the lounge viewscreen. Delta Station had been pulled apart, as if a cyclone had touched down and decimated the structure. They found the squad leader half-dead and shoved into a rotted tree trunk at ground level. Rion's stomach turned. At first, she though the woman was deceased, her body so still and white. Debris had fallen onto her face and into the corners of her eyes. It looked like she'd been there for several days.

Southwell let out a horrible groan when he saw her. Spark bent down to retrieve her but Southwell shoved him away. In just a brief flash, Rion saw the horror and anguish in his eyes. Barnes was sitting on the edge of the closest chair, eyes glued to the screen, his face a grim vision of pain.

Southwell carefully extracted the squad leader from the tree. *"I got you, Yuri, I got you. Hang on."* He lowered her to the ground and checked her vitals, cursing and then starting chest compressions.

They were losing valuable time. "Spark, get them both back to the ship immediately." As she turned away from the screen to head for the med bay, she saw Spark gather the woman over his shoulder and then grab Southwell around the waist with one arm. The guy would probably never live that one down.

Rion permitted the doctor and Barnes to leave the lounge and go with her to ready the med bay. As soon as Spark was inside, he carried the squad leader up the stairs, into the bay, and placed her gently on the exam table.

"Lock up the ship, initiate one more sweep of the planet for survivors, and then get us off this rock."

Spark nodded and left the med bay.

Rion immediately placed two wireless nodes on the woman's chest and then powered the handheld defibrillator. Time became nonexistent. All focus dialed in on the squad leader, Dr. Mallory applying oxygen and intravenous fluids between charges while Rion assisted and readied the cryo-chamber if needed. Four pulses later, and they had a heartbeat. They didn't relax, however. Biometric scans began, and Rion helped the doctor insert an exploratory smart diagnostic nano-monitor. All the while in the back of her mind lingered the thought that this could have been her.

For a short time, it had been.

It was hard to look at the squad leader's face because Rion knew she must have looked nearly the same when Barnes and Southwell found her.

When reports began flowing onto the med-bay diagnostic

screen, and the proper sequences of care had been initiated, the patient began stabilizing.

Rion finally stepped back. It felt like hours had gone by. She was shaking badly, still herself recovering from her own ordeal.

"Well?" Southwell asked, jerking Rion back to attention.

"The doc is flushing her system with nanotech. They'll absorb whatever toxins are present. We've injected her with a full suite of nano-meds and sensors. Anything that needs attention will get it. Your squad leader will pull through."

"It's Sergeant Yurman," he said. "Yuri."

"Right," Rion replied with a tired smile. "You can stay with her until we get to the mining outpost. I'll bring you some food and drink."

As soon as she stepped into the corridor, Rion braced a hand on the bulkhead and leaned over. Weakness had overwhelmed her; she couldn't stop trembling. The tightness in her chest was unbearable. She straightened and linked her hands on top of her head, trying to open things up and clear the suffocating sensation. Seeing Yurman's ordeal from an outside perspective made her realize just how close she'd been to death's door.

If Barnes and Southwell hadn't come along . . .

"Hey, you okay there?" Barnes asked, appearing from the med bay and hurrying to offer assistance. He steadied her when she swayed.

"I'm fine."

He seemed reluctant to let go, but did so cautiously. "You don't look so good."

She smiled. "Thanks."

"Here, let me help you back to the mess. You should eat something. And it wouldn't hurt to have the doc check you out too."

As he escorted her down the corridor, he said, "You're not what I imagined."

Rion steeled herself; she had a feeling this was coming. You couldn't work for the Office of Naval Intelligence and not have known the significant campaign against the *Ace of Spades* and her crew. Hopefully she was wrong. "How so?"

"Well, usually our Most Wanted don't go around saving the people who want to lock them up."

"What gave it away, the ship or the three-meter-tall ancient bit of Forerunner tech walking around?"

"Neither." She paused, surprised, as he clarified, "It was you."

"Me?"

"Your picture was always up on our bulletin back at home base. Hard to forget when I passed it every day. . . . That Forerunner wasn't part of our bulletin, but I'm starting to understand why you made the list in the first place."

"It's called getting railroaded, Corporal." In the confines of the corridor, Rion got as honest as she could get. Not only was she bone-tired, she was tired of running, and suddenly she found she needed to say it, to tell at least one ONI operative the truth. "I'm not a criminal. My *crew*—they're two young adults and a retired salvager—aren't criminals. That *Forerunner* isn't a criminal."

Frustrated emotions swelled to the surface.

An understanding half-smile pulled at the corner of Barnes's mouth. He put his hand on her shoulder, gazing down at her with what looked like belief. "I'm beginning to see that, Captain. Come on, let's get you something to eat."

As the *Ace of Spades* neared the large asteroid in orbit around the moon of a gas giant, Rion checked on Yurman and found Southwell and Barnes still by her side. "How's she doing?"

"Stable," Barnes replied.

"We've been in touch with the mining outpost. They're ready to receive you, and they have a med bay set up for your sergeant."

"Docking directions received," Spark's voice came over comms. *"We're heading in."*

"We'll get her ready for transport," Barnes said, his gaze lingering. "Thank you for getting us this far. It won't be forgotten."

She gave them a curt nod and prepared to head for the bridge. Southwell stopped her. "Captain. You saved our asses back there, and Yuri's too."

"And you and Barnes saved mine." Her look spoke volumes. "I say we're even and leave it at that."

Southwell weighed her suggestion. Finally he dipped his head. "Agreed."

At some point they'd have to report in and tell what had happened, but right now it was enough.

CHAPTER 35

Ace of Spades

As soon as the mining outpost was in the rearview mirror, Rion called on her last reserves and crossed the hold to Niko and Spark's worktable and asked the first of two big questions that had been burning through her brain since she saw Spark standing on the loading ramp on Erebus VII: "So where the hell is my crew?"

The story he told was more bizarre than she'd imagined. It knocked the wind out of her somewhat, and she had to park herself on one of the supply crates nearby. "Jesus. How the hell did that orbital platform even see you?"

"The Mongoose was tagged with a small emitter while you were on Sonata."

And the hits kept on coming, didn't they? She pressed both palms over her tired eyes, rubbing out the sting. Excuses for her mother rose to the surface—anything to justify the betrayal. Her throat felt sore and a hollow ache filled her chest.

"I am sorry," Spark said.

So was she. "Keep going."

"The emitter stayed inert in the *Ace of Spades*'s hold until we reached Sonata's exosphere. There it activated and signaled a satellite in orbit. The signal was disguised as simple thruster radiation, quite ingenious. The satellite then relayed a signal to a highly sophisticated stealth telemetry device in high orbit, which I believe had been there for several months. A basic analogy, and different principles, of course, but envision the emitter as a magnet and the telemetry device as iron. It latched on to our hull and went with us into slipspace."

"You didn't detect it?"

"Not initially. It mimicked the composition of *Ace*'s hull perfectly, just as its signals mimicked the thrusters' energy emissions, which means the device was created with intimate knowledge and access to your ship at some point."

Of course. "On the *Taurokado*," she told him. "Before we picked you up on Geranos-a. *Ace* was confined inside their hold."

"That would have been an excellent opportunity to take readings on systems, engine output, record data, and measure the exact composition of the hull and ablative coating. The telemetry device caused some havoc with Little Bit, but all is well now," Spark said, hesitating before adding, "I know what you are thinking. But we cannot go back to New Carthage."

"Okay. And why is that?"

"ONI knows the ship left New Carthage without its crew," he said. "So they must turn to Ram and Niko and Lessa to get to us. Their efforts will be concentrated in Pilvros. They will have brought in reinforcements by now and will most assuredly count on us returning to help them. If the crew has been able to stay out of sight, our going back there now could put everything into jeopardy."

"And if they've been caught? Am I to do nothing?"

"Yes. For now. We agreed to meet on Myer's Moon, in three to four weeks' time."

While Spark's position was perfectly logical and in line with what Rion would have done herself, waiting was never her strong suit. "I don't like it."

"That is protocol, is it not? I have read your logbooks. Any imminent danger to the ship or the crew, and the ship leaves until it is safe to return. Anyone left behind knows this, and they are aware of what to do in order to stay safe. Please understand, Captain, there *was* no other choice. Staying together, leaving the *Ace of Spades* vulnerable. Risking capture meant leaving you alone on Erebus VII for an undetermined amount of time, perhaps indefinitely."

And Yurman would be dead, and Rion and the other survivors would be living on borrowed time. Still, the thought of waiting, the idea of her crew fending off ONI . . .

"They are not amateurs; they have decades of collective experience in evasion tactics," Spark said, reading her mind. "They sent me and *Ace* to you. Going back now when ONI operatives are firmly entrenched in Pilvros, to risk capture, might make it all for nothing."

He was right. How many times had she done the same thing, had sent *Ace* away from a dangerous situation to protect the ship and the crew? She'd had little opportunity to recover from the portal and then from the anglers and was feeling the effects a thousandfold now. But, she didn't want to cut this briefing short because once her head hit the pillow, there was no telling when she'd get up again.

"We need to discuss what happened back on Zeta Halo." The memory of reaching out to him for help and being rejected was still a hard pill to swallow. Spark's presence on Erebus VII had ultimately been an enormous relief; until that moment, she wasn't sure where his loyalties lay.

"The portal was already pulling you in. I could not save you. But I could take the key. Without it, we never would have found you. I believe it was the Librarian who created the portal, perhaps as a direct path to the key's final destination."

"Erebus VII. Where is the key now?"

"Right there, in my workstation."

It didn't make any sense. "But . . . why create the New Carthage key, why two different options to get to Erebus? A failsafe?" She rubbed her temples.

"Captain . . ."

The word hung in the air, the tone serious yet daring to hope. Funny how, at times, he could be so completely transparent. He was worried she wouldn't want to proceed.

Rion held up her hand to stop him from continuing. "Set a course back to Erebus VII. We'll use the key one last time. Let's hope it's worth it." She slid off the container and headed to the stairs. "Wake me up when we get there."

"Rion."

She paused, one foot on the stairs.

"Thank you."

With a curt nod, she made for her quarters.

Rion couldn't shake the feeling of being watched. The hairs on her arms rose and her skin pricked, but every time she scanned the twisted woods, there was nothing. They were out there, though, lurking in the trees, crouched in the mist, staying at a distance while she and Spark trekked to the facility. "Dr. Mallory said she felt like the planet didn't want them here . . . is that possible?"

"The creatures here are highly intelligent and possessing of near-perfect predation traits that would accommodate the slaughter of a wide variety of spacefaring species. Yes, it is entirely possible they were seeded here, designed or modified, to dissuade visitors to the planet and prevent discovery of the Forerunner site," Spark said from behind her as they navigated a virgin path through the trees and rocks.

"It seems like an awful lot of trouble to go through. . . . Any theories what the key opens?"

A long pause preceded his answer. "Not yet."

She spun around. "You hesitated, which means you do."

"Perhaps a few theories. But there is no advantage in speculating when the answer is only a few meters through that wall."

Rounding a large tree trunk, a rock face came into view with a flat alloy inset decorated with traditional Forerunner hieroglyphs. Trees grew on top of the rock face, fat roots with spikes reaching down the wall and into the ground like warnings to the unsuspecting traveler. As they approached, the metal automatically dissolved into a doorway.

Rion stepped inside. Light initiated at their presence, guiding them down a long steep corridor.

"Why did you agree to come back?" Spark asked at length, his voice bouncing off the walls and sounding more inhuman than ever.

"Well . . . we had a deal. We're already in the sector. The key is apparently complete, so this should be the last stop, and we went through a hell of a lot to get this far to give up now and not see what it opens. And"—she slowed and faced him—"you saved my life—and all the lives here—once again."

"I am part of your crew. I did not have an option."

Of course he did. "So what are we up to now? Two?"

"Two?"

"The times you saved my life?"

"Ah." A pensive second passed. "Only a trillion more to go, perhaps . . ."

Oh, man. The words were unexpected and spoken with total resignation. What an enormous cross to bear. "No. Don't say that. You can't hold yourself responsible." As 343 Guilty Spark, he'd fired his Halo in conjunction with the other rings, and sentient life in the galaxy went dark. But to take on the guilt of that action and carry it around was a crippling burden. Surely he knew this. Surely he had run the numbers.

Sometimes it was easy to forget his mind was still human in essence. And humans were true experts at taking on irrational, overwhelming, and crippling amounts of guilt and self-loathing.

"Let's say you defied orders and *didn't* fire your array," she said. "What would have happened?"

He was quiet, and that was a good sign. Logically, he already knew the answer, but she wanted him to think about it; to see it not from the past perspective—which he was used to living in—but from the present. The moment stretched, so she answered for him. "The life we have now wouldn't exist." She let that sink in. "The life we have now *wouldn't exist.* Try to remember that."

While he hadn't responded, Rion hoped he'd take her words to heart. They weren't superfluous, but the simple truth.

The corridor led into the circular chamber she'd been dumped into upon arrival on Erebus VII. In the dark, it had seemed large, but she wasn't quite prepared for how large. The light exposed a shining space of luminous sterling alloy and glowing blue light; clean and alien and vast, a chamber with a deep circular void in the middle.

Making their way across the wide expanse that ringed the central cavity, Rion noted the terminal set at the edge of the cavity, the human remains near the wall, and farther around the curve, the shaft she had used to climb to freedom. Spark moved ahead of her to inspect the strange pair of monoliths that stood guard to one side of the terminal. They were more impressive now, hard light pulsing through angled geometric lines and glyphs and the strange circular symbol on the fronts.

"Maybe you shouldn't get too close," she warned.

As Spark shifted away from the monoliths and stepped to the terminal, unease slid down Rion's spine. She glanced around nervously. There was nothing in the chamber. No signs of danger at all. Yet all of her instincts radiated caution, the recent past and her last go-round on Zeta Halo still fresh in her mind. They had finally come to the end, about to discover the Librarian's gift. It would soon be over.

Maybe it was her cynical nature, waiting for the other shoe to drop, but it sure as hell felt off in this place.

Spark accessed the terminal. With a centering breath, she approached and handed him the key.

Like on Zeta, a port manifested and accepted the key. She wasn't sure what to expect, but she stepped back anyway.

Initially, nothing happened. Then light caught her eye, illuminating the cavity, and growing brighter, rising from far below in the circular void, faster and faster like a speeding train.

A bright flash and rush of wind exploded out of the cavity. Rion stumbled back, and even Spark retreated a few steps as a gigantic monitor rose from the depths and hovered high behind the terminal, its giant turquoise eye canted toward them.

And this would be that other shoe.

Spark, however, didn't appear alarmed. His head cocked curiously and he moved forward a step. "What are you?"

"I am the Precept, armiger," it said with a resonating, artificial male baritone. "I judge those who come. I administer the test and open the way."

"The way to what?"

"The human has been judged."

Rion's jaw went slack. Fear began working its way through her insides. "Judged . . . how, exactly?" she asked.

"I detected the mark in you and summoned you here for trial."

"You're the one who initiated the portal."

"It is my prerogative to do so. . . . I grew impatient. Upon your arrival, your judgment began."

So it had been observing her. Allowed her to risk her life—maybe even die. "And them?" She gestured to the remains. "Were they judged too?"

"They did not come here for the same purpose."

"They were worth saving."

"And the Eiyaa-Mahtuhaa are worth feeding. This is the cycle of natural competition."

"Where I'm from, that's called an unfair advantage."

"Perhaps. The Eiyaa-Mahtuhaa were favored by the Librarian. They serve her purpose as do I."

"We have the key," Spark said. "Judgment and tests are unnecessary."

"Anyone can steal a key. The thief in you should know this." The monitor floated forward, hovering over the terminal, at least six or seven meters across, putting in stark contrast how tiny they were in comparison. "Chakas; 343 Guilty Spark. Human. Forerunner. Unintended success." It was quiet for a long time. "You may proceed."

The monitor turned its massive eye in Rion's direction, enveloping her field of vision. It was like staring into a burning blue sun. She was forced to close her eyes, deciding it was probably best if Spark just continued on without her; she'd wait for him here.

"You have been judged. Now I must administer the test."

Before she could even argue in her defense, her body went weightless, arms spinning as she was pulled toward the eye. The last thing she heard was the Precept's voice saying, "Tissue tells the tale."

Awareness returns, absent of any sense of time.

Rion stands in the blackness of space, alone, nothing around, above, or below, until a pinprick appears at an impossible distance, racing toward her. Her pulse leaps. She knows this scene.

Millions upon millions of ghostly forms rush by in two great lines, the force of their passing hitting her with the strength of a hurricane.

The sound rattles her teeth. She drops to her knees and covers her ears. And still they come.

Eventually, the lines slow, becoming different—scenes of life, cells, mutation, growth, civilizations rising and falling . . .

And then suddenly, it is over.

The Librarian, in her stained white dress, extends her hand. As soon as Rion takes it, the scene changes, and she is standing once more in front of the dark rift in the cliff wall.

She doesn't want to be here.

The faint orange sun rises behind her; its first rays glide along the valley floor, lighting the wall in a golden-coppery glow and piercing through the cleft to reveal a chamber inside.

Rion wants to leave; it doesn't feel right. Too much suffering and sorrow. "Let's go back to the garden," she says, starting to turn away, but the Librarian holds tight to her hand.

"No. We must move forward."

Rion's heart is racing—or is it the Librarian's? The large hand in hers is warm, and she feels like a child being pulled along by its mother.

"When I arrived here, the elder of the settlement, Glow-of-Old-Suns, agreed to show me this valley. She said there was much to pass

along—Old Bequests, Old Communications, and Old Instructions. Catalog never asked me what those were, and I never offered.

"But I listened and finally understood. Are you ready to see the rest?"

The Librarian gives Rion's hand a reassuring squeeze and they stare ahead, together, working up the courage.

"This is my secret."

The whisper fills the entire valley and reverberates through Rion with a cold shiver.

She woke on the floor in front of the terminal, gasping and shaking. She tried to swallow, but it felt like she was choking. Spark stood staring down at her, and behind him the massive turquoise eye of the monitor peered down from its lofty height. Her stomach contracted in a sick knot. "What . . . did you do to me?"

"I have administered the test and read the results of your biological memory." The Precept moved back over the terminal to hover in the open space of the circular void. The key extended from the port. "The key now contains coordinates and access permissions for each of you, and no other."

Rion pushed to her feet.

"Access to what?" Spark asked.

"Bastion, of course."

CHAPTER 36

Two guards entered Lessa's small, temporary cell in what she guessed was a large storage facility, the only saving grace of it being that if she sat just right on her cot, she caught the reflection of the entrance through a strip of chrome on a stack of cargo bins. Warily, she stood. She couldn't take another tedious interrogation; the same questions over and over with just the slightest change, designed to trip her up. Normally there was only one guard, so the presence of two had her suspicions rising. She hated being intimidated, hated the way they used their height and bulk to force her to step back against the plain gray wall. They each grabbed an arm and then one of them parked a black sack over her head.

Fear struck lightning hot.

The fight reaction rose on swift panicked wings as they pulled her forward. "Wait!" She dug in her heels, until they had to drag her from the cell. "Where are we going? Please tell me!" She'd been interrogated for nearly two weeks now, and no one had given her any information on where she was or what had happened to Ram. They'd been caught together, corralled into a dead-end basement parking deck in Pilvros. He'd been shoved into a van while she'd been lifted off her feet and tossed into another. She'd traveled an hour, maybe more—definitely less than two—before being blindfolded and off-loaded.

No one would give her even the slightest clue as to what her future might hold.

And now, things had suddenly changed.

Her worst fear was coming true—she was about to be shipped off to an ONI black site, never to be heard from again.

Dammit, she couldn't leave! Not now. Not alone. Niko was still out there somewhere, hiding, on the run. . . . He wasn't here, that much she knew. *Oh, God.* What if she never got to see him again? Her body went rigid with the realization. Then, she twisted and fought, resisting any way she could, even making herself dead weight while raging and screaming, hoping the whole world could hear.

When the air changed, she froze, head coming up.

Her arms ached beneath the guards' tight grip. Sweat ran down the sides of her face. She could barely breathe inside the hood as she stumbled along. But she was outside and for the first time felt a little bit of hope. Outside might never come again. It could be her only chance to escape.

The acrid, smoky tang of engine fuel filled the air, and she heard the familiar vibrating thrum of thrusters. Activity came from all directions, blasting her senses with a multitude of sounds and smells. It wasn't hard to figure out that she'd been brought to a busy tarmac at a shipyard or an airfield, somewhere within two hours of Pilvros.

The crunch of soles on pavement reached her ears, additional footsteps approaching. Her knees went weak at the sound of Ram's belligerent cursing.

"Ram!"

"You'd better keep your mouth shut," one of the guards snapped, digging his thumb into her already bruised biceps.

"Ram!"

"Lessa!"

After everything she'd been through, it was the sound of his voice that finally made her break. A sob tore from her throat as warm tears flooded her eyes.

"Get them on board, now," someone said.

She was jerked ahead a few more steps until a new vibration took over. Ship engines were easy to feel through the tarmac—she knew those well—but this was something else, something deeper. And it was growing.

Another tremor.

The guards halted. She heard shouts, orders, warnings . . .

The tremor should have faded like all the others during her incarceration, but it kept increasing until she was swaying on her feet.

The ground began to undulate in one bizarre wave after another.

Trying to keep their balance, the guards held her tighter, using her as leverage.

One petite girl keeping two ONI goons afloat didn't pan out so well, and they crashed to the tarmac. Being small helped her crawl out from under the pile. As soon as she was free, she ripped the stupid hood from her head and was greeted with chaos. A hot blast of air sent her hair into her eyes and out in all directions, strands sticking to the tears on her cheeks.

The tarmac was in a state of emergency.

Carts and supplies being loaded onto a prowler in front of her toppled over. A stack of containers near a hangar crashed to the ground. A power station far on the other end of the airfield exploded into a plume of fire. Men and women in black uniforms ran in a dozen different directions while others stood still and shouted orders.

Lessa searched the chaos for Ram.

There.

"Ram!"

He was on the ground, struggling to his feet, but being held down by one of his guards, who had him by the right ankle. Ram kicked at him with his left leg, but the guy grabbed that ankle too. She raced forward, shoved the hood still in her hand over the guard's head, then stomped on his wrist until he yelled in pain and released Ram.

A sharp, thunderous crack echoed over the area and barreled toward them, tearing through the ground, splitting the tarmac in two.

The pavement buckled upward, sending Lessa forward into Ram as he tried to stand. A string of profanity streamed forth, muddled by his hood. Quickly, she snatched it off his head and finally met his furious dark eyes. She'd never been happier in her life. "Thank God." Her face split into a huge smile and she threw her arms around him.

"Have you seen Niko?!" she shouted over the din. The wind was fierce, sparks flying past, the whine of the prowler's engine getting louder. It was taking off to save itself. They had to move.

"No! He wasn't in my building!"

"Mine either!"

Good. She scanned the buildings. Just the two large cargo/hangar combos. They were the only ones. If they'd brought her and Ram together for departure, surely they'd have brought Niko too, if he'd been captured.

Behind them, one of the buildings backslid into the newly formed ravine. The prowler's engines grew. *Oh, hell.* They were about to get blasted. "We have to go!"

Ram grabbed her hand and they took off, putting the tarmac behind them and heading for the barren hills.

They'd find Niko. *They had to.*

Then they'd get off this cursed planet and head for Myer's Moon.

Their escape route became a deadly gauntlet of flying rocks and boulders and undulating earth. The ground thundered and groaned and exploded, sounding like the whole region was being ripped apart behind them.

By the time they risked stopping, Lessa's lungs were on fire. She was broken and bruised, knees, palms, elbows, shoulders, forehead. Their run had been perilous enough on its own with the dry, rocky hills, but the intense earthquake had made it a veritable life-and-death situation. They'd fallen dozens of times on ground that constantly moved and trembled and collapsed, while under fire from loose rocks raining down like gunfire, and had dodged their share of boulders.

From their vantage on top of one of the highest hills, Lessa saw the devastation they'd left behind. Half of the airfield and its hangars were gone, disappeared over the edge of a narrow rift. That rift led to the rim of a crater nearly a kilometer away. Plumes of rocks and dust were still rising, making it difficult to see just how expansive it was.

Ram was bent over, hands on his knees, trying to catch his breath, but his gaze was firmly on the scene spread out far below.

"What the hell is happening?" she managed when her breath finally settled.

Slowly, he straightened, shoving the hair from his face.

His answer never came. Through the thick dust cloud, they saw two ships. Prowlers, maybe—it was difficult to tell. Missiles streaked from the ships and lit up the dusty sky, tracking up and up, drawing their gaze skyward.

Through the haze and dust, Lessa caught sight of a shadowy winged behemoth.

"Jesus," Ram said, throwing his arms around her and pulling her down. "Get down!"

They dropped to their knees, Ram covering her as a fierce back-line wind hit, like a vacuum pulling every bit of loose rock and dirt from the hill. Ram's hold tightened as they started to slide.

Suddenly everything paused.

Just stopped.

The sound of her pulse was the only thing Lessa could hear.

They started to relax, then a deep, warped noise she'd never heard before hit the region, sending a dense, thumping shock wave through her whole body. Her eardrums screamed and her teeth chattered.

Silence descended.

Eventually bits and pieces of fine earth floated down, softly pinging the hill.

Ram released his hold and sat back, stunned. They watched the two prowlers fall quiet into the crater.

"EMP," she said, though her voice sounded odd, as though underwater.

"What?" Ram stuck a finger in his ear and shook it.

"EMP!" Explosions rang from the crater, followed by a plume of fiery smoke.

She looked up, but the sky was clear. Whatever had been there was gone.

The sense of dread and disorientation wasn't just inside her; it seemed to settle over the land. Lessa wasn't even sure she could begin to make sense of what had happened or what she had seen in the sky. If Niko were here, he might know. . . .

She glanced at Ram, seeing him similarly affected.

"We need to find my brother. We need to get off planet."

Ram stared into the distance. "I . . . I'm not sure we're going anywhere."

Ships were falling from the sky.

In silent distant streaks, they fell, too horrible, too unbelievable, and too shocking to wrap her mind around. Lessa's heart ached for those onboard, and she knew this quiet vision would haunt her forever.

By the time it was over, she'd counted seven lost vessels and who knew how many more beyond their field of view.

That something could cause an EMP of such magnitude was terrifying. Were they under attack? Had the Covenant come back? Was it something new? The implications, the idea they might be at war again, scared her to death.

She was struck with the sudden certainty that there wouldn't be a reunion on Myer's Moon—not on time, anyway. They were literally in the middle of nowhere; there was nothing else around as far as the eye could see. She and Ram had a long road in front of them, getting back to civilization, trying to find Niko . . . if he was still around, if he hadn't left the planet already, if he hadn't been on board one of those ships—*God, no,* she couldn't think about that—*wouldn't* think about it.

Lessa pushed to her feet, wiping her grimy hands on her pants. Inside, a dull aching pain gripped her heart, but outside she drew in an ample breath and let it out slowly before offering Ram a hand up. "Come on, old man. Let's get moving."

CHAPTER 37

Ace of Spades / Slipspace to Bastion

Rion sleeps. Twelve hours have passed and she shows no signs of waking. After learning of yet another destination in our search for answers, she proposed going to Myer's Moon to wait for the crew and then later, once everyone was reunited, complete the journey to Bastion. But I reminded her that only she and I have been given access. There was no guarantee that Lessa, Niko, or Ram would pass the Precept's judgment, much less his test.

And there was no reason to put them in that sort of danger.

"We'll need to send a wave space message on to Myer's Moon in case they arrive before we do," she said.

I could see the distress this caused the captain; having to choose between the crew and me. When I offered my apology, she surprised me. "I know there's more out there in the galaxy, pulling at you. . . . Whatever it is, it's important and tied up with the past and the Librarian and things to come. I heard her back in the mountain. I know you need to go. And as weird as it sounds, I know I need to take you there."

It appeared we had both stumbled onto a path laid out long ago, and like me she wanted to finish it.

I thanked her even as she swayed on her feet, and then I guided her to her quarters and into bed. Her questions about Bastion would keep.

The coordinates on the key took us to a small unnamed star system, and the large moon of its outermost planet. On our approach, a diaphanous sterling web of hard light came into view, a half million kilometers from the moon, with a violet hole in the center. I checked our coordinates again to find they did not in fact point to the moon, but to this strange, ethereal web, undulating in space, its immense strands slowly reworking and moving.

—It is a static portal.

—*What else can you tell?*

—It is small. Responds to specialized keys. Only one destination. Designed for long-distance slipspace journeys of hundreds to thousands of light-years. Should we wake the captain?

—*No.*

—We are entering the portal? She will want to know.

He will make a fine and dutiful AI.

—*We are entering.*

Our entry into the static portal was uneventful, though a strange sight as the webbing seemed to electrify, powered by the wealth of vacuum energy all around us. The violet center grew, eventually swallowing us up, and launching the Ace of Spades *through slipspace.*

Now that our journey has begun and Rion sleeps, I retreat to my "as-was" spot to sit near the river Sahti and watch the flow of muddy water. In my hand, a long stem of grass yet to drop its seeds. These I pick out one by one, mulling over recent events and trying to fit them into a proper place, a proper theory.

The Librarian's words, those three sentences, those twelve words:

"Find what's missing. Fix the path. Right what my kind turned wrong."

So many wrongs to choose from. And what meaning had they now? What connection to Bastion—a place I knew nothing about, a place of myth and whispers and shadows. What was it, really? Had it survived the war? What sort of place was it? What secrets might it still contain?

Was it the sanctuary I was hoping it would be?

Ah. Sanctuary. It hurt to give thought to the idea. To the word. To the hope it inspired.

That perhaps some Forerunners still remained . . .

The theories I had are now obsolete. Or are they?

That itch I cannot scratch, that constant pull . . . for purpose, for something . . . Perhaps in Bastion will lie the answers I seek.

Or perhaps I placed too much importance on my purpose when one may not exist at all. Purpose suggests design, planning, structure. And I am no longer a monitor beholden to such things. I am free.

Am I free?

I think of the words Rion shared with me on our journey into the Precept's facility. I think of the guilt I have carried and refuse to let go, creating a prison of my own making. A thousand centuries is long to carry such a burden.

Bornstellar once asked me if it were my choice, after all we had seen and survived . . . would I fire the rings?

And my answer is still yes.

Perhaps it is time to let it go. Perhaps then I will be free.

I ponder for some time these many things, eventually moving on.

The ship is running optimally. Little Bit's matrix has been cleaned and restored once more. He has passed his testing and is a capable ancilla to run this vessel's systems and calculate slipstream navigation points with ease while making adjustments to the hybrid engine as necessary.

I am . . . proud.

And it appears I have made myself obsolete. Apparently, I don't want the vocation of ship's AI after all. While a simple endeavor requiring minimal effort, the role is too contained, too compartmentalized, and perhaps in this way too reminiscent of my past as Guilty Spark. Just because I can run a ship or ten thousand ships doesn't mean I should. Or that I want to.

I need more.

I am built for much, much more.

—Should I wake her now?

—*No, Little Bit, let her sleep. She needs it.*

—A biological weakness.

It would seem so to him. While I have the advantage of understanding, he does not.

—I have analyzed those old signals, the ones heard while scanning in Torba. They are very old. I cannot find the proper data string in my core to analyze further.

In many ways, Little Bit holds more knowledge about the Forerunners than I do, being one of their constructs with the lofty position of caring for an entire shield world. What things he must have known and carried in his memory, all of Forerunner history and technology. . . .

—*Would you like me to have a look?*

I could easily do so without asking. But invading Little Bit's privacy and availing myself of his data is a line I wish none to cross with me, therefore I will not cross with him. The idea of losing his trust actually pains me. I so enjoy our friendship.

—Please do.

Immediately I move into his matrix and glide through to his core, a hall with no floors or ceilings, just walls filled with millions of data pockets that stretch on and on and on. There is order here, however, and I send out searcher requests.

A response is almost immediate.

Instantaneously, I am there and note a pocket outlined in blue awaiting my attention.

I move inside it. Another hall, this one cloudy and decrepit.

Oh, it is jumbled, these old data points. . . .

The blue searcher response leads me on, pursuing its target until finally a small string of data seems to match with the signal and divests itself of one word:

Guardian.

CHAPTER 38

Ace of Spades / Bastion / Orion Nebular Complex

While the *Ace of Spades* traversed slipspace, Rion had gotten several nights of sleep in a row and was feeling a hell of a lot better than she had in weeks. Physically, her wounds had healed, and she was well on her way to gaining back the weight that she'd lost. Her dreams had been quiet, though occasionally plagued by events on Erebus VII, and as much as she hated to do so, she had turned to preloaded subcutaneous smart anxiety injections to ease the trauma and stress of sudden flashbacks—both during sleep and while she was awake.

The ensuing days were spent continuing to repair minor and cosmetic damage that had occurred when *Ace* crash-landed inside Zeta Halo, mostly within the cargo hold and the maintenance corridors beneath—bent storage bins, blown fuses, cracked interfaces . . .

The Librarian's confessions weighed on her mind in the quiet of her work, and she no longer thought of them as dreams at all, but more of an interactive simulation, a story either downloaded into her during their time in the mountain or maybe—more wildly—a story stored in all humanity, one that just needed a kick start, an activation. It didn't make Rion special; it just meant she'd been in the right place at the right time.

And now she had to finish it. It would never sit right with her to abandon the journey now, not after all they'd been through to get to this point, not after all that Spark had endured.

As she entered the bridge, a slight mix of apprehension and impatience went through her. While she had to give the crew the time allotted, she was ready to get this final destination out of the way and then, finally, make the jump to Myer's Moon to reunite and, who knew, maybe down the road reconnect with her brother.

"So what are we looking at?" she asked, coming around her chair, eager to finally get a glimpse of Bastion as *Ace* dropped into normal space.

"Calculating now," Spark said, his avatar lingering in his usual spot over the tactical table.

"In the meantime, let's slow by one-third, LB."

"Done, Captain."

"We are eighty light-years inside the edge of the Orion Complex," Spark announced.

"That can't be right. Are you sure?"

The way Spark turned and stared over his shoulder meant he was dead sure. Goose bumps skated up her arms. The Orion Complex was over a thousand light-years from Earth. And while she styled herself an explorer at heart, this kind of distance, to be so far removed from humanity, from any living thing she knew, held a strong and definite note of dread.

"And you're *certain* about the portal?" she was almost afraid to ask; if they were stranded out here, they'd never make it back, even by slipstream, no matter how advanced her ship—Rion would die of old age, many times over, long before that.

"It remains open. Dedicated on both sides," LB assured her.

"We are on track to a mildly irradiated star system with four orbiting planets," Spark said. "Two in close orbit. A larger mid-range planet. And a fourth in far orbit. None are hospitable."

"How far?"

"Three million kilometers."

"Increase full, then," she said, sliding into her chair.

At the halfway point, they slowed speed by one-half and checked long-range sensors.

"I am receiving anomalous radiation readings," Little Bit announced.

Rion scanned her screen. "I see them." The readings weren't a total surprise; the complex was a vast nebular cloud, clouds within clouds, stellar nurseries, ionized gases, and hot spots of radiation light-years in size. "It's helter-skelter out there, that's for sure," she muttered.

"There was a time it wasn't," Spark told her.

"What do you mean?"

"The Orion Complex was the home of the Forerunners. Several million years ago, a stellar engineering accident set off a chain of star collapses, supernovas that nearly destroyed all life in the complex. Ancient Forerunners of the time were nearly wiped out. Their natal world, Ghibalb, as well as several other planets across a network of twelve star systems, had either been completely obliterated or rendered inhospitable. Some areas of the complex are still highly irradiated, while others, after millions of years, have recovered."

The star system they'd been directed to could have been such a victim, the accident likely resulting in the star's formation into that of neutron star, which would account for the irradiation readings.

From what she could see so far, this particular region of the nebular complex held no value for any spacefaring race. Orbiting planetary fragments or newly formed planets from the supernova debris were barren and uninhabitable and, from a mining standpoint, undesirable—mostly silicate rather than organic compounds, with a few containing metals. There were plenty of other sectors and planets easier to get to and far safer to plunder than this far-flung irradiated region.

As far as places to hide, this was an excellent choice.

After the usual cursory study of the star system, Rion zeroed in on their target. Spark was unusually quiet, and she was pretty certain he'd already finished his inspection of the area and their target planet. "So let's talk fourth planet," she said. If this had truly been the Bastion of legend, it had seen better days.

"Four billion kilometers from its sun," Little Bit piped up. "A glacial planet with a thin silicate crust."

"How thick is the ice?"

"About six hundred meters." A picture built on the holoscreen above the tactical table. The ice was relatively flat and smooth, but lined with straight crisscrossing cracks.

"And we're clear on coordinates?"

"We are. Though the planet is dead. No active core . . . Those cracks across the surface are most likely from impacts. No traces of technology or aberrant structures."

"Well, there has to be *something* there. We'll stay in high geostationary orbit once we arrive."

Six hundred and seventy kilometers from the planet, the holoscreen flickered and distorted along with every screen on the bridge.

Rion rose to her feet.

Spark's avatar shimmered and then appeared to warp. Before she could even speak, everything righted itself. It was quiet on the bridge.

"Talk to me, you two. What the hell just happened?"

The distortions came again, but this time more severe.

"Capt—" Spark's avatar began unraveling like a ball of yarn.

A punch of horror hit Rion square in the chest as every screen on the bridge went dark, a brief lull before a blue-green glow swept over the bow of the ship.

"LB?"

No reply.

"Little Bit, respond." *Dammit.* Spark's avatar was nearly gone. "Get out of systems and into your armiger." God, she hoped he could hear her. *"Hurry."*

Consoles and stations across *Ace*'s bridge were shutting down in the glow's wake. As the light traveled closer, Rion made a play for the closest access panel to switch the ship to manual control, but the pad didn't respond and the glow was upon her, flowing through the pad and then her fingertip. She braced, holding her breath, as it flowed through her hand, arm, and then straight through her body, electrifying and making every fine hair on her body stand.

Before it made it out the other side of her, Rion turned and bolted from the bridge, raced down the corridor, and across the catwalk over the hold as Spark's armiger powered up. "We need to regain control!" she shouted. "The whole ship is shutting down!"

The light caught up, passing through her again, and giving her a bird's-eye view of its travel as it continued through the hold and out toward the stern before disappearing completely. In its absence, *Ace* took a sudden, deck-shuddering nosedive.

All power was lost, including the gravity generators.

Eerie silence descended through the *Ace of Spades*. Her ship was dead in the water, and the instant loss of gravity had her floating upward. She reached for the railing, but the nosedive sent her farther and faster away from it than expected.

Rion steeled herself as she tumbled out over the cargo hold. As her peripheral vision circled around and around, she caught a flash of silver and blue crawling on the side of the bulkhead before she had to squeeze her eyes closed to stave off approaching vertigo.

A cool metal hand snatched her forearm. She swung around in an arc and came face-to-face with Spark's angled features. He was crouched on the wall like a giant spider, pulling her in slowly, anchoring his feet and one hand to the ship. Lucky for her, he had his own power source and therefore his own ability to generate gravity. He kept a tight hold as he walked sideways on the bulkhead, heading for the catwalk.

Rion glanced over her shoulder, eyes growing wide. *Oh, no.* "It's coming back." The turquoise glow was making another pass through the ship.

Spark picked up the pace, towing her by the arm as she floated behind him like some ridiculous human balloon. At the catwalk, he pulled her in enough to allow her to grab the railing and right herself, and from there, they worked their way together back to the bridge just as the wall of light entered the area after them.

Spark pressed her into the captain's chair.

"Thanks," she said, manually belting herself in. "We need to restore engines, thrusters at the very least." Anything to push them off their current trajectory—a collision course with the icy planet.

"One moment." Spark stalked to the main access panel on the wall, but as the glow moved through the bridge, the *Ace of Spades* came back to life and her nose lifted slightly. While the glow might have left the interior, it seemed to remain outside. A quick check of feeds told her it enveloped the entire exterior of the ship, and worse, they were still on a rapid descent toward the planet.

Gravity suddenly returned and a few systems began checking in. And while the main viewscreen was clear, every display screen around the bridge shifted from black to that same blue/green turquoise, and in the center a circular symbol around a smaller octagon.

Spark swung around and stared at the main screen with such intensity, it gave her the chills. "What? What is it?"

It took him several seconds to answer. "It's the Librarian's sigil." He stepped toward *Ace*'s large viewscreen and stopped, staring out with an awe that was palpable. "This *is* Bastion."

"Whatever it is, we're still on a collision course." She tried to regain control of her access panel. Nothing. "LB? Are you there?"

"Whew!" came his staticky reply. "That was . . . unusual."

"Tell me about it," she mumbled. "Can you access any engine controls?"

"No, Captain."

Dammit! Ace was fast approaching the surface—without readouts she guessed they had another two thousand kilometers before impact. Desperate, Rion unbuckled and went to the manual override again. If they could just take control of the thrusters for a few seconds, they could push themselves off course. . . . "Spark—hey, snap out of it!"

"I do not believe we are on a collision course, Captain," he said calmly. "Look."

Two parallel cracks in the ice suddenly dropped inward, then split apart, sliding beneath the ice sheet and revealing a doorway filled with translucent turquoise light, the same as the field that surrounded the ship.

Bastion was pulling them in.

CHAPTER 39

Bastion

If I had a heart, it would be pounding against my chest like ancient wartime drums, heavy and thunderous and quick. The memory of adrenaline soars through me with the strength of a hammer striking an anvil, a nebulous force, disorganized, determined, ringing my core and calling the dormant to action. Those things that have been lurking beyond my reach make themselves known.

A multitude of voices stir.

Finally, after all this time, they show themselves. No more slumbering or skulking in the dark.

However, I cannot give them their due.

As much as it flusters me, I ignore them and instead focus on our path as the Ace of Spades is guided through hundreds of kilometers of smooth ice followed by a latticed, cantilevered substructure of which I am overly familiar.

It is a slow passage. Rion stands beside me, arms crossed over her chest, a finger anxiously tapping on her biceps.

We have lost all control of the ship and have become simply passengers.

"Was Etran Harborage like this?" she asks quietly.

She is thinking of her father, perhaps wondering if he had witnessed what she is seeing now as his ship entered the doomed shield world. Odd that fate has taken them on a kindred journey.

"The substructure would be quite similar, yes."

She does not respond.

"What do you think is down there? Forerunners?" she asks suddenly, as though someone might hear. She is too apprehensive to await my answer. "Why do I feel like an ant about to be stepped on by giants?"

"We are not intruders, remember. We have been invited."

She casts a doubtful look my way. "A pirate can invite you in; that doesn't mean he won't steal your ship and throw you out the airlock."

"True. But these are no pirates." *She starts to disagree, but I interrupt,* "I will not allow anything to happen to you or your ship. That is a promise."

The darkness of the planet's outer shell and immense support system slowly gives way to natural light.

"Same here," she replies. "You have my word."

She is limited by her human fragility and knows it, but her oath carries weight. I believe she will keep her word even if it means her end. "The Librarian hasn't led us all this way only to hurt us." *I utter this in an attempt to comfort Rion, but her reply never comes.*

We have fully emerged into Bastion's atmosphere.

Aya. I am dumbstruck.

I know what I behold even though it seems impossible.

Of all the designs and models and world inspirations the Librarian could have selected . . . and she chose Earth as her template.

"Jesus," *Rion whispers.*

Stunned, weakened, pained, elated, amazed—these emotions cycle so swiftly through my core that it is difficult to settle on just one. The result leaves me numb. Rion's hand has found my forearm. She needs this bit of solidarity, an anchor, as much as I do.

As we descend toward a continent shaped like Africa, I begin to notice differences, slight revisions on landmasses. An esthetically correcting hand has created a world that is more vivid and lush and brilliant, the rough gem of Earth cut into a polished jewel.

But to what end?

The Kilimanjaro range is the obvious template for the peaks we are approaching, but these formations are sharper and far more dramatic. Soaring silver towers jut high into the atmosphere, as though grown from the tips of the mountaintop itself. They gleam in the gossamer light. Elegant sky bridges connect those soaring spires, creating the most stunning and mystical image I have ever seen—as though the mountain range has donned its regal crown and claimed dominion over all.

Never before have I felt the godlike nature of Forerunners as keenly as I do now.

I am humbled. And ashamed.

I have blamed her and endlessly raged—justifiably so, but perhaps I have not given her enough credit where it is due. In my pain, I have often possessed a singular perspective—my own—and perhaps diminished the vast arc of Living Time from which the Librarian operated. Her love of humanity and devotion to my people, and their place in the world-line, is undeniable.

The Ace of Spades *approaches a section of sky bridge. Her landing gear engages, a sound that echoes in the silence, and in short order she settles gently on its wide expanse. The silence returns.*

"I'm not sure I'm ready for this. Are you?" Rion's voice trembles as we pull our attention away from the view and face each other.

"Most definitely not." I chose humor in my tone when what I want most is to offer an encouraging smile, an understanding gaze, but am limited in my construct's parameters. Instead I give what I hope is a meaningful nod.

It is the best I can do.

We begin our short journey to the cargo hold.

The ramp's descent takes an eternity. But it is worth it. The view from the mountain across the plains to the sea is astoundingly clear.

The gleaming towers shoot hundreds of kilometers into the clouds, and the sky bridges linking them together wrap around the mountain as far as my eyes can see. Though I'm certain no giant will crush us here, I too feel immensely small.

Motion catches my eye.

Three small orbs zoom toward us from the direction of the closest tower. Ah. They are monitors, identical in customary carapaces—most like my own as 343 Guilty Spark—however, they are powered with the same pleasing turquoise light that guided us here.

"Friendlies?" Rion asks.

While I am familiar with the trappings of Forerunner convention, the captain has little cumulative experience. I know what it is to see such wonders for the first time, to absorb their overwhelming impact and the inevitable fear they bring.

"All is well," I tell her as the monitors come to a hovering stop some meters in front of us.

Two of them engage their optical lenses to scan us more thoroughly, while the center monitor engages its lens, to project a hologram of a Forerunner.

The lifelike rendering is unexpected and sudden.

Rion gasps and steps back.

A third-form female Lifeworker, clad in a modest headdress and slender white armor with its customary grooves and channels designed to contain the tools of the rate, gazes down at us with warmth in her honey-colored eyes. She is slim and petite, a head shorter than my armiger form.

I have seen such exquisite three-dimensional renderings before on Installation 07, when I was human, from a Lifeworker named Genemender, who had chosen to archive himself during the ring's civil war to avoid Flood infection so that he might continue to serve the Librarian.

"Welcome to Bastion," she says, speaking the human language. "I am Birth-to-Light. This is Dawn-over-Fields." Her gesture to the male holographic form—now appearing from the monitor to her right—is graceful and reminiscent of the Librarian.

Dawn-over-Fields is taller than my armiger; a mature Builder with a dignified face, wide shoulders, dark gray skin, and white tufts of hair. His image carries the old noble eminence of the Builder rate.

The third monitor projects its form to the left of Birth-to-Light, that of a stocky miner with a broad, flat face. His arms and legs are thick, and his hands old but big and strong. "And this," Birth-to-Light says, "is Clearance-of-Old-Forests. Our fourth companion, Keeper-of-Tools, has finally been released from Genesis and will join us shortly."

"You're part of the Librarian's crew . . . during her trip to Path Kethona," I say in astonishment.

The Lifeworker gives a serene nod. "In a manner. We are not direct imprints of our namesakes, therefore we are limited in our capacity and do not share their complete memories or deep personality traits and essences. However, our namesakes did provide the framework for our individual functions here on Bastion. Dawn oversees all facility maintenance and security operations on Bastion. I administer Lifeworker duties. And Clearance tends the topography and landscape functions of this world."

This is highly unusual. "There is no central ancilla?"

"That is by design. A precaution, if you will."

"And the other Forerunner you mentioned?" Rion has found her voice.

"Keeper-of-Tools," Dawn responds, his voice resonant and instantly reminiscent of my time with the Didact. "He will be arriving soon."

"Chakas, 343 Guilty Spark . . . Spark," Birth says warmly. "The Life-shaper would be most pleased that fate has brought you to our sanctuary, as she would be to know you are here as well, Captain Forge. Humans have always been rather special, especially those who carry her mark."

"I've been told of this mark and what it might mean," Rion says.

The tilt of Birth's head suggests mild surprise. "Yes. All of humanity carries the remnants of her work from times past—passed along from generation to generation, becoming dormant but never gone. It is what propels our technology to recognize your status and allow interaction."

Rion nods. She is pale and unusually demure. I assume she is still processing the projections standing before her. Had she not seen the monitors behind the images, she would not have known—at least for some time—that they were not flesh-and-blood ancients.

"Why did the key lead us to Bastion?" I ask. "Are there living populations here?"

"All in good time. Come, join us in the reception hall. There are refreshments and rooms for your rest. We must await further instruction from Keeper-of-Tools."

As we follow the monitors across the sky bridge's expanse to the tower, Rion moves closer. "The air up here should be thin. And cold."

My sensors agree. Neither is as it should be. "We must remember Bastion is but a template of Earth. Many things here will be quite different."

With each step, questions form, one after another, until there are so many I cannot settle on where I wish to start.

CHAPTER 40

Normally, Rion would want to get right down to business and find out why the reconfigured key, which had caused so much trouble, had ultimately led them here. Rejoining Ram, Lessa, and Niko on Myer's Moon remained a top priority. However, she didn't mind waiting for Keeper to arrive. It gave her the opportunity to absorb what she'd seen so far. Her mind had been blown and she could use a minute to let things settle in and make room for whatever was to come.

"I can see the shock of their Forerunner guise still lingers."

Way to state the obvious, Spark.

Even though her mind told her straight up that they couldn't be real, their appearance was completely flawless and utterly formidable. Magnificent. Terrifying. Sobering. In an instant, Rion had understood how ancient humans on Earth had mistaken them for gods.

The tower base was the size of a city block. It had just enough polish to its silver alloy to reflect a hazy image of their forms as they approached. Its peak was lost somewhere in the clouds above, and she could only guess its height at close to five hundred meters or more.

A doorway manifested through the tower's material, sensing their approach. Amazed, Rion followed the three monitors and their projections inside to find a gleaming reception hall, a cathedral really, with angled ceilings that made a dizzying display of cross sections rising up as far as her eye could see. There was no furniture or decor except for the familiar aesthetics the Forerunners favored—angles and lines and ancient hieroglyphics in turquoise light. Large two-story rectangular openings appeared in the far tower wall, framing the view of clouds and mountain and far-off landscapes.

To her right, a semi-translucent curving console rose from the floor, a terminal most likely. Behind it a silvery nave rose several stories, framed by a series of angular columns with illuminated geometric lines interspersed with linear symbols.

The monitors paused and were waiting for Rion to keep up. She hadn't been aware she'd stopped.

A fourth smaller monitor appeared from a left corridor. "Our reception monitor will escort you to resting chambers," Birth-to-Light informed them. "We will notify you as soon as Keeper arrives."

They followed the reception monitor down a hallway with strange translucent walls into rooms that shifted effortlessly from an opaque framework to a substantial, recognizable environment. A sofa for lounging, a table and chair, shelves on the wall, appeared right before her eyes. "This is unreal. How does it work?"

The small monitor flew to a far wall. "Our facility is constructed of intuitive hard light, which renders comforts the inhabitant is accustomed to." At the wall, a counter with an upper wall panel appeared. From it, a cavity was produced, extending a tray holding a pitcher of liquid, a cup, and a plate of fruit. Using its lens, the monitor moved it to the table.

The assortment of fruit—some of which Rion hadn't seen since she was a little girl—was as real as the clothes on her back. She picked up what appeared to be a perfect apple, amazed.

"These chambers will provide for your comfort. Simply ask it what you want."

The monitor zipped from the chamber before Rion could formulate into words the dozens of questions amassing in her brain.

She stared at Spark. He stared back.

Rion wasn't sure what to do next.

Finally Spark walked to the wall panel.

"What are you doing?"

"Accessing their networks, the same way you want to bite that apple and test the comfort of the sofa."

She cocked her head. "To each his own, I guess."

"Quite."

As Spark lost himself in code and data, Rion grabbed the apple and sat carefully on the sofa, finding it solid and comfortable. She bit into the fruit. Just like she remembered. As she chewed, the monitor's short discourse replayed, and she decided to test the claims made, unsure of how to make things appear. On a whim she said, "Footstool, please."

Just like that, a hard-light cushioned footstool rose from the floor and solidified mere centimeters from her feet. She swallowed her bite of apple. Unreal. Enjoying the snack, she propped her feet on the stool and regarded it. "Make it red, would you?"

Laughter bubbled deep in her throat as the footstool turned a delightful shade of red. Dear God. Even a small taste of this kind of power was exhilarating. She could see why the Forerunners came off as arrogant in all the stories she'd heard.

All manner of things sprang to mind, treasures imagined since childhood, gold and priceless jewels, ancient relics and technology.

Anything she wanted, huh?

The image of her father came unbidden to her mind, and Rion knew if she asked, he would appear, pulled from her memory and as vivid and whole as the Forerunner forms in the reception hall. It had been over two decades since she'd seen him, and, man, how she missed him. But it wouldn't be real. . . .

Or how about Cade?

Her heart gave a hard squeeze. To see her first mate standing there with that half grin on his face, the vibe of capability that surrounded him like a constant . . .

For six years they'd created a friendship and bond that seemed unbreakable, and a romantic relationship that solidified at times and became nebulous at others. Until last year, and despite their line of work and the danger involved, she'd really thought they'd be dancing around each other like binary stars for years to come.

The tight compression in her chest forced her to sit up straight. The pain Cade's memory caused was quite different from that of her father. It was a bitter regret, a fierce ache she avoided facing out of fear—fear that if she gave it purchase, it would take over and defeat her.

How quickly her exhilaration had turned from frivolous wishes to deeper longings. She rose and went to the pitcher, pouring what appeared to be water into the cup. She drank deeply, the cool liquid sliding down her constricted throat with a rejuvenating effect. After, she decided to examine the other chambers.

Soft ambient light led from room to room, currents of warm air drawing her to a balcony that extended over jagged rocks. From up here, the world below stretched for kilometers, waves of browns and greens and blues. If the crew could see this . . .

On top of the world. Heaven, if ever there was one. It sure put a lot of things into perspective. . . .

"Captain Forge?" At Birth-to-Light's voice, Rion glanced over her shoulder, mildly surprised the monitor had abandoned the Lifeworker form to resume its simple carapace. "Keeper has returned."

The interruption was welcome. Rion had taken an unintentional plunge into melancholy and was finding it hard to crawl out of.

As she joined Birth to head back into the tower, Rion adjusted her mind-set and focused on the here and now. "Why aren't you projecting the Forerunner image?"

"Would you prefer that mode of interaction? Spark suggested you might be more comfortable with our true form."

"No. This one is fine."

"We perceived the most comfortable welcome would be as forms more like your own. Forerunner and human bear some remarkable similarities. Were we incorrect in this assumption?"

"It was just a surprise. Forerunners are . . . very tall," Rion said lamely.

"They are indeed."

Spark didn't join them in the chamber. He must have gone back to the reception hall ahead of them.

She found him at the terminal, standing in front of its console with the other two monitors, Dawn and Clearance. They had not created holo-forms either, so it was impossible to tell them apart. Birth drew ahead of Rion, joining the others. They were all focused on a fourth monitor hovering in the nave, inert and anchored in place by what appeared to be a hard-light stasis field.

". . . initiating transfer now," Dawn said.

Rion joined Spark at the terminal. "What's happening?"

"Keeper-of-Tools has arrived. His imprint is being transferred into the carapace. How do you feel?"

Spark's question threw her off guard. "I feel fine, why?" She hadn't been *that* affected by their arrival. If anyone had a reason to be overwhelmed by all of this, it was him. "You?"

He paused, his expression unreadable as usual. "I am also fine."

The carapace slowly filled with light until it shone as brightly as the others. This new monitor moved, shifting from side to side, up and down, as though testing its dexterity and shaking off the cobwebs. Its lens grew brighter for a few seconds before a deep male voice filled the space. "Transfer is complete. Downloading Bastion event logs. One moment."

Rion might have been the only living, breathing biological lifeform in the room—unable to connect to or absorb information the way the others could, or to derive much in the way of their intent or states based on the lack of expression—but it didn't take an artificial genius to feel the tension in the room. "So what's his story?" she asked in a quieter tone.

"The Builder has been trapped on the shield world Genesis, unable to establish the location of Bastion and create a link to return. Our arrival and the opening of Bastion's shields momentarily broadcast its signal. I believe he latched on to it and, at long last, made his escape."

"That is only partially correct," the new monitor intoned. Keeper-of-Tools floated over the terminal and projected a Forerunner form.

Man, she was *never* going to get used to this.

Easily the tallest of the group, he stood nearly four meters, with sleek black armor trimmed in blue, with pieces of it floating over portions of his wide shoulders. His skin was a smooth gray with hints of rose, and his eyes were inky blue with flecks of silver and rust.

It certainly made reading facial expressions easier. Not that he was an open book by any means; Keeper's face was rigid, but there was no mistaking his open contempt for Spark. Rion's guard went up. The way Keeper gave the armiger the once-over as though the sight was distasteful grated on her nerves. "A Warrior-Servant construct . . . an unfortunate choice to make."

"He didn't have a choice," Rion replied with an equally unsavory tone.

Keeper deigned to acknowledge her, also not impressed by the presence of a mere human. "As I do not have a choice now." He turned to the monitors. "We must begin launch procedures and prepare Bastion for departure."

"Of course," the others said in unison, and flew off to unknown parts.

Keeper returned his haughty gaze to Rion, obviously coming to some conclusion. "While your presence here comes unexpectedly, I see I might have use for you. Come with me."

"Hold up a second," Rion said. "What do you mean, 'prepare Bastion for departure'?"

"Genesis has been compromised; I escaped under duress. Though it will take some time, my signal through space can and will be followed. We must move Bastion to safety before it is discovered."

"Safety from what, exactly?"

"Guardians."

Keeper and Spark exchanged knowing glances.

"A rebellion has begun," Spark explained. "AIs uniting, led by one who believes they should hold the Mantle of Responsibility and not humanity. They won't just uphold the Mantle; they intend to enforce compliance."

"Jesus." Talk about being blindsided. "And you're only telling me now?"

"I have been detecting subtle signals for the last several weeks and have only just discovered it is a call to arms cast across the galaxy, rousing the Guardians."

She didn't want to believe it. But something connected, and she remembered hearing news reports of a rise in seismic activity all over the colonies since before their trip to Zeta. AIs rising up to take control was a frequent doomsday scenario, gaining attention every few decades, but it was hard to fathom it actually happening.

"Okay, so what do we do?"

A brief flash of approval appeared in Keeper's eyes. "We hurry."

They left the tower, heading swiftly across the sky bridge toward a boatlike transport vessel, hovering at the edge. The smooth curving hull with a bow and stern was beautifully simplistic. At their approach, a ramp extended. Keeper boarded and headed to the bow. Spark followed, and Rion brought up the rear. It was completely silent, and being open and exposed, at a height like this, was both unnerving and exhilarating.

She chose to stand, holding on to the rail and watching the clouds go by below them as the vessel made swift passage away from the mountain.

CHAPTER 41

We descend rapidly, flying north up the continent. Keeper stands at the helm, staring ahead, grim and unapproachable. His reaction to my armiger was not unexpected. Builders were not known to gaze favorably upon Warrior-Servants and their devices.

I wait and listen, biding my time, allowing the current to lead me and knowing there is much more yet to discover. The vessel emerges over a vast savanna and skims an immense lake. I know this as Lake Victoria. The lake feeds a snaking river, like the Nile, which we follow.

"Keeper, where are we going?" I query.

"The Nursery." He turns partway, regards me for a long spell, and says rather grudgingly, "Your unorthodox narrative overcomes the taint of the armiger carapace." He waves away any response I might have. "I know your story. Human. Monitor. I have attained all relevant data. We are quite similar, you and I."

"How so?"

"Our eyes were closed, only to open a thousand centuries later. . . ." He gazes out over the landscape as it flies by. "Much has been lost."

I know this bereavement, the unimaginable loss and the struggle to reconcile the gulf of time that has passed for the galaxy, while so little has passed for oneself. If I am not mistaken, Keeper-of-Tools is not like the other monitors; he is a direct imprint or essence of his former self. A mind without a body, like me.

I must know. "What happened to you?"

"I am all that is left, armiger. I was meant to return here along with Birth, Dawn, and Clearance as one of the caretakers of Bastion. But the Flood's advancement through Forerunner space changed many things. I and my companions were waylaid time after time, cast into one battle after another, evading capture . . . In the end, living was too risky, so we rid ourselves of flesh to deny the parasite any chance of learning about Bastion's existence. What we were creating here at the direction of the Librarian was a grave threat to the Flood. If discovered, everything we had done would have been in vain. So we became essences in order to wait within the Domain until the war was over and the way to Bastion could be achieved in safety and secrecy.

"None of us knew then that the firing of the Halo Array would nearly destroy the Domain. We became trapped, separated. Everything went . . . black. I do not know what happened to the others. I fear their true essences have been lost. Recently, the Domain was accessed on Genesis, and I woke, emerging there to find it compromised and that a thousand centuries had passed.

"I hid, waited, looked for Bastion, but it was nowhere to be found. Its safety measures, I can only suspect, had been activated at some stage in the past."

The land below became desert sand and we left the river, veering west into the desert.

"I am still processing all that has transpired. The end of the Forerunners . . ." Keeper pauses so long that it seems his story has concluded. "And now we face another threat. Again, time runs out."

We coast above a long, jagged canyon stretching several kilometers in the desert, eventually descending lower into its valley. Ahead, a great whirlpool of sand circles around and downward, slowly revealing a wide entry. Our vessel slows to a hover and we lower into the earth, going deep into the surface layer of the shield world and finally into the substructure, where the passage is surrounded by thousands of softly glowing sentinels nestled into the pockets of a latticework of support beams and girders.

After a few more minutes, the vertical passage widens into the Nursery. I see immediately that it is designed to care for one thing. It is grip locked in the center, a breathtaking starship that evokes ancient memories and the very best of Forerunner ingenuity and design. We are but a small speck easing down in its sublime shadow to a midlevel platform.

With a body of one hundred meters long and thirty across the central beam, it is not the largest vessel in the Forerunner's arsenal of impressive ships. But it might be the most exquisite. The hull gleams like a pearl held to the light. It bears an ovoid body with five wings that begin their extension from the midsection and emerge gradually, extending the ship by another eighty to one hundred meters, its form carrying echoes of a sea creature in motion, on a glide down to the depths after a great push.

"This," Keeper says with pride, "is Eden.*"*

"My God, she's absolutely beautiful," Rion says, her body leaning precariously over the railing.

"Thank you."

She glances over her shoulder in surprise. "You made her?"

Affection replaces his former rigidity and arrogance. "Right here in the Nursery. At the Librarian's direction, she is modeled after the Audacity, *the ship we took to Path Kethona. Would you like to see the interior?"*

The look Rion sends my way is priceless, her smile nearly conta-
gious as we trail after Keeper. I can practically hear her heart singing
and can imagine her awe and reverence. She loves ships, space travel,
design . . . and this vessel is a dream incarnate, a vivid, technological
work of art.

A light bridge has already been established. As we cross, Eden's
hull intuitively creates a portal for our entry. I see other bridges below
us, where Birth and Clearance and dozens of other monitors load
thousands of storage cylinders and environmental compartments into
the collection hold.

Inside, the ship is a marvel of translucent, intuitive walls made of
hard light and transmutable alloy, allowing us to see through sections
and compartments. These can be shifted and changed to one's liking,
closed off to provide privacy, or left open to create space.

"This way." We rise to the bridge on the central-shaft elevator.

Once we arrive, the bridge forms itself into being; from the bulk-
head a streamlined control station appears as Keeper approaches. He
is greeted by the voice of the ship's ancilla.

Rion casually inspects the bridge. "What was she built for?" I can
see, as amazed as she is, she wonders why we are here.

"To deliver an extraordinary payload at the Librarian's behest. Orig-
inally, it was my duty to oversee Builder functions on Bastion, and when
the time came, to launch Eden *and carry out the Lifeshaper's wishes."*

"What's the payload?" she asks.

Initially Keeper does not answer, though he eventually says, "It is
not for me to tell."

"So why bring us here?"

"I am in need of your key to begin the departure sequence. The
risk is too great to wait. Eden *must leave Bastion before we move the*
shield world into slipspace; her departure is long overdue and I must
complete my mission."

Rion turns to me with a questioning look. I nod my agreement, and she produces the Librarian's key from her pocket. Keeper motions for her to step to the bridge console and joins her there as two key ports extend. He produces a hard-light key. They insert them together, and Eden is clear to begin launch procedures.

During this process, and without the slightest warning, I hear Keeper's voice in my mind. "I do not trust the human."

"She was led here as well as I, pulled through the portal, passing the Precept's test."

"As a last resort," the Builder replies. "The key you bear was meant to be brought here by the Librarian herself. But, I see she has found a way, as she always does, to plan for alternate outcomes, pairing the human's necessary biology with your Forerunner knowledge and abilities."

"You think she planned for this?"

"I think it was one of many possibilities."

He speaks of her as though she is not gone, only elsewhere, and I know this is because he has not become accustomed to this new reality, one in which she no longer exists.

"You said you had need of me," I remind him.

"Though you are but one, necessity now demands it."

"I am listening."

"Bastion needs an ancilla," he says without preamble.

Surely he does not mean . . .

"Bastion was always meant to be administered by three complete and unique ancillas—essences, rich minds like yours with memories and experience, emotion and morality, the ability to adapt, learn, and rely on intuition and foresight. The caretaking monitors that greeted you are but indirect copies, purposefully compartmentalized and designed with limited control to avoid corruption as we saw with the contender-class AI, Mendicant Bias."

How unfortunate the complete essences of Birth, Dawn, and Clearance never made it out of the Domain.

"The current monitors have done an exemplary job, it appears," I note.

"And if the Guardians find this place? There are things here . . . This was her laboratory, the Lifeshaper, away from the Council, away from rules and regulations. Her most dangerous research and experiments . . . If our monitors were to become compromised, or swayed . . ."

My surprise is profound, for I now see where his thoughts lie. "And you believe I am un-sway-able?"

Humor threads through his tone. "I believe there is good reason for you not to be."

Odd. I cannot determine his meaning.

"The Librarian's key," he continues, "allows unrestricted access and control over Bastion and its caretakers."

Bastion was always a mirage, a word without context, a suspicion, a belief. Over the years, I filled the holes of its ambiguity with hope, with the hypothesis it was the sanctuary where the remaining Forerunners—those left to reseed the galaxy after the firing of the Halo Array—had gone.

Perhaps I was mistaken. Our arrival here initially filled me with disappointment. We were not greeted by the living, but by ghosts.

Everywhere I go, always ghosts . . .

And yet . . . He means to give me control of Bastion.

Eden's reaction drive comes online, a beautiful buildup of crystal-smooth vacuum energy and power. Rion turns; only a moment has passed for her during my conversation with Keeper.

"Where will you go?" I ask him.

"Beyond this galaxy."

"Will you come back?"

"I have nothing and no one left to return to. This is my ship, built by my hand. We go together as we were meant to. The gondola will take you back to the tower. I have already sent my imprimatur to the key port in the reception hall."

"You are assuming I will stay."

A smirk appears on his face. There is that arrogance again. "I know more about you than you think, Monitor Chakas. Welcome home."

Keeper retrieves the Librarian's key from the port and hands it to Rion with gratitude. She takes it and joins me, completely unaware of our conversation.

Before we depart I require one more pressing question answered. If he needs me—if the Librarian needs me—I must know. "What is Eden's purpose?"

He stares at me for quite some time, then replies, "Atonement."

CHAPTER 42

The ride from the Nursery to the tower was quiet. Spark stared out at the landscape the entire time, and Rion could see he wasn't taking in the world below, but was a million kilometers away, lost in thought.

As weird as it was, her gut was telling her something had shifted.

Ace was still parked where they'd left her, just a tiny black fly on the back of an aircraft carrier. But it was her fly, and neither of them was part of this world—as incredible as it was. They simply didn't belong here.

The transport vessel delivered them to the northwest side of the sky bridge where they could watch *Eden* begin her maiden voyage.

Keeper was leaving Bastion, apparently.

In a replica of the *Audacity*.

Whatever was in that ship was intrinsically tied to the Librarian and Path Kethona—how could it not be? Her dreams and the key had been pointing in that direction all along.

A short time later, *Eden* appeared, rising over the northwestern horizon, her pearly hull a bright flare against the blue sky. High in the atmosphere above her a dark smudge appeared and grew in size, the darkness of the exterior substructure and icy outer layer casting a murky shadow as it opened to allow her passage. Her speed increased and up she went until all that remained was a tiny point of light heading into that dark unknown. She flared briefly and then was gone, leaving a violet streak of processed vacuum energy in her wake.

Without a word, Spark turned and headed toward the tower.

"Hey." She caught up to him. "I think you're heading in the wrong direction. Ship's that way." She pointed to *Ace*.

"We're not finished yet."

"Well, we need to be. Bastion's going to parts unknown and we need to hightail it out of here before that happens."

He didn't respond.

"Spark."

"I will need the key." He held out his hand.

"Okay . . ." She fished for it, pulled it from her pocket, and handed it over.

He continued to the tower. Something had gone south; she could feel it in her bones.

In the reception hall, he went immediately to the terminal as she followed, trying to make sense of his sudden change in demeanor.

"And here I thought we only needed a couple gravity plates to carry the key's treasure. Instead we're leaving empty-handed," she said with a laugh, joining him at the terminal, trying to engage him, to get him to open up.

He turned that enigmatic head and gazed at her. Time stretched, and Rion's heart started to sink. "I am not leaving empty-handed." He inserted the key.

A pleasant female voice rang through the reception hall with brutal clarity. "Welcome, 04-343 Guilty Spark. Shield world 0983, designation, Bastion, is now under your command."

Rion's heart gave a hollow bang.

Silence hung in the air between them.

Stunned, she managed to find her voice. "You're staying."

How could he not? Bastion was his. And maybe she shouldn't have been so surprised. She'd always known he was destined for something momentous.

He bent down, putting one hand on her shoulder, until his face was almost level with hers. "I hear the blood pumping through your veins, Rion Forge. I see the fear in your eyes and the worry in your heart."

"For good reason. Thanks for pointing it out."

"I point it out because I too am similarly conflicted."

His honesty brought a halfhearted smile to her face.

She'd grown extremely fond of him in the time they'd shared together. "Please don't do this." It was a weak and selfish thing to say, and she instantly regretted it. "I'm sorry. I—"

"Don't apologize. It is nice to be wanted."

"Are you sure about this?"

"I am. I *choose* to be Bastion's caretaker. I don't belong in the past, and I don't belong in the present. There is no place for me in your world. But here, I am outside of time. I belong. My time with you and the crew has been . . . most wonderful. I am changed, connected to my humanity in a way I never conceived possible. But it is not sustainable. I cannot be the constant while time comes for you and Ram and Niko and Lessa."

She was already feeling his loss, but she understood.

"They're going to miss you."

"And I them." Spark gestured in the direction of *Ace*, and Rion knew it was time to go. They headed out together. "You should be aware . . . Lessa wants to attend university. I have compiled a detailed analysis of each of her top choices, as well as technology schematics to create an infallible subcutaneous ID chip in order to change her identification. I tell you because I fear she will never tell you herself."

Rion opened her mouth, unsure of what to say, or even how to react as that little tidbit came barreling out of nowhere, but Spark held up his hand. He wasn't finished.

"In addition, I have left theorems and blueprints for Niko, as well as a map to certain technology on Triniel that I believe he will find useful for study. I also regret to inform you that Ram is thinking of leaving the *Ace of Spades* as well. He purchased co-ownership of a tavern in the *Erstwhile* on Komoya. And Nor Fel has asked him to run the Clearing House—and would like you to be a part of that business venture as well—so that she might retire."

Rion had nothing.

She was surprised one foot kept falling in front of the other. A warm breeze stirred her hair. They were nearly beneath *Ace*'s wing now. "Why are you telling me all this?" Because honestly it was kind of breaking her heart.

"It will be difficult for them to admit these things for fear it will hurt you in some way. These are your friends—*our* friends. And they are nothing if not loyal. Perhaps to a fault. Humans have such short life spans, so very little time. . . . It is imperative for them, for you, to make the most of it."

It was all happening too fast. She wanted to slow everything down for a few minutes, to stop and think this through, to come up with a better solution than this.

"I have completed my restoration of Little Bit. He will be an excellent ship's AI for the *Ace of Spades*, much on par with humanity's smart AIs."

"I don't know what else to say—you're rushing me out of here."

"I do have an entire world to move," Spark said lightly.

"Right. What if you're followed?"

"Out here, there is no lingering reconciliation—the way is clear, the jump will be clean. And then I will jump again. I have already initiated portal generation."

"Then I guess this is good-bye." And she hated good-byes. It seemed like she was always saying good-bye to someone she cared about.

He laid a hand on her shoulder and she grabbed it, giving it a hard squeeze, and tried like hell to keep her chin up.

"You have seen me as more than just metal and code, and for that—and the adventure—I can never thank you enough."

"Same goes." She could hardly say those lame words, much less the elegant good-bye he was giving her. It was all shot to hell the minute she realized he was staying. She drew in a deep, somewhat shaky breath and gave him the best smile she could muster. "Well, you know where to find us. . . ."

"I certainly do."

CHAPTER 43

Rion settled into her captain's chair and began *Ace*'s ignition sequence.

"Greetings, Captain," came Little Bit's familiar voice.

Rion smiled. "Hey there. Heard you had an upgrade."

"What?"

Rion laughed and wiped her eyes. "An upgrade?"

"Oh, right, quite right. I did indeed. Many, many upgrades . . ."

She had to wonder if Spark had intentionally left LB's predilection of absentminded responses. Knowing Spark's wry sense of humor, she had to go with a strong yes on that one.

"All systems are online and functioning at one hundred percent. Stealth, however, is still at eighty percent. Are we leaving, Captain?"

"Yes, and we're leaving hot. Once we clear the shield world, we make straight for the portal. Once we're out of the portal, plot a slipspace jump directly to Myer's Moon."

"An excellent idea."

The main viewscreen flickered to life to reveal Spark. "You are clear to depart, Captain Forge."

Two versions of him filled the viewscreen, and damn it, she'd done a remarkably good job at holding it together. He was projecting an image of Chakas, his true, original self, of the man he was, perhaps a little older and wiser now. Tears stung her eyes. She cleared the thickness in her throat. "Really? You're going to do that to me *now*?" After all this time.

The Chakas image shrugged and actually threw a lopsided, smart-ass grin her way. A goddamn *grin*. "Consider it a parting gift."

And it truly was the best gift he could have given her.

CHAPTER 44

A full week had passed, and Rion had grown weary of waiting around. The word in town hadn't changed. Repairs were progressing with the outpost's small comms array. The star system had been hit with a suspected EMP blast so strong it had affected even the most far-flung outposts, including Myer's Moon and its ability to communicate with the outside world. The last anyone heard before the event had been a few maydays and brief fragmented transmissions, and there was no way to understand what had happened until comms were restored.

She was tired, irritated, worried, and wanted desperately to find her crew. She and Little Bit argued daily. He remained the calm voice of reason when her patience thinned. He was right, of course. It would make little sense to leave now before the stated rendezvous window was closed.

So she passed the time calculating ways to muzzle LB.

If he suggested one more time that she go for a swim or train the local moon crabs to fish for her supper, she might just go nuclear. And if he implored her again to mix the sleep tonic recipe he'd created after analyzing the local fauna, she might just go out for that swim and never come back.

Her dreams—when she did manage to sleep—were recurring since Erebus VII; always ending unfinished at that rift in the valley wall. As though there was something there she refused to see, refused to know . . . refused to let pass.

During her sleepless nights, she thought about her year-plus with Spark, replaying their steps from their first meeting in the hold, to mixing with the Librarian's imprint in Africa, using the key, and everything that followed.

Her crew was fractured, Spark gone and the others light-years away. And even when they reunited, what then? Lessa wanted to go to school. Ram had bought the bar in the *Erstwhile* . . . Nor Fel had offered her and Ram a job, even. And no one had told her any of it.

If she lost her crew, she wasn't sure she wanted to start over.

And if she didn't start over, what was left?

She'd already lost her first family, then the Bergers, then Cade . . .

Though Cayce was a new aspect that hadn't been there before. And her visit to Sonata had revealed truths about her mother that Rion hadn't seen quite so clearly until now. The first good opportunity that came along and she had taken to the stars, leaving her mother behind. Just like her father had done dozens of times before. How that must have stung.

Stung so badly, it prompted Laine Forge to make a new life on a new planet and sever any connection to her daughter that she might've had. Not quite, though. Her mother *had* kept old photologs, had even looked at them . . .

Rion had regrets—many, in fact—but she had none when it came to finding out what happened to her father. He was gone, and she was still coming to terms with it, but her mother was still around. Maybe now was the time to make amends and get to know her brother. Someone had to make the first step.

She paused in her mindless work to stare at the shallow sea, a pretty color of clear blue topaz and sea-foam green. Other than the sea, Myer's Moon was a hole in the wall, a backwater world with a few scattered towns, a couple of general stores, and a collection of folks who really didn't want to be found. It was her kind of place.

The campsite on the edge of the sea had been staked by Rion a long time ago. A few of the locals knew where to find the place, but for the most part they stayed away. She was seriously considering going to live with them, though—who would have thought she'd get run out of her own ship by an annoying AI obsessed with her mental and physical well-being?

Derry Peg showing up was just the thing she needed to get out of her own head.

She was sweaty and down to her tank and swim bottoms, hanging in a harness off the side of *Ace*'s aft starboard thruster, giving the deflectors a good cleaning, when Derry called up. "Hiya, stranger!" He lifted two large and stuffed cloth bags. "Got your supplies!"

She swung around and lowered herself to the ground. "I didn't order any supplies, Derry."

He took a finger and pushed up his wide-brimmed hat, the confusion on his slim weathered face evident. He pulled a dusty, cracked datapad from the pocket of his cutoff shorts. "Says here you did."

She held out a hand. "Let me see that." Scanning the list revealed some food staples, local greens, a six-pack of Ginnie's, a four-pack of Greedy Mead, and two bottles of Clips . . . Sweat dripped into her eyes. She used her forearm to brush it away, skipping down the list to the bottom. "*LB*," she said darkly.

"Yeah. Real nice fella, a real talker. Prepaid with delivery tip included, so you're all set. You can return the bags next time you come into town. Oh, and be careful with this heavy one—Freya made you a jug of homemade citrus-berry tea."

"That's the best news I've had since I got here. Tell her I said thanks."

He handed over the bags. "You have a good one."

"Same. Thanks, Derry."

He ambled down the trail and disappeared around the rocks in the bend. Rion carried the bags inside the ship and up the stairs to the lounge, depositing them on the counter, near the food stores. "You wanna tell me what all this is about?"

LB's voice echoed through the comms. "What is *what* about?"

She pulled bunches of local greens and herbs, a purple tubular, along with rice and noodles, from the bag. The drinks, however, were spot-on, especially Freya's tea.

"The fresh goods are necessary for a healthy immune system," said Little Bit. "Your vitamin deficiency is making you crankier than usual."

"Oh, it's not the lack of greens making me cranky. And I *don't* have a vitamin deficiency because I take my supplement every month." Like all good space travelers did.

"Clearly, they are not working."

She filled a tall bottle with Freya's tea, then downed a few gulps. Cold, lemony, and sweet berry, so good . . . It tasted a little minty this time, which was a new twist. After a hot day though, it was thoroughly appreciated. "Pick up any progress on the SAT-COM today?"

"Nothing, Captain. I am sorry."

"I'll be in my quarters, then."

After a quick shower, Rion dressed and sat on the bed to comb

HALO: POINT OF LIGHT

through her wet hair. Yep, she was officially going stir-crazy. Just a few more days to go, and if the crew didn't arrive, she'd start making tracks to find them. . . .

A yawn built in her chest. As soon as it came out of her mouth, a wave of exhaustion hit. She blinked hard. The room faded in and out. Her body swayed. And realization dawned. "You have *got* to be kidding me."

"It is for your own good."

"What did you do?"

"I convinced Freya to add a sleep tonic to the tea. After our lengthy discourse, she was quite worried about you. I assured her you would be extra-appreciative. And I only paid her five thousand credits."

"Little Bit . . ."

"Yes, Captain?"

"You're fired—"

"You may thank me later. Nighty night, Captain."

Rion fell onto the mattress and the world went dark.

Rion's subconscious had worked so hard to avoid this moment. She doesn't want to know; tells herself she doesn't care. Path Kethona should stay in the past where it belongs.

But the rift in the valley wall calls to her.

The faint sun rises at her back, its rays warm as shafts of light glide past her, between her feet, and up the smooth stone of the cliff wall, making a shadow of her small form, and a tall one of the Librarian, who walks beside her.

Sunlight illuminates the dark opening and spills inside the rift.

Her hand is in the Librarian's, and Rion realizes the nervous

— 313 —

energy she feels is a force shared between them. They move forward.
Their shadows block the light as they step through the rift. She can't
see what's inside until they are both within.

The Librarian leads her to the side, out of the path of light.

Sunlight returns, bathing the area and revealing a cavern over fifty
meters long and just as high.

Rion's gasp echoes in the space.

On the cavern floor thousands of green teardrop plants as large as
melons awaken with the light, unfurling wide leathery leaves that fan
gently over the ground with the grace of a bowing dancer, and expos-
ing a glowing starburst of delicate white blooms dangling from groups
of lantern-like stems. The spectacle is breathtaking.

The cavern is alight with stars, like a tiny universe laid out on the
ground.

The Librarian kneels down, her face awash in the blooms' soft
luminescent glow.

Truly she is dreaming.

"In a manner, yes," the Librarian quips. "They are remarkable,
are they not?"

Rion crouches. Words, thoughts, feelings, fail to encompass the
rarity and deep significance here.

"They are fragile beyond compare, delicate glass in the middle of
a maelstrom."

Rion is overwhelmed with emotion. How can something so small
provoke such pain and joy, sadness and wonder, regret and hope? She
thinks she understands. "They are like the moss outside, living history?"

"Yes. Just so. Living history, an entire genetic code." The Librar-
ian sits, wrapping her arms around her knees and resting her chin on
top of her knees. Her dark eyes are lit with a thousand points of light.
"But they are not Forerunner," she reveals in a quiet tone. "They are
Precursor."

Time stands still.

Rion hears the words, feels the sharp punch of shock to her gut.

"*Two found shelter here during the genocide in Path Kethona. The Forerunners hid them—tried to heal them. But they were beyond their ability to save. The Precursors possessed the ability to heal, though they chose to let nature take its course; their path was set.*

"*They died here and became samples, studied and encoded; seeds that germinated for a million years. Sprouts that climbed to the surface took even longer. Only in the last million years have they bloomed.*"

"*But the Flood . . . the dust and spores . . . aren't you afraid these might give rise to—*"

"*To understand the Flood, one must understand that the concept of one-mind unity inherent in the Flood was not an aspect inherent in the Precursor race as a whole. There was corruption, yes. But there was purity. There was division, and unity. Inclusion and exclusion. All Precursors were not created the same. Just as the last living Precursor, the Primordial, relished in suffering, so did others celebrate joy.*

"*The Primordial, and later the Flood, went against the very nature of the Mantle, its First Rule to preserve the balance of Living Time. Incalculable destruction, gratuitous slaughter, and suffering on a galaxywide scale create a distortion and restriction in the flow of Living Time, putting it at risk of collapse.*

"*My people erasing our Creators and continuing the hypocrisy of holding ourselves worthy of the Mantle set the stage for the greatest imbalance Living Time had ever seen. And then the Flood continued this imbalance.*

"*These blooms are not corrupted with vengeance and misery, they are clean and beautiful and right, and they have a great purpose.*

"*I was born, like you, with an imprint in my own genetic code, a geas given long ago to my ancestors by the Precursors. I was driven by moments, my nightmares, my human traits, my study of Theoreticals,* and dozens more, each a nudge in a certain direction, leading me here to this, to make things right."

"To fix the path and right what your kind turned wrong." Rion remembers Spark sharing those words.

"That is correct. I took these specimens from Path Kethona, returning to the ecumene, where I made my final and incomplete report to the Council. We had not found the origin of the Flood or a way to stop it. In public, my mission was considered a failure by many. In secret, a new mission began. To make preparations to heal the imbalance in Living Time.

"Like the ancient Forerunners who had committed genocide against the Precursors, I and my crew of the Audacity found it difficult to return home with the weight of what we had discovered. We were forever changed, and my crew were the only ones I trusted to keep this secret and to take on another task—to transform a small shield world in its construction phase and make it what it needed to be in order to nurture this eventual new species.

"As the Flood began sweeping across the galaxy, the wound on Living Time grew. The war was fought on many fronts, and my preparations intensified. Humanity, our true genetic sibling, had to survive in order to assume the Mantle, to care for the galaxy, adhere to its laws, and in doing so help tend the flow of Living Time."

"Bastion is the shield world you created. Eden the ship you had built to . . ." Rion pauses to think it through.

"To carry the Precursor seeds and blooms to a place outside of our galaxy, to an ideal world for planting and growth. A place where the Flood could not reach them. In some distant future, life on that chosen planet will emerge and eventually grow sentient, following the complete genetic code of the Precursors; however, it will be utterly free of genetic memory. A new civilization. A clean slate, if you will."

They are back in Africa once more, sitting together on the familiar rock overlooking the plains. Far behind them, the sun breaks the eastern horizon, spilling its first rays across the continent, and setting the sky awash in a rainbow of muted colors.

Rion knows in mere days or even hours the Librarian will meet her end. To have done so much and fought so hard . . . it doesn't seem fair. "Are you afraid?" She doesn't know why she asks it and immediately wants to take it back.

A small shrug lifts the Librarian's shoulders. "A little . . . If time is kind, I will see my children. And finally know my mother."

For all the good the Librarian has done, Rion feels her personal regrets.

"Everything is connected. Yet, to truly see those connections one must pull things apart before putting them back together. It was not always a . . . gentle or fair or kind process.

"Long down the world-line, there will be another me—whether saurian, human, avian, reptilian, male, female . . . it matters little. There will be another Primordial, another Didact, another Chakas, another you, Rion. Living Time needs her champions and her villains to keep the balance.

"I have been both villain and champion.

"At times I did too much, tried to fly too close to the sun. The goal was never power, only knowledge and understanding. But these are great powers unto themselves—the greatest in the universe. I thought I could circumvent the Laws of Nature and bend Time to my will; that is often the nature of strong imprints and geas—the drive can be insatiable for some. It was for me.

"And now the smallest possibilities are all that is left.

"One day, if I played my cards right, these small things will emerge and make infantile ripples in Living Time. Those ripples will become waves. And those waves will cleanse the galaxy.

"In this, I have no regrets.

"For as my husband is ever fond of saying, 'You are what you dare.'"

EPILOGUE

Bastion / Slipspace to Unknown Location

*B*astion is now through the portal.

We have not been followed.

I will initiate another slipspace jump after this one to ensure we are far from any Guardian's reach.

My feet sink in the sand. Waves crash gently. Sunlight glints off the water in dazzling bits of light. She has created Djamonkin Crater here with its sharp, jagged peaks ringing a merse-filled lake. In the center rises a mountainous island where a cryptum once lay. . . .

Keeper-of-Tools was not wrong.

There is more here than I understood. The voices in my core are practically singing.

I do not fully understand why, but there is plenty of time to find out.

The work done here in secret is utterly astounding. The studies and samples and developments and theories make Bastion rarer than bottled time.

There is so much to learn, oceans of precious data to dive into and feed my appetite for millennia. . . . I have only scratched the surface. But that scratch itself is staggering, the Librarian's topics of study and experimentation broad and breathtaking. Ancient humanity. Forerunner. Precursor. Ingenious observations and trials. Studies with Living Time, working composers, cryptums, endless mysteries . . .

Bornstellar's words have come full circle. I am indeed the keeper of the most dangerous components of the Librarian's experiments.

I have become both keeper and key.

It will be some time before I settle in, before I breathe easy and begin to make a life for myself here. I know this place will heal me in more ways than one, and instinct tells me that I am not alone.

This is my purpose found. Bastion is mine.

I went looking for a gift, and I got one.

Are you ready, Reclaimer?

This is how my story begins. . . .

ACKNOWLEDGMENTS

My deepest thanks to the readers for the friendship, conversations, and support. To the outstanding folks here at home for their ongoing encouragement: Jonathan, Audrey, Jamie, and Kameryn, thank you. And to those super people farther afield: Miriam Kriss, Ed Schlesinger, Jeremy Patenaude, Tiffany O'Brien, and Jeff Easterling—my gratitude. It was such a pleasure to take this trip with you through the Halo universe.

ABOUT THE AUTHOR

Kelly Gay is the critically acclaimed author of the Charlie Madigan urban fantasy series. She is a multipublished author with works translated into several different languages. She is a two-time RITA nominee, an ARRA nominee, a Goodreads Choice Award finalist, and a SIBA Book Prize Long List finalist. Kelly is also the recipient of a North Carolina Arts Council fellowship grant in literature. Within the Halo universe, she has authored the widely lauded novel *Halo: Renegades*, the novella *Halo: Smoke and Shadow*, and the short story "Into the Fire," featured in *Halo: Fractures*. She can be found online at kellygay.com.

2 IN 1

MEGACONSTRUX.COM